A CAPED FIGURE STEPPED INTO THE NARROW ENTRANCEWAY TO THE VAULT.

The security guard's eyes went wide. It was him! Dammit, it was him! Except it couldn't be him! It mustn't. Tully made frantic noises in his throat, trying in some way to warn him off.

Batman either wasn't listening or simply didn't understand. He moved quickly to Tully, freed his hands, and tore the tape off the man's mouth. Pain roared through Tully's face, but that didn't stop him from getting out the words, "It's a trap!"

The safe door slammed shut before even Batman could turn. Before the resounding clang of the heavy metal barrier had even begun to fade, Two-Face's voice issued from a speaker hidden somewhere within the vault.

"Good evening, Mr. Bat," he said. "Your mission, should you choose to accept it—or not—is simple. Die!"

Batman and Tully were hurled to the floor as the safe jerked forward, starting to move.

"We have a problem," said Batman.

WARNER BROS. Presents

VAL KILMER   TOMMY LEE JONES   JIM CARREY   NICOLE KIDMAN   CHRIS O'DONNELL

A TIM BURTON Production   A JOEL SCHUMACHER Film "BATMAN FOREVER"   MICHAEL GOUGH   PAT HINGLE   Music Composed by ELLIOT GOLDENTHAL

Executive Producers BENJAMIN MELNIKER   MICHAEL USLAN   Based Upon Batman Characters Created by BOB KANE and Published by DC COMICS

Written by LEE BATCHLER & JANET SCOTT BATCHLER and AKIVA GOLDSMAN   Produced by TIM BURTON and PETER MACGREGOR-SCOTT

Directed by JOEL SCHUMACHER

BATMAN™
FOREVER

NOVELIZATION BY PETER DAVID

BASED ON A SCREENPLAY WRITTEN BY
**LEE BATCHLER & JANET SCOTT BATCHLER
AND AKIVA GOLDSMAN**

BATMAN CREATED BY BOB KANE

WARNER BOOKS

A Time Warner Company

WARNER BOOKS EDITION

Copyright © 1995 DC Comics. All Rights Reserved.

Batman and all characters and related indicia are trademarks of DC Comics © 1995. All Rights Reserved.

Cover design by Rachel McClain

Warner Books, Inc.
1271 Avenue of the Americas
New York, NY 10020

Ⓦ A Time Warner Company

Printed in the United States of America

First Printing: June, 1995

10 9 8 7 6 5 4 3 2 1

BATMAN™
FOREVER

THEN . . .

I.

The rain poured down in sheets, with such ferocity and intensity that it didn't seem as if it were originating from the skies. Instead—at least to the young man who was running through it, one arm pumping, the other clasped against his heaving chest—it seemed as if the rain were coming from everywhere at once. From above, below, to the sides . . . everything was a source of violent precipitation, as if all reality itself were in mourning. . . .

He had run from the house, a house that was no longer a home. Something compelled him to turn and look back over his shoulder at it. The ground, however, did not cooperate with the intention, and his feet went out from under him as the mud gave him no traction. It was like ice-skating on dirt.

He tried to catch himself but didn't succeed, and the impact rattled his teeth. He didn't care about it particularly, though. Indeed, it had been a while since he cared about anything.

His suit pants were thick with mud. There was mud under his fingernails, mud in his hair, in his mouth. His feet felt heavy and leaden, filling up with filthy water. For just a moment, like a small winged creature, a thought flitted through his mind:

Dad's going to kill me.

Then he remembered once more how moot that concern

3

was and—for the hundredth time, it seemed, in that day alone—the floodgates in his eyes threatened to burst. But he kept it in, as he had managed to do thus far and had every intention of continuing to do. Previously it had been a matter of willpower. This time, he was so consumed by misery that he had to bite down on his lip to repress it. But he did so, and kept on doing it until the last vestiges of the urge to sob had subsided. He was unaware of the blood trickling down his face from the bite, giving him an appearance similar to that of a vampire from an old horror film. There was a distant stinging in his mouth, but he ignored that. Pain was something that he'd been training himself to disregard. Physical pain, at least. And within moments, the rain had washed the blood away from his face, although the mud had become a bit thicker.

He hauled himself up, turned, and looked back and up at the house. That's all it was now: a house. Not a home. Home, after all, is where the heart is. But the young man's heart was elsewhere: It was scattered in small, bloody ruins on the filth-ridden ground of a place recently dubbed "Crime Alley" after its most recent atrocity. His heart lay intermixed with the blood of two people, pouring from them, darker, much darker than he'd imagined blood to be. There had been warmth coming off it, for it had been a very chill evening. Life had gushed from them with a deep, abiding warmth, the heat rising, wafting away two lives and three souls. Leaving behind two corpses and one living creature that only wished he were dead.

And a leering, chortling monster of a man, glowering down at the boy and saying something that made no sense:

"Tell me, kid . . . have you ever danced with the devil in the pale moonlight?"

The boy had frozen. Not out of fear for himself; that was long gone. No, frozen as he'd sensed the blood of the people cooling in the evening. Frozen as his soul, it seemed, had left him.

Then had come the sirens . . . and the lights . . .

The lights now flickered at him from on high. Lights from the police cars were washed away in his awareness by the illumination from the house. The windows flickered like so many glass eyes, blinking down at him from the cliffside above. Like the eyes of God looking down at him, but not kindly. Not divinely. Not sympathetic to the miserable child, but instead with a sort of cold, distant interest of the type that a scientist might possess. It made him feel like a creature in an experiment. A lab rat. A lab rat flown from the lab.

The rain was coming down harder, which he would not have thought remotely possible. It was getting tougher for him to see. He rubbed his eyes, and only succeeded in smearing more dirt on his face. From the nose up, his face was a solid, dark mask of mud, with two small white orbs peering out through slitted eyelids. He held up an arm to try to ward off the rain, but it was like trying to hold back the Atlantic Ocean with a mop.

His father had told him, sternly and repeatedly, to stay away from the area where he presently trod. It was at the outer edges of the property. The ground was uncertain. Even under the best of weather conditions, the young man could fall and hurt himself. And he'd be so far away from the house that help would not easily find him. "You could break your leg," his father had said and then, with a smile, added, "and, of course, if that happened, we'd have to take you out and shoot you."

His father had never been one for jokes. Oh, he fancied that he had a sense of humor. Everyone thinks they do, particularly those who don't. Still, the remark had been amusing enough that the young man had actually laughed. And because of the rareness of such an occasion, the boy had taken care to attend his father's words.

But his father had no more words.

And the young man had no more father.

Somehow, words of advice as to how to take care of oneself lose their impact when the advisor isn't able to keep himself from being killed. It seemed to undercut the entire premise.

What, indeed, was the point? What was the point of any of it?

In the distance, vaguely over the roar of thunder, the young man thought he heard something. A voice, an anguished voice, calling his name over and over again. But it was far away, and perhaps even his imagination.

Of course, it might be . . . **him.** The family servant who seemed to have outlived the family. But the young man couldn't stand the thought of seeing him right now. He couldn't stand seeing that gentle, sympathetic face, offering a shoulder to cry on, because he would be damned if he'd cry.

What difference did it make? He was damned anyway.

He had no clear idea of what he was going to do, or where he was going to go. He only knew that there were too many ghosts in the mansion. That if he had to deal with one more mourner or high-muck-a-muck or captain of industry or president of some massive conglomerate . . .

One more sad word or pat on the back or "Stiff upper lip, son . . ."

One more quick glance in his direction . . .

One more bit of guilt . . .

One more . . .

No more . . .

There was nothing he wanted to deal with, nothing he wanted to face, nothing he wanted to **do** except to get away, to escape, to hide. Hide from the mourners and the ghosts of his parents. Hide from the things he'd learned. Hide from himself.

The embankment that he scampered down was sharply angled. About a hundred yards off was a precipice which, if he tumbled over it, would send him plunging to the roaring water below. His parents had always loved the view from the mansion on high. His mother, something of a romantic, had likened it to living in an Emily Brontë novel. But the warning for her son to keep away from precisely the area he was now wandering about in had been just as strident as the admonitions of the young man's father. Just as strident, and—at this moment—just as ignored.

The young man skirted the edge, still at a safe distance. Whatever shouting might be coming from the direction of the mansion was now drowned by the roiling surf far away and far below.

That's when there came a crack of thunder that seemed to explode directly over his head. The young man let out a yelp and jumped, and once more his feet went out from under him. But this time he was at a sharper angle than he'd been previously. This time he didn't just fall to the ground. He skidded, trying to slow himself down as he tumbled, the world spinning out around him. He was completely disoriented. He had no clear idea how fast or how far he had gone. He knew only that not too far ahead, the edge of the embankment was waiting for him.

Half of him welcomed the notion.

But another half . . . that which powered his will to live, his need to survive . . . refused to accept that it was all to end in a heels-over-head plummet into icy waters. For a split second the two sides of him warred, and ultimately, it was his determination to live that won out.

That is to say, it won out in the mental argument. The ground, however, which slid away under his grasp, was not cooperating.

The young man's descent toward certain doom was accompanied by an eerie silence. One would have expected a long, terrified scream, but there was nothing. A gasp of surprise, perhaps, but nothing beyond that. He was developing a stoicism that bordered on the superhuman, and were he allowed to live to manhood, there was no telling where such resolve might take him.

At that moment, as if by some meteorological miscue, the clouds parted. The rain did not abate in the slightest, but nevertheless there appeared, pale and unwavering, the moon.

Something fluttered across it.

The ground around the sliding young man was illumined, and he had a brief glimpse of just how close the drop-off was.

It couldn't have been more than twenty feet.

The young man tried to dig his heels in, tried to slow his descent by a few seconds so he could come up with something.

As it happened, it took far less time than that, although it wasn't something for which he could exactly take credit.

All he knew was that, abruptly, he was no longer sliding. Ten feet from a one-way ticket to oblivion, the young man had gotten a reprieve.

Of sorts.

He was no longer hurtling toward certain doom on a cliff-side.

Instead he was sinking to an uncertain doom below.

It was as if the earth had decided to end the suspense and bury him right there and then. Before he fully realized what had happened, the lower half of his body had simply vanished, sucked down into a cascading pit of dirt and muck. His legs pinwheeled, seeking ground like a drowning man hoping that, by some miracle, his feet would touch bottom. But there was nothing. For all the young man knew, and for all his frantic mind might allow him to envision, he was about to plunge into a tunnel that would drop him straight into the center of the earth.

He sank lower, up to his armpits, the dirt covering his head. Even so, his hands clawed at the soft loam, hoping against hope that he might still be able to save himself.

Instead he dropped through the hole and vanished from sight. All that remained on the surface that affirmed his existence was the mournful calling of his name by a British manservant, desperately trying to maintain his reserve but—moment by moment—felt himself giving way to desperation and even despair.

The moon hid behind the clouds once more, waiting.

*   *   *

The young man tumbled, Alice down the rabbit hole, plummeting to that place where a grinning creature solemnly announced, "We're all mad here." Or so, at least, it seemed.

And then he landed.

It was a rather abrupt stop as he thudded to the ground. It seemed to him that he'd been falling forever. But it was hard to tell how much time had actually passed. It might have been barely seconds. He might have fallen six feet or twenty or two hundred. It was impossible to say. He was inside a small cavern an indeterminate distance underground, with no clear idea of how to get out.

Not that he was being given a lot of time to think. Dirt and mud continued to rain down on him. He rolled out of the way and scrambled to his feet, his eyes trying to adjust to the gloom. The cascade of earth continued for a few moments more and then slowly came to a stop.

Moonlight streamed through the hole above him, briefly supplementing his own vision, which was actually fairly acute in darkness—so much so, in fact, that his father had once commented that it almost seemed as if he were born for night.

Thoughts of his father, the doctor, prompted him to do what his dad would have done in this situation: methodically check himself over to make sure there were no broken bones. He flexed his elbows and knees, patted himself down . . .

And then realized that *it* was missing.

It had fallen from him during his plunge. It had to be somewhere in the pile of dirt nearby, beneath the hole. He ran to it, shoved both his hands in deeply. It was all he could do to stifle a sob. Losing his footing, losing his life . . . these were things with which he could cope. But losing *it*, losing that which was his last connection to his parents, was a calamity that threatened to overwhelm him.

He shoved deeper and deeper into the dirt, hot tears mixing with the mud that caked his face. Then, finally, his questing fingers seized on a small, solid object, and he pulled it to himself with a heartfelt gasp of joy. He lay there like that for a moment, sprawled on the dirt, clutching the object that had come to mean so much to him. Then he rolled over onto his back and looked up.

The ceiling was moving.

Not down toward him precisely, but more side to side. As if it were stirring somehow, alerted to his presence.

He squinted upward, trying to make out precisely what would cause such a phenomenon. And then he started to distinguish small, hanging forms, like . . . bananas . . . but that made no sense. Whatever kind of bizarre cave he'd landed in, the concept of tropical fruit growing there seemed fairly unlikely.

At that moment, high above, the moon emerged from behind the clouds once more. Faint streams of light poured through the hole that had been the young man's unexpected entranceway.

Now he was able to make out just what precisely was above him.

Bats.

Hundreds, thousands of them. Hanging, dangling from every crevice, their wings flexing slightly, their eyes glittering.

The young man froze, afraid that the slightest motion might set them off. But even as that concern implanted itself in his mind, he realized that it made no sense. He had plunged squarely into their midst through the most disruptive of means. That alone should have been more than enough to set them off, send them hurtling through the air, filling the cave all around him with the beating of their wings and their high-pitched squealing.

But there was nothing. Beyond the slight stirring of their leathery wings, there was no movement.

Slowly, ever so slowly, the young man eased himself away from them. At one end of the cavern there was an opening outward. He heard a distant dripping and . . . no. More than a dripping. A rushing of water. There was some sort of underground stream nearby, which probably fed directly out to the ocean.

He made his way toward the hole and peered through and down. He couldn't quite make it out fully, but he had an impression of massive scope. A vast cavern below him and, sure enough, far below a stream. But he quickly sensed that there was no easy way down. The wall was too sheer. He'd have to get spelunking equipment, more lights if he wanted to explore this vast area.

You'll have to build stairs . . .

It was as if another voice had spoken within his head. A voice that sounded like his own but colder, deeper, a dispassionate whisper.

The bats began to stir. It was as if they had heard it, too.

Stream's wide enough . . . You could put the boat there . . .

There it was again . . . the voice that chilled him, that sounded so alien and yet so familiar.

Then there was a gentle scraping from below him . . . below . . . as if something was coming up toward him.

He tried to peer down at it, and no, he wasn't imagining it . . . there was something there. Something large, the size of a human, but he knew immediately that it was anything but. It was climbing up the sheer rock wall toward him, small clicking noises coming from the scrape of its claws against the stony surface.

Automatically he backed away from it. Behind him, above him, all around the bats were becoming more and more agitated. It was as if they had made no motion until now because they were waiting for something. For some thing. And that thing, whatever it was, had now arrived.

He retreated further until he stumbled against the mound of dirt. And there he froze as the thing pursuing him climbed up and into the small cavern with him.

He could make out nothing of it, for it seemed clothed in darkness, as if it were pulling shadows from everywhere within the cavern and wrapping them around itself. It stood there for a moment, as if contemplating the young man. And at that moment, the young man wanted nothing but to be as far from this place as possible. To run from it, fly from it, forget that he ever saw it . . .

That's not the way it will be, came the voice once more. He couldn't tell whether the obscured form shambling toward him was the source, or whether it was from within his own head.

"Let me out," said the young man as the thing came nearer, nearer still. It seemed to be limping sightly, as if walking was an alien practice.

Let me in, came the response, and the creature lifted its head to gaze at him. Its eyes were burning red, its ears tall, and it was covered with dark, matted fur. It spread its wings and they just seemed to keep going and going, encompassing the whole of the cavern, leaving no place to run.

The rest of the young man's thoughts were a torrent, and it would not be until years in the future that he would be able to pick out any of the individual notions tumbling through his mind. A bizarre cascade of images, past, present, and future, all leading toward something greater than himself . . . something less sane than himself.

There was fire in the creature's eyes, fire in its heart, a massive bat image that was enveloped in flame, and it surrounded the young man. And finally, finally, after everything he'd been through, the young man did emit a genuine, wholehearted, unstinting shriek of pure undiluted terror. "I'm in Hell!"

You're home. Same thing.

The creature drew the struggling young man to him as the moonlight held steady.

Everywhere now, the bats were shrieking, as if roaring approval . . . or joining in a song of celebration.

And then the young man's struggles ceased, and suddenly the world made sense again.

Bats flew through the light from above, their shadows cavorting against the walls, like some sort of flapping signal to the future. Hundreds, thousands of screeching voices came together in unison.

And with the cries of the leathery creatures providing an ungodly orchestral tone, the young man danced with the devil in the pale moonlight. . . .

EDWARD NYGMA

II.

"Hey, Eddie . . ."

Edward Nygma looked up at the hulking lummox and his snickering cronies who stood nearby. The eighth-grade lad blew air impatiently from between his lips. It was library study hall, and he was working on his fifth crossword puzzle in the last fifteen minutes. Edward had thick brown hair that he was constantly pushing out of his eyes, and an expressive face that didn't seem to be made of flesh so much as rubber. Behind his eyes there was a fiery intelligence that did not suffer fools gladly. "Got something on your mind, Raymond? A thought, maybe? And you're afraid it'll die of boredom?"

"Got a riddle for you."

"A riddle, Raymond?"

"Yeah. That's right. You're always doing puzzles and stuff. A riddle."

Edward glanced around, but there was no teacher anywhere in sight. Typical for this dump. He put the puzzle down and sighed. "Okay. What's the riddle?"

"What has four wheels and flies?"

Edward looked at him pityingly. "A garbage truck," he said.

Raymond's face clouded. "You heard it."

"Just a wild guess. A shot in the dark which, by the way, I wouldn't mind taking at you."

"Is that supposed to be funny?"

"Wanna hear another riddle? It'll go over big, Ray-

"No, this is. Wanna hear a knock knock joke for morons?"

Raymond glanced at the others, who shrugged. "Okay."

"Fine," said Ed. "You start."

"Okay. Knock knock."

Ed propped his chin on his hand and replied, "Who's there?" Then he batted his eyes.

Raymond's mouth opened, and then it closed. "Huh?"

One of Raymond's cronies started to snicker. Raymond looked at him suspiciously. "What? What's so funny?"

"The joke," said the crony. "Well . . . kind of funny."

Raymond still looked utterly befuddled. Knowing that he was already pushing his luck, nevertheless Edward said, "Maybe you'll understand it if you try it."

"Okay," Raymond said gamely. He turned to the kid standing next to him. "Wanna hear a knock knock joke for morons?"

"I'm sure he does, Raymond," Ed said brightly. "Why don't you start?"

"Okay. Knock knock."

"Who's there?" came the reply.

And once again, Raymond stood there.

Ed looked back down at his puzzle and commented, "That's what we love about you, Raymond. Your train of thought is powered by the little engine that couldn't."

He snickered slightly, but his private amusement was cut short by Raymond's rough hand grabbing him by the back of the hair and snapping his head back. Ed gasped.

"How'd you like me to bend you into a question mark, funny guy?"

"Ohhh, I don't think so," Ed grunted.

"I was really tryin' to be nice. The shrink, and the guidance counselor, and the parole officer . . . they all say I should try and be nicer. Talk t'people that I'd just like t'beat the crap outta and be int'rested." His face grew darker. "But it's so much easier to pound . . ."

"Wanna hear another riddle? Legit!" he added when Raymond growled in response. "Really! A famous one! Real old!"

"This better be on the level," Raymond told him.

"It is! I swear!"

"Go on."

"What walks on four legs in the morning, two in the afternoon, and three in the evening?"

Not letting up on the pressure, Raymond nevertheless sounded curious. "I dunno. What?"

"Raymond!"

It was the stern, angry voice of a teacher, heading their way. He wasn't especially tall, but he carried himself with a confidence that seemed to add a foot to his height. He had a newspaper tucked under his arm. He peered up and over his thick glasses at Raymond, who promptly eased up the pressure.

"Hi, Mr. Pike," said Raymond. "Problem?"

Edward was rubbing the back of his neck. "What's the matter?" he asked derisively. "Run out of comfy sofa space in the teachers' lounge?"

"You're not funny, Edward."

"Yes, well," and he glanced up at Raymond, "that seems to be the consensus today."

"We were just talking," said Raymond sullenly.

"Talking doesn't usually require students twisting someone's head in a painful manner."

"Right," Edward said gamely. "Leave that for the teachers."

Impressively, Mr. Pike looked even less amused than before. Edward quickly put up his hands and said, "Right. I know. Not funny."

"What's the answer, Eddie?" said Raymond.

"Go find your own answers, Raymond," said the teacher. "Now."

Raymond seemed to study him with a manner of sullen glare that Pike sensed probably extended back to Neanderthal times. Then Raymond and his pals moved off. Mr.

Pike turned to Edward and said, "I was helping *you,* Edward. A little less smart-mouthing would be in order."

"Yes sir," Edward said in his most contrite voice.

"And you shouldn't be sitting around doing puzzle books. This is the library, for crying out loud. Read one of the books."

"Already have, sir. All of 'em. I have an unquenchable thirst for knowledge."

The comment sounded so pompous that Pike assumed Edward was screwing around again. But then he saw the intensity with which Edward Nygma had spoken, and thought, *Son of a gun means it.* After a moment, he tossed the newspaper down in front of Edward. "Here. Read today's paper yet? *Gotham Globe?*"

"No sir."

Pike nodded once, and then walked away. Edward immediately picked up the paper and started flipping through it. He didn't have to read it. Not immediately, in any event. His mind would snap pictures of each page, to be digested at a convenient time later on.

The paper was in sections. He went through the sports section in a heartbeat, moved to the science section. This he took marginally longer with, but moved rapidly past that and picked up the news section.

And stopped dead at the front page.

The headline was somewhat sordid. THOMAS WAYNE MURDERED. ONLY CHILD SURVIVES. Subheadings above the article read, PROMINENT DOCTOR AND WIFE SLAIN IN ROBBERY. UNIDENTIFIED GUNMAN LEAVES ONLY CHILD UNHARMED.

It was the child who had caught Edward's eye. The boy seemed roughly Edward's age. There was a huge picture of the crime scene plastered all over the front page, and on the right-hand side of the picture, the "Only Child" was staring straight into the camera.

Edward's gaze flicked to the caption, which described the photo's subject as "the grief-stricken Bruce Wayne."

"No," whispered Edward. "No . . . they got it wrong. He's not stricken with anything. Look at that. *Look* at that."

He saw, there in Bruce Wayne's face, an intensity that mirrored his own. An anger, a frustration at the hand that fate had dealt him. There were no tears on Bruce's face. Instead there was a smoldering intelligence that Edward intuitively sensed was on a par with his own.

There was something in Bruce's eyes, something in that gaze. There was Bruce, in a moment of raw emotion, his parents just having been cruelly taken from him. And there was no self-pity. Just cold, hard anger.

It was the sort of anger that Edward himself felt virtually every hour of the day, trapped in public school, imprisoned in classes where he was bored out of his mind because he was light-years ahead of the other kids. But his anger was free-floating, nebulous, indulging itself in games, riddles, and parlor tricks. Bruce Wayne was focussed. Bruce Wayne was not intimidated.

Bruce Wayne, in Edward's snap opinion, was one hell of a guy.

Ed still had the newspaper with him when he was walking home from school. Not that he needed it to read; the contents were safely locked away in his skull, thanks to his photographic memory. But he wanted to clip out the articles and pictures about Bruce Wayne. He found the young man fascinating, as if he had discovered a soul mate of sorts.

They were very different, of course. Wayne, born to the purple, as it were. Rich boy, all the breaks. Best schools. Best education. Best everything.

Edward Nygma was born to a lower–middle-class family. No breaks. Inadequate schools. Least of everything. By all rights, he should have been wildly envious of Wayne's financial and social situation. But the circumstances surrounding Wayne's newly orphaned status placed him, for once, in an unenviable predicament. And the equanimity with which he was reacting to the stress garnered Edward's admiration.

Suddenly the newspaper was yanked out of Edward's

hand. He spun to find himself facing Raymond and one of Raymond's main henchmen, a pasty-skinned fool named Gil.

"What's the answer to the riddle?" demanded Raymond without preamble.

"What, can't you figure it out for your—"

Raymond grabbed him by the front of the shirt. "I was tryin' t'be nice and I still don't like you jerkin' me around. There's no teacher around now. You better tell me."

"Why? So you can tell other people and feel smart?"

"Yeah."

"Awright, awright! The answer is . . . man."

"Man?" said Raymond in confusion.

"Yeah. In the morning of his life, man crawls on all fours. In the afternoon of his life, man walks on two legs. And in the evening of his life, he walks on two legs, with a cane for his third leg. It's the riddle of the Sphinx."

"It's stupid," Raymond said.

"It's not stupid."

"Yes it is. What's babies and old man have to do with days?"

With tremendous frustration, Edward said, "It's a metaphor! It's—"

"I don't care what it's for. It's stupid!" Raymond said more emphatically, and he threw Edward down with tremendous force.

Edward's skull struck the curb with a sickening crack. He lay there, unmoving, but his eyes stared skyward in disjointed confusion.

"Get up!" shouted Raymond. "Get up, ya wimp! Ya stupid . . ."

"Oh God," Gil said. "Raymond . . . look . . ."

Blood began to trickle out of the side of Edward's mouth. Edward still didn't move, didn't make the slightest effort to wipe it away.

"I think you killed him," whispered Gil.

Raymond looked down in confusion. "No I didn't. Lookit him. His eyes are open. He's faking."

"He's faking *bleeding?*" Gil pulled at Raymond's sleeve. "C'mon. Let's go. I mean it, let's go."

Raymond paused in confusion and then, with a final defiant bit of anger, he tossed the newspaper down next to Edward.

Edward, from a place very far away, heard the pounding of their feet as they ran off. But they seemed almost incidental to him. Two creatures of little to no consequence.

He turned his head slightly to see the newspaper on the sidewalk next to him. The picture of Bruce Wayne stared back at him. Blood oozed, turning the picture into a dark, red splotch.

Why had this happened to him?

Why had the world put both himself and Bruce into such untenable positions?

Why were brutes in charge of things?

How could he improve his personal situation?

When would matters improve?

Who was he? Who was . . . anybody? And why . . . why had he not seen things clearly before?

Suddenly everything made perfect sense.

Suddenly his life's mission stretched out before him, his ambitions clear. He was bleeding, and might be very sick, or perhaps even about to die. But none of that altered the fact that everything made perfect sense.

Questions filled his mind . . . and he had all the answers. . . .

III.

Harvey Dent, district attorney to Gotham City, stood on the flat roof, looking out over the array of similar buildings that spread out before him like an ocean made of tar paper.

It was a low rent section of Gotham, a housing project funded by the Wayne Foundation some years back. As the night air cut through Dent's overcoat, he pulled it more tightly around him. The moon had risen, and he looked at his long shadow, cast against a nearby roof door, his coat flapping around his calves. Not too far above, the North Shore expressway was rather devoid of cars. Not surprising, considering it was the middle of the night.

Dent was fairly tall, squareshouldered, and solidly built. His face was craggy, his black hair shortly cropped and graying slightly at the temples. His thin lips were pursed and he licked them briskly as the cold air dried them out.

He found his thoughts wandering to the first occasion he'd had to meet Bruce Wayne, the head of the Wayne Foundation.

Wayne had seemed a nice enough guy. A little distracted at times, as if his mind were a million miles away. Harvey Dent had been part of a city council project seeking funding for the project, and Dent—along with several other politicos—had had a lunch with Wayne to discuss it. Wayne had arrived forty-five minutes late, and hadn't even apologized, apparently uncaring or simply unaware of his tardiness. Dent had done much of the talking and, as he had done so, found himself fascinated by Wayne's steady gaze. It seemed as if Wayne had been looking straight through him, to a point at the far end of the room.

"We don't want people to have to live in fear of crime . . . in fear of their lives," Dent had said. It had been that comment that seemed to rivet Wayne's attention, for Wayne's scrutiny had swung back to Dent at that moment, focussing on him and—Dent felt—dissecting him.

"You really care about people, don't you?" Wayne said.

"No two ways about it," replied Dent.

"Tell me more," Wayne had said, as if truly paying attention for the first time. Not that that was necessarily the turning point in the conversation. For all Dent knew, Wayne had intended to contribute to the project all along.

What Dent had not been expecting was the amount of Wayne's contribution. A dozen donors had garnered the group about half the money required to accomplish the project. To Dent's astonishment, Wayne had single-handedly kicked in the other half.

Now, though, as Dent stood on the roof, he wondered if his promise had been all that sincere. Crime hadn't seemed to take all that much of a downturn. In fact, if anything else, it had become . . . well . . . stranger.

Indeed, that was part of the reason that he was here tonight.

He looked out again across the rooftops. He could easily understand why his . . . caller . . . wanted to meet here. Surprise was impossible. No way, on this flat terrain, could any cops be hiding, or any sort of trap sprung. It would be seen coming a mile away. . . .

Dent's shadow moved, but Dent didn't.

Harvey had caught it out of the corner of his eye, and his head snapped around to catch sight of the silhouette moving out of Dent's shadow. The figure stood to its full height, the scalloped cape flaring out, dark eyes invisible behind the mask and pointed-eared cowl.

They stood there for a long moment, taking the measure of one another.

"I could gasp *'Batman!'* if it will make you feel more impressive."

He got no response. He cocked his head slightly and continued, "I suppose telling a vigilante such as you that you're under arrest would be a waste of time."

When the caped figure spoke, it was in a low voice, just above a whisper. Dent doubted it was his normal speaking voice. It was impossible to determine whether he did it for disguise or effect.

"That's correct," was all he said.

Dent started towards him. Batman made no attempt to step backward. Harvey took a few steps, and then stopped. "As an officer of the court, I must advise you to report to the nearest police station and submit yourself to arrest."

Batman studied him a moment. "If you're referring to that business with the Penguin, his gang can tell you everything you need to know."

"Well, they've disappeared," replied Dent. "We're looking for them, but—"

As if Dent hadn't spoken, Batman continued, "They're holed up in a warehouse at 73rd and Grand. There's a secret room through a revolving wall on the northwest side." There was a slight glitter from his nearly invisible eyes. "I'm presuming you can get the truth out of them."

"If you knew where they are, why didn't *you* go get them?"

"Are you advocating vigilantism?" There was just the briefest flash of a smile, and then his face grew serious again. "I wanted you to be able to take credit for the arrest. And I wanted to show you I'm capable of working with the authorities. Gordon knows this already. You don't seem to."

Dent stared at him, puzzled. "Why do you care what I think?"

He didn't reply immediately. And then he said, "The local polls place you fairly low in public opinion. You're not planning to run again for D.A., are you?" He had a habit of phrasing things as questions, but they came out as flat statements.

"I'm strongly considering not doing so, yes," said Dent. "I feel as if I haven't been able to keep the promises I made to the people of this city. Plus I have a fiancée . . . we're talking about starting a family . . . with all that, yes, I've been thinking about returning to private practice. Sometimes you dream about doing something, but once you're out there doing it, it doesn't seem to accomplish your goals."

"I know," said Batman, in a tone of voice that immediately caught Dent's attention. But it was as if the dark figure had inadvertently let something slip . . . something closer to him than he'd have liked to admit. Immediately the shadows seemed to enfold him, even though he didn't move an inch. He paused and then said, "I think you're selling yourself short. You could be the best D.A. this city has ever known. I can be of help to you. My investigations can give you leads, point you in the right direction. We have the same goal, you and I. We're just two sides of it."

"Two sides," echoed Dent. "Let me get this straight. I'm thinking about getting out of this rat race, and you want me to stick my neck out further?"

"Yes," Batman confirmed. "But I won't let anyone chop it off."

"You'll protect me, you're saying, from any dire consequences of your 'investigations'?"

"As much as is humanly possible."

Dent sighed. "I'll check out this lead. *If* it pans out, and *if* it results in the arrest of the gang, and *if* they can be 'convinced' to give us an account that vindicates you, and *if* I don't come to my senses, then *maybe* we can come to some sort of accord. But that's a lot of ifs, maybes, and what-have-yous to stake your mask to."

"It's good enough for now," said Batman. Then, without even seeming to move his feet, he drifted backward and melted into the shadows.

"Hey!" shouted Harvey Dent. "Why are you working so hard to convince me to stay in office, eh?"

"Because together we can be more effective in putting crooks behind bars," floated back a voice from the darkness. "And because . . . I care." And then there was a brief rustling that could have been a cape, or perhaps it was massive wings . . .

. . . and he was gone.

. . . Now . . .

Then she thought she saw something—a quick flash—c

CHAPTER 1

Doctor Chase Meridian firmly believed that all the stories about how dangerous (make that Dangerous) Gotham City was were just that: stories. This wasn't the wild West, after all, a place where rules were bent, broken and tossed out the window, where anyone could do whatever they wanted, and all citizens were on their own.

As Dr. Meridian walked briskly down the street during a busy lunch hour, she felt the pulse of humanity around her. It was a cool October day, and clouds were rolling in. There had been light drizzle on and off, and one would think that such weather would somehow make the city feel washed clean. No. It just made the dirt shiny. And with the sky darkening, the rest of the afternoon didn't look much more promising.

Still, enveloped as she was by walls of moving life on all sides, Dr. Meridian had her thesis reinforced for her. This was a city, a bustling metropolis. Gotham City, not Dodge City.

Nevertheless, she found the mind-set endlessly intriguing. Here was a place where people lived and worked, hoped and dreamed, and tried to deal with the fear that pervaded every moment of their existence. Some hid from it. Some fought it. And some . . .

Some hid and fought back, all at the same time.

Then she thought she saw something. A quick rustling of a

cape, maybe, high above on a ledge, yet hidden in the shadows.

She stopped, looked up . . . and saw not Batman, but a small flock of pigeons arc skyward. Her imagination working overtime.

What Dr. Meridian had forgotten, in her brief distraction, was that in the crowded bustling of the city, people take on the aspects of sharks. That is, they have to keep moving or they're dead. The moment she stopped moving, the good doctor became an immediate target.

A man in a hurry to an illicit affair bumped into her, staggering her slightly. "Excuse *me*," she muttered to deaf ears, before being bumped in the other direction by a woman running to catch a bus. Dr. Meridian tried to regain her balance and equilibrium, and it was at her most distracted that she was the most vulnerable.

The purse snatcher seemed to appear from nowhere. Before Dr. Meridian even knew what was happening, he had snagged her brand-new leather Gucci bag and was hightailing it on foot. His long, unwashed hair streamed out behind him, his dirty watch cap pulled down low over his face. Clutching the bag tightly under his arm as if he were charging down the field for a touchdown, the thief barreled down the sidewalk. He slipped in and out of spaces in the flow of humanity with a skill born of long practice.

"*Stop him!*" shouted Chase Meridian. People looked around in confusion, not sure who was shouting, where the shout was coming from, or whom the plea for intervention applied to. The thief was so slick that, even as a flustered pedestrian became aware of his presence, he was already gone.

Chase started after him, but she was wearing a fairly tight skirt that came down to her knees, not to mention high heels. Neither was conducive to speedy pursuit. She made a game try, but after half a block she stumbled. Her right heel snapped off with a sound like a rifle shot and it was nothing short of miraculous that she didn't break her ankle. She kicked off her shoes, snatched them up, and continued the pursuit in her stocking feet. But it was more out of a sense of wounded pride than any hope of accomplishing anything. She knew there was no way in hell she was going to catch the little cretin.

The thief saw a break in the crowd. His victim's cries were echoing behind him, but becoming fainter by the moment as he put more distance between the two of them. And now he was going to be home free.

He darted around a hot dog cart, around a derelict, and now there was no one between him and the entrance to a subway station. This was his particularly favorite station, since there were four different passages to assorted trains waiting at the bottom of the stairs.

The woman had been well dressed and definitely grade-A prime. Probably had a ton of cash, and every major credit card. He'd easily be able to get in some early Christmas shopping before she managed to cancel all the cards.

"Stop him!" came the voice again, and he glanced behind himself to make sure that no one was after him.

As a result, he didn't see the obstruction until it was too late. Then again, even if he'd been watching, there was a good chance he wouldn't have seen it because the figure was a blur.

There was a parked car next to a lamppost. At the exact moment that the thief's attention was diverted, a slim, muscular youth darted across the roof of the car. He grabbed the lamppost and, using it as his axis while never slowing down, he swung his legs around and slammed his feet squarely into the thief's head.

The thief wasn't entirely clear on what had just happened. One moment his way was clear, and the next he was on the ground, with blood pouring from his nose. He looked around in confusion and then saw his attacker: a sawed-off runt with dark hair and a smug expression. He was clutching the purse tightly to his chest.

"Ya little creep!" shouted the thief as he got quickly to his feet. The boy didn't back down, but instead glared at him with the air of one who was either supremely brave or remarkably stupid.

"Stop him!" came a female voice from behind.

And from off to the left came another voice, male, deep, and alarmed, shouting, *"Richard!"*

Angry and upset people converging on him was enough of a cue for the thief to realize that this little endeavor was finished. With a low growl directed at the interfering boy, he darted around the youth while at the same time trying to impede the flow of blood from his nose. The boy took a step to block his flight, but apparently realized after a moment that he'd be pressing his luck. So he froze as the thief reached the subway station and safety. He flipped the boy an obscene gesture. The kid stuck his tongue, out in return.

"There he goes!" came a woman's shout, as the thief vanished down the stairs to the subway.

The teen turned in the direction of the cry and held up the purse. "S'okay!" he called. "I got it back!" His mouth continued to hang open as the woman emerged from the crowd into view. She was attractive, extremely shapely, with a rounded face, lovely blonde hair, and an air of total dishevelment because of her run that he found very fetching. "Calm down. Here you go," he said.

From another direction came a tall, muscular man who bore a striking resemblance to the young man. The man saw the boy, the woman saw the purse, and both of them said, "Oh, thank God!" at the same time.

"Is this your son?" she asked.

"Yes, it is."

"He's very brave, Mr. . . . ."

"Grayson. I'm John. This is Richard."

"Mr. Grayson. I'm Dr. Chase Meridian. Richard . . . you've earned a reward."

"Great!" said Richard, already envisioning the largesse that a wealthy doctor might be capable of.

But his father immediately said, "No, that's . . . quite all right, Doctor. The benefit should be in the act itself. Isn't that right, Richard?"

He had a firm hand on his son's shoulder, and it squeezed ever so gently . . . and ever so ungently. "Absolutely, Dad," said Richard through gritted teeth.

"Are you sure?" asked Dr. Meridian.

"I guess we are," said Richard. "I just . . . did it for the thrill of the action. And because it was the right thing to do."

If Dr. Meridian picked up on the sarcasm, she didn't give any indication of it. Instead her interest seemed piqued. "You know," she said thoughtfully, "I'm doing some studies of people who think exactly along those lines. Would you . . . I hate to ask, you've done so much . . . would you be interested in spending some time the next few weeks in a series of visits . . . ?"

John Grayson didn't appear to understand at first, but then he caught on. "You're a psychiatrist," he said.

"That's right."

"Well, Doctor," and he glanced down at his son, "I admit my son's actions might seem a little crazy . . ."

"Oh no!" said Chase quickly. "I never implied, or even thought that. It's just that I have this study about—"

"It doesn't matter," said John. "We're not in town all that long. Just passing through. And, as a matter of fact, we're late for an appointment. I'm glad we were able to help you out. Good luck to you," and with that he trundled Richard away as quickly as he could. Chase watched them go and scratched her chin thoughtfully.

"I wonder what that was about," she said. Then she shrugged, slipped her shoes back on, and hobbled off to try to find a shoemaker.

"Were you out of your mind?" demanded John.

"I dunno," said Richard, as they walked briskly down the street. "There was a shrink there. You could've asked her.

And why'd you tear us outta there so fast? She was pretty nice to look at. What was the hurry?"

John slowed up and sighed. They were walking along the edge of Gotham Park, and John dropped down onto a bench. "Because I've run into people like that from time to time," said John Grayson. "And the moment they find out we're trapeze artists, they want to start getting into our heads. Get into the entire 'Cheating death' business. I don't need the aggravation, and neither do you. And you," he said firmly, "you're the major issue under discussion. Jumping into the middle of a crime situation. That *was* crazy."

"He could have gotten away with the purse."

"He could have pulled a gun! Did you think of that?"

Dick grinned lopsidedly, not looking especially disturbed. "But we're in the 'cheating death business.' You said so yourself. We always have been."

"Richard," said his father, taking him firmly by the arms, "there's an element of truth to that. But we do everything we can to minimize the risk. What you did *maximized* it. Risking death is one thing, but staring it straight in the face and saying 'Take your best shot' is something else again."

"And that's what I did, huh?"

"Yes. That's what you did."

"But what about that time with Chris? Remember?"

"Yes," sighed John.

"You told me how brave I was! When the wire broke—"

"Yes, yes, I know, Richard. And it was brave. And it was very likely even more dangerous than what you just did. But your brother's life was at stake. Laying it on the line when it's life or death is not remotely the same as taking chances to save somebody's handbag. The stakes are different."

"The stakes are different, but the idea is the same: helping people."

"It's degrees, Richard. It's . . ." Then he shook his head. With a gruff sigh, and ruffled his son's hair. "Just don't do it again, okay? If you go and get yourself killed, your mother and I would have to go and make another baby to be in the act . . . wait for him to grow up . . . the whole business would just take for*e*ver. So be careful, okay?"

"Sure, Dad," said Dick, grin still firmly in place.

There was a distant rumble of thunder and John looked up in concern. "Come on," he said. "Let's pick up those costume items your mom wanted and get back to the circus. I think a storm's rolling in and, from the look of it . . . it's going to be a rough one."

CHAPTER 2

The crack of lightning momentarily drowned out the screams from within Arkham Asylum. But barely had the thunder rumbled away before the shrieks could be heard once more, unabated.

Arkham had a long and impressive history. Of course, so did war, pestilence, famine, and death. The mere existence of that tradition was not enough to instill confidence.

Arkham, named for its founder, was a dark and terrifying place. It had not always been that way. Once, in the dim past, it had merely been a dark and fearsome place. Time had a way of taking the various psychoses and illnesses that infested the human mind and upping the stakes.

To the normal asylums and institutions were consigned those who were merely a danger to themselves. To the abnormal asylums and institutions went those who were a danger to themselves and to society.

It was said that Arkham got those who were a danger to God.

This was an exaggeration, of course.

But not by much.

Arkham sat behind a massive fence with the Asylum's name etched in great twisted metal letters over the gate. The building itself didn't sit on the hill so much as squat there, like a great spider positioned and waiting for prey. The storm that had been threatening the area for some days had finally arrived, and it seemed as if it had settled directly over the gothically styled building. This wasn't unusual. Arkham always appeared to be a sort of lightning rod for every disruption and abomination that nature could possibly conceive of hurling at humanity.

The building was filled with people who were desperate, on edge, over the edge.

And that was just the staff. . . .

The orderly's name was Richter, and Richter was in deep, deep trouble.

He slowly pushed along a cleanup cart, looking nervously right and left. His bald head was thick with sweat. His legs felt rubbery, and he was leaning on the cart as much to stand as to push the cart along.

Despite the thunder and lightning, the screams and the flickering lights, the overall stench of disinfectant and fear . . . despite all that, Richter's mind was nevertheless on anything but his job. He was dwelling on the people to whom he owed money. A lot of money. More money than he would see this month, or even this year.

If only the damned horse had paid off. It should have. Why should Richter be held responsible for the stupid horse's leg breaking in the middle of the race? It wasn't fair. . . .

And then there was that lousy run of luck at the card game. How could he have been expected to know that the other guy could beat an ace-high straight? It wasn't his fault . . .

And that night playing craps . . . he'd been on a roll. The money had been flowing and he'd had a hot hand, that rare feeling when you touch the dice and they're yours to command. By all rights, he should have been able to recoup all his losses and more, pay off the loan sharks, buy the wife that coat she'd been wanting, maybe even get enough in the bank that he could quit and survive for a year or more while looking for a good job, a decent job.

He couldn't have known that the hot hand would evaporate, just like that, leaving him cold bones and even deeper in debt. How could he have anticipated it? Just like that, just like that. It wasn't his fault.

He rolled past the guard at the maximum security point, the wheels on the cart squeaking. The guard, whose name was Irvin, nodded slightly. Richter returned the nod and continued on his way.

He went past cell after call. He was no longer looking around. Instead his focus was utterly on the door that was up and to the right.

Room 22.

He stopped there, waiting for someone to say, "Hey! What're you doing!" But no one did. He drummed his fingers for a moment on the cart.

Next to the door was a keypad. The combinations were changed electronically and automatically every day. But Richter had managed to sneak into the head office and pick up that day's combo. He punched in the numbers and heard a soft click. The electronic lock had unlatched. He took a deep breath, and then eased the door open, pulling the cart in behind him.

There was a single stream of light in the cell, coming from a barred window overhead—nowhere near enough to illuminate the entire cell, even as small as it was. Nevertheless, the single occupant of the cell was partly visible. His legs were casually crossed, and Richter could hear something whirring through the air rhythmically. Something small and metallic, tossed in the air and then landing in the occupant's hand.

"M . . . Mister Dent," said Richter. "I'm . . . it's me. Richter."

"We know it's you," came the voice of the man Richter called Dent. He was only distantly related to the Harvey Dent who had met with Batman on the rooftops all that time ago; nominally, they shared a body. But that was all. The mind was something else again.

"I brought what you asked for." He stopped and fidgeted. "You probably want to see it, don't you?"

No sound, save for that up and down of the metallic object.

Richter reached down into the cleaning cart, to the hidden compartment he'd rigged up. He pulled out a pair of goggles and an acetylene torch. "Cut through the bars in no time."

"Put them down where we can see them," said Dent.

Richter stepped forward and did so. Then he paused and said, "You . . . you remember the deal."

"We remember it."

"The money . . . the money you promised me . . . half a million, if I helped you escape . . . you . . . you do have the money . . . ?"

There was a two-second silence.

"You read the newspaper stories, just like everyone else," came Dent's voice. "You know we have two million stashed away. Half a mill of it is yours . . . unless, of course . . ."

"Unless what?"

Another two-second pause, and then something was thrust into the light.

It was a coin. It was a special commemorative coin, issued to celebrate the 100th anniversary of "Lady Gotham," a statue situated in Gotham Harbor. Lady Gotham was depicted in profile on both sides. The coin gleamed in the shaft of light and then, with remarkable dexterity, he turned the coin to reveal the other side. Richter then saw that—whereas Lady Gotham had been pristine on one side—on this other side her head had been disfigured, slashes made through it.

"Would you be interested in . . . double or nothing?" came Dent's calm voice. "A flip of the coin decides."

Richter's immediate impulse was to say "No." No, not just say it. Shout it. Scream it. Scream, "Are you insane? I'm risking my career, my freedom, violating trust, breaking the law . . . and you're asking if I want to chance winding up having nothing to show for it except an empty cell, a mountain of debts, and some guys who would rip my insides out just for kicks, much less for the amount of money I owe them?"

All of that very correct, very understandable response, rattled around in his head. But during that time, the twinkle of the coin sparkled in his eyes.

A million bucks . . .

(It's crazy.)

But a million bucks . . .

(You've been hanging around in this nuthouse too long.)

The gambling instincts pounded through him, thudded in his temples until it was all he could hear. A half a million dollars would put him in the clear, sure . . . but a million . . . he'd be set for life . . . forever. Not only could he clear off his debts, but then he and the wife could blow town, go to some small island in the Bahamas or something, live like a king and queen on what was left over.

For years . . . for so many years, she'd considered him a loser, a nowhere bum with dream but no drive. Wouldn't the expression on her face be worth the risk?

Hell, for that matter . . . the Bahamas beckoned him, and she didn't necessarily have to be part of the equation. Wouldn't *that* be worth the risk?

The night erupted in light and sound, and the coin looked like a hellish ember.

"Well?" said Dent. "Decision time, Richter. Time is money."

"All right . . . you're on."

Barely were the words out of his mouth before the coin was airborne, flashing in the light. "Call it," said Dent.

He thought of the grotesque, scarred head. "Clean side," he decided.

The coin seemed to hang in midair, alternatingly beautiful and frightening. Then it spiralled to the floor and landed. It spun for a moment. Richter stepped closer to see for himself what the result was.

It hesitated, carried by its momentum, and then settled. Richter stared down at it.

Scarred side up.

"Too bad," said Dent.

There was a sudden, swift movement that Richter barely even had time to register. Then he felt a sharp pinch at his throat, and a warmth trickling down it. Automatically he put his hand to the source of the warmth, and came away with a hand coated with his own blood.

"Would you like your palm read?" asked Dent. "Oh . . . too late. It's red already."

Richter went to his knees. His already-blurring eyes managed to make out what Dent was now holding in his other hand: A double-edged razor blade. His mouth moved, forming the word, "Why?" but his vocal cords were traumatized and he couldn't produce the sound.

Nevertheless, Dent was able to make it out. "Why?" he said, sounding genuinely puzzled. "You're asking why? But . . . isn't that obvious? It was double or nothing. Nothing means no money . . . no life . . . nothing. Null. Void. Two times zero . . . is zero."

Richter's final thought was, *I . . . I didn't know . . . it's not my fault . . . it's not fair . . .* and then he crashed to the floor, the last sound he would ever be responsible for making. Without bothering to glance at him, Dent—still hidden by shadows—stepped over him and picked up the acetylene torch. As he placed the goggles over his face and fired up the torch, he said to the man who could no longer hear him, "This has been a productive evening, Richter. Thanks to you, we not only escape . . . but we save half a million dollars. We're doubly grateful."

He fired up the torch, pushing back the darkness.

The right side of his face was much as it had been back when he had had his meeting with Batman.

The left side of his face looked like a relief map of purgatory . . . except, in this purgatory, there would never be any redemption or forgiveness.

There would just be more, and greater, insanity.

*   *   *

Dr. Burton, the chief psychiatrist of Arkham Asylum, was not particularly looking forward to this session. Meetings with Harvey Dent were not only an exercise in futility, but self-control as well. Staring into that face, that . . . face . . . was a test of Burton's ability to maintain his own grip on sanity.

He walked the old hallway, glancing around and making mental note of places where plaster was falling, where cracks were forming. They needed money to maintain the place, but the city budget was cut to the bone and it was difficult to get private donations. Arkham Asylum wasn't one of the "sexier" places where people could contribute.

He stopped at the entrance to the maximum security wing and flashed a high sign to Irvin. The guard returned the gesture, and then was almost deafened by a thunderclap overhead. Dr. Burton was somewhat less thrown. He, instead, was counting, as he had been much of the night. The rain had concentrated on Arkham, but the lightning had still been some distance away. Just like his father had taught him when he was little, Burton had been counting off the seconds between the flash of light and the thunder.

It had drawn closer and closer, the count going from ten to five in a dazzlingly short period of time.

"Hell of a night, huh, Doc?"

Burton chucked a thumb and said, "Hell's in here."

Irvin nodded in silent agreement. "Want backup, Doc?"

Burton considered it a moment. Then he nodded. Irvin promptly informed the central guard post, via his walkie-talkie, that he was accompanying Burton. Within twenty seconds a replacement would be there, the exit covered. Irvin's full concentration would be on making sure that Harvey Dent didn't try any funny stuff.

Burton approached Dent's cell, which was securely closed, as always. He punched in the release code and then gently pushed the door open. "Mr. Dent . . ." he called, feeling some degree of comfort about Irvin's presence directly behind him.

He saw Dent's shadowed form seated in a chair. He garnered some relief from that. If Dent was visible, it meant he couldn't spring out from hiding.

"Counselor . . ."

No answer. Burton was now completely in the cell, and he stepped toward the unmoving figure, cautious and even a little worried. "Harvey . . ."

Lightning flashed as the body slumped over. It was Richter. The front of his uniform was covered with dried blood.

As if on cue, the inmates in surrounding cells began shrieking. A hideous cacophony of laughter, howling, and demented cackling filled the air.

Irvin was already on the walkie-talkie, but Burton didn't hear his voice. Instead he looked up . . . up to the grating that had been burned through, iron supports twisted and open.

Lightning came and, reflexively, Burton counted in his head. The thunder rumbled two seconds later, and from the fading light, Burton was able to see something scrawled on the wall. Then it vanished. He moved toward it, his mind still numb.

Lightning and thunder crashed together, and there were the words in blood—Richter's blood—etched on the wall.

THE BAT MUST DIE

This time, when the inmates screamed, Burton's voice was raised in chorus with them.

CHAPTER 3

More and more, Bruce Wayne had been harder to see during the day.

His business associates and employees knew that seeing him in the morning was problematic. Early afternoon the odds rose to about fifty-fifty, and by late afternoon one was far more assured of catching his ear.

Consequently, there had been a subtle shift of hours at the Wayne Foundation. There was no company policy or official memo, but . . . slowly but surely . . . it became acceptable to arrive late and stay late. Wasn't that bad a deal, really; it was a nice way to avoid rush hour traffic.

Although when it came to beating traffic, it was hard to top the resources at Bruce Wayne's disposal.

The granite-and-glass towers of the Gotham City skyline shimmered in the autumn sun, hanging low in the western sky. The helicopter sliced through the air smoothly, the pilot being extremely reluctant to jostle his passenger. It was, after all, his boss. His boss, and the boss of a couple thousand other employees.

"You okay back there, Mr. Wayne?" he called, just to make sure.

"No problem, Rudy," Wayne replied.

His voice was pleasant, as indeed was his entire demeanor. His thick brown hair was neatly coiffed, his square-jawed face annoyingly flawless (annoying to "mere mortals," as one newspaper gossip columnist was fond of observing). His suit was Savile Row, dark pinstripe, tailored and perfectly pressed.

And his attention was not remotely on the pilot's query, or the quality of the helicopter ride. Instead, his concentration was squarely on the video screen situated directly in front of him.

There was a photo of Harvey Dent . . . Dent as he had been, a lifetime ago, illuminating the upper right-hand side of the screen. And the newscaster, appropriately grim, was saying, "And in Gotham City last night, ex–District Attorney Harvey Dent escaped from Arkham Asylum for the Criminally Insane. Dent, once Gotham's leading contender for mayor, was horribly scarred by underworld kingpin Boss Maroni during an indictment hearing. Dent, whose resulting left-brain damage transformed him into a violent criminal, launched a grisly crime spree before being captured by the Batman. Reported to have sworn revenge on the Dark Knight, he is extremely dangerous. Repeat . . ."

Words.

Just words. Words that covered the surface aspect of the situation, but didn't begin to approach the depth of what had happened. Didn't come close to the core of guilt that Wayne carried with him to this day.

It was one of those moments where he had done everything right . . . and it had still gone horribly wrong.

There he'd been at the indictment, seated some rows back, in disguise (since he didn't want the high-profile Bruce Wayne to be a presence at criminal proceedings. He always preferred to err on the side of overcaution).

The collaring of Maroni had been the latest success in the private little arrangement between Batman and Harvey Dent. The improvement in Batman's ability to operate had been fairly immediate. Commissioner Gordon had been a long-time supporter of the Batman and his "questionable" activities. But the mayor and the city council were far more political animals, and were concerned about how the Dark Knight's shadow cast itself over Gotham.

It had been Harvey Dent who had swung the balance of public opinion (not to mention behind-closed-doors and smoke-filled-room opinion) toward Batman. Dent had been the first to go on record that Batman apparently had been framed by Oswald Chesterfield Cobblepot, dubbed "The Penguin" by the same media that had crucified Batman until Dent spoke out on his behalf. And Batman, in turn, had saved Dent when the D.A. came up against the demented villain known as "Poison Ivy."

With all of that, with all that history, there had developed a bond and trust between the two. And so, on the bigger trials, Bruce felt a need to be present, even if Harvey was unaware of it. It felt . . . right . . . somehow.

A hundred, a thousand times since then, Bruce Wayne's mind had replayed that moment. It had seemed to stretch out into infinity. Boss Maroni stepping out of the witness box, a substantially changed man from when he'd first stepped into it. He had been swaggering and confident when Harvey Dent first started questioning him. Harvey's courtly, gentlemanly demeanor could be very disarming if one wasn't prepared, and the overly assured Maroni was as far from prepared as one could get. His lawyers had warned him, but he hadn't listened.

But as Harvey Dent had slowly and methodically torn him to shreds, watching Maroni had been like watching a deflating balloon become smaller and shriveled and pathetic. By the time Dent had finished with him, it had seemed like there was nothing left.

There had been, though. There had been the desperate act of an infuriated man. It was as if somehow Maroni had had a premonition of how things might, in some unimaginable reality, go. And he had decided before setting foot in the courtroom that if he did go down in flames, there would be some final, furious act of defiance. No one, but no one, was going to get away with embarrassing and humiliating Boss Maroni.

"Hey! Dent! Cross-examine *this!*" he'd shouted, standing in the witness box. His hand had dipped into his pocket and he had yanked out a small vial. His throw had been smooth and flawless.

If Harvey had just stepped back . . .

. . . or ducked . . .

. . . or *anything,* then the vial would have wound up as glass shards, its contents bubbling away viciously but harmlessly on the courtroom floor. It would have been a simple charge of "attempted assault" tacked onto the lengthy criminal indictments already facing him, and that would have been that.

But he stood bolt still, surprised, a deer in the headlights, as the vial's contents splashed all over the left side of his face.

There were certain sounds that Bruce Wayne would always carry with him. Sounds like his parents' screams, or the tinkling of his mother's broken pearl necklace falling to the ground.

The flapping of wings and the screech of bats, although somehow the memories of the circumstances themselves were somewhat blurred.

The crack of Catwoman's whip.

A couple of other sounds . . . and now this. This hideous, unspeakable moment, and he would never forget the sound of the acid bubbling and burning and eating away at Harvey's face. Harvey's scream was almost secondary, as had been the panicked cries of other people in the courtroom. He'd heard screams before, and certainly enough sounds of a confused and shouting mob. But he'd never, before or since, heard the sound of flesh just being *eaten* away.

That night he'd come to the hospital as Batman. It seemed to him that Harvey was beyond pain. Instead Harvey was looking up at him with his one good eye, and there was something in there . . . a look of hate and betrayal and anger. . . .

Batman knew that look all too well. It was the look on his

face every night when he slid the mask down that covered his features.

It was disturbing to see it turned back at him. Disturbing and something that boded ill for the future.

"Nice protection," was all Harvey said, and then turned away. He said nothing more.

The next time Batman would see him would be weeks later, after Harvey's devastating crime spree with his new *nom de guerre* of "Two-Face." There was Batman, Dent's former ally, now his pursuer and, eventually, captor. "We made it that much easier for you to operate in this town," Two-Face had growled, "And now you leave us . . . double-crossed. We will not forget that. Not ever. *Not ever.*"

Bruce Wayne was jostled from his thoughts by a slight dip in the helicopter's angle. He looked out the right window and saw the glowing sign that topped the towering headquarters of Wayne Enterprises.

"There's home," he murmured.

"Home?" said the pilot. "With a mansion like you got, Mr. Wayne, you think of an office building as home?"

"Actually, I guess not, Rudy," said Wayne after a moment's thought.

"I'm not surprised. Actually, with all the houses you got across the world, and offices and stuff . . . guess it's hard to imagine *where* you'd actually consider home."

An image fluttered across Bruce's mind, of a dark cave and a black costume.

"Very hard to imagine," he agreed.

"Isn't it incredible!" Edward Nygma said for what seemed the three hundredth time that day, leaning out of his cubicle and addressing a passing coworker. The coworker, who'd been the recipient of this particular piece of enthusiasm a mere twenty times since 10:00 A.M. barely nodded before walking quickly past.

"Bruce Wayne! Here!" continued Edward as if his co-worker was still around, hanging on his every word. He retreated back into his cubicle, which was a clutter of computer parts and scattered paper. And whatever space was left over was occupied by puzzles: Rubik's cubes, assorted games, dozens of puzzle books published by an outfit who had a green-suited sort of "mascot" called "The Guesser" on all their publications. The Guesser was always poised with his finger pointed at the reader, demanding, "Have you got what it takes?"

Edward Nygma always had what it took. The problem was, he was the only one who knew it. But that was going to be changing very, very soon.

And the man who was going to be changing it was headed his way.

Edward would certainly know him when he saw him. He'd spent enough time anticipating the moment, after all. For on the opposite wall of his cubicle was something that could only be considered a "shrine" to Bruce Wayne. There was an assortment of photographs, articles, magazine covers. He had been fairly scrupulous throughout the years.

He'd even included, down and to the right, the first article, the very first. It was old and stiff and there were still blood-stains on the face of the young man staring into the camera.

Nygma had it all planned out. Finally he was going to be meeting Bruce Wayne face-to-face, and he had every moment of the encounter scripted. He knew what he would say and, more important, he knew exactly what Bruce would say. He'd rehearsed it to perfection in his mind for weeks upon months, and there was no way that there could be any possible deviation. He simply knew Bruce Wayne far too well to have miscalculated.

Someone else was walking past now, and was doing so very quickly. But it wasn't fast enough. Edward was on his feet immediately, calling, "Mr. Stickley!"

Fred Stickley, who wore his state of harassment with as much familiarity as other people wore backward baseball caps, stopped in his tracks. Without looking, he said, "Yessss . . . Edward . . ."

"When are you planning to bring my project up to Mr. Wayne?" he asked. His adult face still had that same youthful impishness that had gotten him into major trouble as a kid. But there was an additional bit of barely controlled zeal that had been present ever since he'd come out of the coma, the coma that he'd been in for three weeks after he'd cracked his head on the curbside—the coma that he'd come to think of as his cocoon time, his chrysalis period, before emerging into the world with a clear and unfettered vision.

His greatest frustration was that there were so many people out there who didn't share that vision. He was constantly trying to rein himself in wherever and whenever he encountered someone like that.

With Stickley, he had to rein himself in quite a lot.

Stickley, for his part, felt absolutely no need to. "Mr. Nygma," he snapped, "what part of 'no' were you unable to grasp?"

Nygma paused a moment, gathering his thoughts, and then began, "You don't understand . . ."

But Stickley was already shoving a finger into Nygma's face. "No, *you* don't understand. I, your department head, have scotched this project. That is my prerogative." Then he gained control of himself and slowly lowered his hand, not wanting to work himself up into a lather on the day of Wayne's scheduled visit. He tried to sound pleasant. "Edward . . . listen . . . you do outstanding work on the projects you've been given. But the stuff you've developed on your own, it's . . ."

"Over the top? Pushing the envelope? Out there?"

Stickley had been going to simply say "crazy," but instead he nodded amenably. "All those."

Nygma grabbed him by the shoulders, his voice almost shaking with intensity. "But don't you see? That's the point! You think when they pointed at bread mold and said, 'Hey! Here's a wild thought: Penicillin!' How many people said, 'That's over the top!' But how many others had the foresight, the intelligence and, I might add"—and he adjusted

Stickley's necktie—"the stunning fashion sense, to see the possibilities?"

Stickley's patience was running out fast. "Edward . . . let me make this as clear and concise as I can. This . . . mind creation of yours . . . the answer is no. No, okay? I can't make it clearer than that. I can't put a fine enough point on it. I can't think of a word with fewer syllables to put it across. The answer is no."

Nygma's mouth drew into a smile that didn't touch his eyes. "Well," he said in a soft and unpleasant whisper, "why don't we let Mr. Wayne decide that for himself?"

"Because he hired *me* to make these decisions!" Stickley said, his voice louder than he would have liked. "You will not ask Mr. Wayne about this! No . . . that's insufficient. You will not speak to Mr. Wayne at all, do you understand? *Do you?!*"

As Stickley's rage had built, Edward had grown calmer and calmer . . . unnaturally so, in fact. He said one word, overenunciating every syllable:

"Perfectly."

Stickley nodded just once, which was all he trusted himself to do, and then he moved off toward his office.

Edward, meantime, turned and looked out the large window at the end of the hallway. He saw a helicopter approaching the building, descending toward the roof.

He knew precisely who was in the 'copter. And he knew with equal certainty that the events of the next couple of hours were destined. It's why he hadn't bothered to argue with Stickley over the project. He knew that very soon, Stickley's opinions . . . and, very possibly, Stickley himself . . . would be moot.

Bruce Wayne would be descending from on high, and he would see Edward's brilliance firsthand. He would point to Edward and raise him up to his social circles, and heap rewards and friendship upon him.

And not even a platoon of Stickleys could stop it from happening. Of that simple fact, Edward had no doubt at all.

*   *   *

Bruce Wayne's office was filled with ornately carved woodwork and simple yet elegantly styled furniture. The only sign of life in it was a telephone array with several lines blinking. Otherwise it sat empty, waiting and silent. It didn't have to wait for long.

The great doors swung inward and the room was filled with noise and conversation, all of it overlapping. Bruce Wayne entered, followed by his secretary Margaret, his CEO, Lucius Fox, and a bevy of aides that seemed to have sprung up like mushrooms. In a slightly distracted frame of mind, Bruce found himself looking at some of these people and trying to remember who they were and what kind of function they served, other than to barrage him with advisories and questions. In fact, it was entirely possible they served *no* other function.

Margaret, reading off a clipboard, said "The president called. You left your tennis racket at the White House. He wanted me to assure you the arms ban will stay on the bill."

As she spoke she crossed quickly to the phone bank. She plugged an earphone into her ear, getting new information even as she finished telling Wayne about the arms ban. Then, without missing a beat, she continued, "The Japanese prime minister again. On two. Holding."

There was a moment of breath taken, and Fox jumped in. "Five minutes to your inspection of the electronics division, sir."

The aides converged. One said, "We need these authorizations yesterday" while the other informed him, with increasing urgency while looking at a watch, "Tokyo's closing, sir. The LexCorp stock . . ."

But they had spoken simultaneously. It seemed impossible that, even with full concentration, Wayne could have been following the conversation. To make matters trickier, he had taken a stack of contracts from one of the aides and was signing them quickly, mowing through them like a thresher through wheat.

Apparently oblivious of any distractions, Margaret piped up, "Gossip Gerty from 'Good Morning Gotham' again. Holding. Must know who you're taking to the charity circus."

Bruce waved off the contract-holding aide with an unhurried, "The rest can wait," and then turned to the other and informed him, "Tokyo's not closing for fifty-eight seconds," as if that supposedly huge time margin gave him an eternity of maneuverability.

Meantime two more aides had staggered in with a large wooden crate. They finished prying it open and wordlessly held up the contents to Wayne. It was an oil painting of a man in full body armor, backed by a battlefield spent by war.

Fox took one look at it and shuddered inwardly. But it wasn't his money on the line. He turned to Wayne and said, "The painting you saw in the catalog, sir. The purchase price is two million dollars."

Bruce stepped back to get a better view of it, and almost bumped into an aide who said brightly, "The circus benefit committee would like you to make a speech, sir."

Wayne moved to the side so as not to trample the aide and found himself bumping up against the phone bank. Margaret was looking up at him imploringly and he sighed. He pointed at the phones. "Who's who?"

"Prime Minister Kikuchi on two. Gossip Gerty from 'Good Morning Gotham' on one."

He picked up the receiver and said, "Hi, gorgeous." Then a moment of silence passed, and his cheeks flushed just slightly as he said, "Oh. Prime Minister."

Margaret looked at the phone lines in a accusatory fashion. They glowed at her unabashed.

In the meantime, Bruce had pushed his way past the momentary embarrassment. "*Ogenki des'ka? Senjitsuwa . . . jidou-kikin eno difu . . . arigato gozaemashta.*" Then he laughed as the prime minister wished him well with whoever "gorgeous" turned out to be. "See you on the golf course. Sayonara."

"Please, sir. The stocks," implored one of the aides as if his life hung in the balance.

Bruce started to address him, but then paused a moment to say to Margaret, "Cancel my dinner tonight, Margaret. Roses, apologies to Ms. Gotham."

"You mean Ms. January?"

"Right." Then he turned and pointed virtually at random to assorted aides and said, "No speeches . . . buy . . . sell." He paused a moment, hoped that he hadn't just snapped orders that would send him spiraling into bankruptcy, and then turned to Fox and said, "Let's start that inspection."

But before he could take a step in the direction of the door, the clamoring for his time rose again like the Red Sea converging on the Egyptians.

"Mr. Wayne . . ."

"One more contract."

"The takeover bids—"

"The circus—"

Bruce raised his hands and called out, "Stop!"

Dead silence. It was like the old child's game of "1-2-3 Red light!" They all froze in midmotion, even midsentence. "Let's all just take a deep breath, okay?" As one, they nodded.

"Good," he said and then, as they all waited for him to decide which immediately pressing problem should be addressed first, he instead turned and walked out of the office. "I gotta give myself a raise," he muttered to himself. The comment was not heard, of course, buried under the concerted chattering and bellowing of his aides as they followed him out begging for just a moment of his time.

CHAPTER 4

Wayne was moved to think of Hansel and Gretel, leaving behind a trail of bread crumbs so that they wouldn't get lost. As he toured the electronics division of Wayne Enterprises, he was able to take comfort in the fact that he'd never had to resort to such measures. He'd always have a line of aides and assistants and assistant aides trailing behind him.

Walking slightly ahead of him was Stickley, the manager. A good man, solid worker, if not always inspired and even a bit of a fussbudget. Then again, that's the sort of person who could get the job done.

"Your inspections are a departmental highlight."

Bruce laughed lightly. "Really? You all need to get out more," he said in a slightly self-deprecating manner. That, of course, was his prerogative. When you're the boss and powerful, you could take yourself down a peg every now and then, always confident that an employee would laugh and say, "Very amusing, Mr. Wayne."

All the aides laughed, and Stickley said, "Very amusing, Mr. Wayne."

Wayne slowed and stopped next to a mechanized pedestal that was slowly turning. Atop it was the metal model of a sleek new airplane. He looked at Stickley questioningly. "We should be further along than this, shouldn't we?" he asked.

Stickley's head bobbed up and down. "The design appears

flawless on paper, sir. But we can't achieve an antigravity field. The model plane should float but it doesn't."

He lifted the plane and started walking with it, turning it over and over in his hands, and began making minute adjustments. Mildly puzzled, he said, "Hmmm. Funny. Should work." He paused and then asked, "Anybody try kicking it?"

Everyone laughed.

Being the boss had its moments.

In his cubicle, Edward Nygma was busily twisting one of the Rubik's cubes. He was murmuring to himself, "We'll probably be dining at Wayne Manor together." He envisioned Bruce sitting across from him, and began to launch into a narrative. "Bruce, could you pass the gravy boat? What's that? I forgot, you have people who do that, don't you?" He laughed and then in pleased surprise, "Yes. Yes. A party in my honor? I should have rented a tuxedo. What?" he couldn't believe it, "One of yours, Bruce?" He gave it a moment's thought and then shrugged. "Why not? We are the same size."

Then he heard something. It was a group heading his way. Chatting and someone would say something, and then they'd all laugh. "Oh my God. It's him," he whispered.

Without hesitation he darted out into the hallway just as the group was approaching from the other direction. Stickley saw Nygma coming, and put a quick hand on Wayne's elbow. Stickley fired Edward an angry glance but kept his voice pleasant as he said, "Well, Mr. Wayne, on to R&D?"

No chance.

Wayne turned to Stickley but suddenly his attention was completely pulled to Edward, who had thrust himself squarely in their path. Edward saw the consternation in Stickley's eyes. Good. Excellent, in fact. Now Stickley was going to see something.

Edward seized Wayne's hand in a viselike grip and started pumping it firmly. Wayne was politely puzzled as he asked, "Mr. . . . ?"

"Bruce Wayne. In the flesh," said Edward, still not quite believing that the moment was happening. He was like a raw, open wound, his emotions laid bare.

Stickley looked as if he were going to have a cerebral hemorrhage.

Bruce smiled easily and said, "No. That's me. And you are?"

At first Edward didn't realize what Bruce was talking about, and then he ran through his mind what he had just said to Wayne. He winced in chagrin. A classic screwup like that hadn't been part of the plan. But he pressed forward. After all, in the grand scheme of things . . . in the fabulous, sweeping intertwining destinies of Bruce Wayne and Edward Nygma, such a slip would not even rate a footnote. "Nygma. Edward. Edward Nygma. You hired me. Personally. Just like I tell everyone."

He saw Bruce's politely puzzled expression and amended, "Well, we've never actually met, but your name was on the hire slip. I have it framed."

He still hadn't let go of Bruce's hand. Bruce said gamely, "I'm gonna need that hand back, Ed."

"What? Ah yes. Of course. I'm sorry! It's just that . . ." He took a deep breath and plunged in. "You're my idol. And some people have been trying to keep us apart."

Bruce looked at Stickley, who had gone dead white. Still, this fervent fellow clearly had something particular to discuss.

Go on, Edward silently urged. *This is where you ask me what's on my mind . . . go on . . . go . . .*

"So, Mr. Nygma, what's on your mind?"

Bingo!

"Precisely!" declared Edward, launching into a spiel that he had been preparing for two months, every day, every night. "What's on all our minds? Brain waves. The future of Wayne Enterprises is brain waves."

Brain waves, Edward? Why . . . tell me more! Although, of course, Bruce Wayne would already have grasped the im-

portance of the sentence. Indeed, he might already have figured out just where Edward was going with it. Still, Edward
was willing to wait for that inevitable demand of *Tell me
more!*

He waited. Patiently.

Wayne was staring at him. At him . . . and then back to
Stickley.

Bruce, you're missing your cue, thought Edward, smile
frozen firmly in place. *If you wait too long, Stickley's going
to simper and . . .*

"I really do apologize, Mr. Wayne. I personally terminated
his project this morning . . ."

This wouldn't do. It simply wouldn't. So Bruce had
missed a cue, a single line. Again, no big deal in the grand
scheme of things. Grasping Wayne by the elbow, Edward
pulled him over to his cubicle. He gestured toward the device
that covered his desktop, looking for all the world as if it had
been designed by Rube Goldberg. There was a small TV
monitor, jury-rigged to transceivers, diodes, and tangled
wires. Connected to the whole thing were two elaborate
headbands, bristling with so many dials and lights that they
looked like props from an old science fiction serial.

"Voilà," declared Edward. He spoke all in a rush. "My invention beams any TV signal directly into the human brain.
By stimulating neurons—manipulating brain waves, if you
will—this device creates a fully holographic image that puts
the audience inside the show. My Remote Encephalographic
Stimulator Box will give John Q. Public a realm where he is
king." He had said the foregoing in one breath, and, taking
another, he continued ingratiatingly, "Not that someone like
you would need it. Someone so intelligent. Witty. Charming.
But for the lonely, the . . ."

"Paranoid? The psychotic?" opined Stickley.

Edward fired Stickley a venomous glance and turned back
to Wayne. "I just need a bit of additional funding. For human
trials. Let me show you . . ."

You've caught my interest, Ed. Let's fire that sucker up and see what she can do.

Bruce's mouth began to move, and Edward held his breath waiting for it.

Suddenly it seemed as if Bruce's attention had been drawn away. He blinked, then refocused on Edward. "Listen, Ed. Let me see your technical schematics on this . . ."

Edward jumped to a line from later in his rehearsed dialogue. "I want you to know, we'll be full partners in this, Bruce. Look at us. Two of a kind."

My God, Ed, you're right. Come join me on the tour. Then we'll go out, grab some dinner, and—

Bruce's glance darted away once more, and then he said, "Call my assistant, Margaret, she'll set something up."

Edward felt his world coming unglued. Anyone could be told to call Bruce's secretary. Anyone. Some bum on the street, some fool, some toady . . . anyone. Not a soul mate. Not a compadre. And not, for crying out loud, not Edward Nygma. He was not remotely able to keep the agony from his voice as he said, "Oh. Call your secretary. Is that *it*?"

"Yes, we'll get together—"

Bruce started to move away, and Edward caught the satisfied, even vindictive gleam in Stickley's face. And he became suddenly painfully aware that if Bruce Wayne walked away without Edward Nygma by his side, then that would be it. It would be finished. All these weeks, months . . . indeed, a lifetime of planning . . . and it was crumbling under him just like that.

He grabbed Bruce's arms and shouted, "No. Don't leave me! My invention! I need you!"

Bruce was thunderstruck as he was pulled partway into Edward's office . . . and then he caught sight of the shrine.

Edward's head bobbed eagerly, like one of those little baseball player statues with a spring-head. Now, finally, Bruce would understand the depth of Nygma's devotion to his idol. He would see how important he was to Nygma. How he stood for so much that Edward wanted to emulate.

And Wayne's gaze zeroed in on the picture of himself as a young man.

The eyes of Wayne the elder locked with Wayne the younger, and when he slowly turned his scrutiny back to Edward Nygma, Edward could feel the temperature in the cubicle drop to subzero.

"Tampering with people's brain waves is mind manipulation. It raises too many question marks."

It was as if Wayne's arm had turned to granite. When Wayne gently dislodged Edward's fingers from around his arm, Nygma made no effort to hold on.

Raising his voice, Wayne called out, "Factory looks great, folks. Keep up the good work."

He stepped away from the slack-jawed Nygma. All the time that he'd been talking with Edward, he had still been making minor adjustments to the plane model. It was as if one section of his brain was perfectly capable of operating separately from the rest of it.

He set the plane back on the pedestal, gave it the slightest kick with his toe, and the pedestal started to glow. The model plane rose, floating, into the air.

Without another word, Bruce Wayne headed back toward his ivory tower as Stickley clapped his hands briskly and said, "All right, everyone, back to work." As he moved forward, he stopped next to Nygma and murmured, "We'll discuss this later."

Edward Nygma was paying almost no attention. Instead he was staring after the retreating form of Bruce Wayne.

"You were supposed to understand," he said. "You were supposed to understand."

And then, in a voice very low and very dangerous, he said, "I'll make you understand."

He stepped back into his cubicle, and never noticed what

Bruce Wayne had suddenly caught sight of in the midst of Edward's presentation.

It was a signal, projected against a low-hanging cloud. A signal that was the emblem of a bat. . . .

Wayne strode into his private office, having given firm orders that he was not to be disturbed. This was a tough order to enforce, since there was a tendency for various aides or employees to knock tentatively or call, "Mr. Wayne, this will just take a moment. . . ."

But this time he'd said it in a tone of voice that indicated he wasn't kidding around. His staff believed him. The tour of the electronics department had been so close to disastrous, thanks to that one demented employee, that everyone figured Mr. Wayne was probably in one hellaciously lousy mood. Now might indeed be a good time to give him as wide a berth as possible.

Still, just to play it safe, Bruce said briskly, "Lock."

An electronic lock slammed into place. A bazooka would have been required to get through.

He plopped down into the leather chair and spoke again. "Capsule."

And the chair dropped out of sight.

The floor under him had slid back to reveal a hidden transport tunnel. Directly below him was a transport capsule, and the leather chair clicked down smoothly into place. The transport tube ran into a shaft he'd had installed that was nominally for a private elevator. He used the elevator on rare occasions. He used the transport tube, however, far more frequently. And it went a lot further than the bottom of the building.

The capsule rolled forward and then angled sharply downward as it eased into the shaft. It built up speed hurtling down the shaft, holding tightly onto the tracks, and then snapping forward to a normal angle and hurtling underground to a preencoded destination. Lights flashed, whipping by at incredible speed.

Inside the capsule, Bruce checked the speed and time readouts, and nodded slightly to himself in approval. On the windscreen, a familiar craggy face appeared.

"Alfred . . ."

"I saw the signal, sir," said the butler. "All is ready."

"I knew I could count on you, Alfred," said Wayne.

Alfred sighed wearily. "Yes. I know you did." He didn't sound as if he considered that to be a badge of honor.

Alfred was waiting patiently nearby the large vault that Bruce Wayne had entered mere moments before. "What to wear, what to wear," Alfred murmured to himself.

From within the vault, Bruce's voice came. "What did you say?"

Alfred paused a moment, and then said, "You don't have to go, you know."

This time when the voice came back, it was different. Just from the tone of it, Alfred knew that the mask had already gone on. "I saw the signal, Alfred."

"You could pretend you didn't."

"Impossible."

"Why impossible?"

Bruce Wayne emerged from the vault, his long black cape sweeping around him, his gauntleted arms folded across his sculpted chest. His eyes glimmered from beneath his cowl.

"I've never been much for pretending," said the Batman.

Alfred made no response, feeling that the irony of the situation spoke for itself.

Batman moved quickly to the long, powerful black car. When he'd first begun his career, he had simply referred to it as "the car." But the press had begun hanging all sorts of nicknames onto his weaponry. The car, for example, had been nicknamed "the Batmobile." It was a term that Batman himself utterly despised . . . and which Alfred, naturally, embraced immediately. To get back at him, Bruce had started referring to the underground hideaway (a place that Alfred personally found a dank and dreary environment) by the cozy name of "the Batcave."

Bruce had retooled the Batmobile considerably in recent months. Not only had he redesigned the chassis to make it more aerodynamic, but he had built in several new computer overrides and fail-safes.

As the Batmobile's engine roared to life, Alfred stepped closer and said, "I suppose I couldn't convince you to take along a sandwich."

In the low, whispered voice that indicated he had fully slipped into his persona of Batman, he replied, "I'll get drive-thru." He paused and then said to the car, "Go . . ."

The cowling slid into place over the cockpit of the car. With a glow that seemed to emanate from somewhere in the bowels of Hell, the Batmobile roared forward. It moved quickly through a series of underground arches, picking up speed. The onboard surveillance systems confirmed that there were no other vehicles in the area, which made sense; Wayne Manor was somewhat isolated, and casual visitors were a rarity.

Moments later, the Batmobile whipped through a holograph of trees that masked the entrance of the Batcave. It screeched out onto the forest road, fallen leaves and dead branches whipping around as the powerful vehicle blew past.

And at the turntable that served as the Batmobile's parking place and exit, Alfred stood long after even the echo of the car's screeching tires had faded.

Alone in the cave.

He thought about how it had been in the beginning. How he had kept waiting, hoping, praying that the fixation would go away. And when it didn't, and when it became clear that if he tried to oppose young Master Wayne's crime-fighting plans, Wayne would just go ahead with them anyway . . . Alfred had become his reluctant accomplice.

He'd been torn ever since Batman's early days. On the one hand, success meant vindication of a project and desire that had consumed Wayne's life. On the other hand, if he failed . . . and presuming he survived the failure . . . then there were so many other, healthier (physically and mentally) avenues that he could pursue. So many chances for a happier life. Except could he be happy then?

Was this dismal cavern truly the only place where Bruce Wayne could find peace?

What sort of bleak fate was that? Living in a cave, underground . . . spiritually, emotionally buried alive.

CHAPTER 5

The guard's name was Tully.

Once he'd been a cop. He'd walked the streets of Gotham city for twenty-seven years. Spent his entire life as a beat cop. Been shot twice, including one time that had put him on a respirator for a week. Won three meritorious service medals and a commendation. He'd never married, never had kids, and devoted his entire life to the force.

And after those glorious twenty-seven years, his medals and commendations were collecting dust on a shelf at home, and his pension wasn't even beginning to cover his simple, meager living expenses. So he'd taken a job at the Second National Bank of Gotham as a security guard.

They'd assigned him to the twenty-second floor of the bank's office building, guarding the company vault containing billions in negotiable bonds, stocks, and other assets of high-powered corporations. Appropriately, it was his second night on the job when he'd found himself in more trouble than he could ever recall being in during his entire tenure as a cop.

Tully was tied up on the ground, bound at his wrists and ankles. Standing around him were six thugs of varying sizes and shapes, but all of one consistent personality type: nasty. Tully was trying not to look at them, for fear was bubbling furiously inside him and he hated the way it made him feel. Instead he was staring out the window at the great signal hanging in the sky. A bat illuminated against a low-hanging cloud.

And then the signal was blocked out by the twirling disk of a gleaming silver coin. It passed the signal by, and then descended. A hand speared out and snagged it easily.

A man stepped into view. He was standing in profile, looking off to the right. He was rakishly handsome, at least on his good side.

Once upon a time, he'd gone by the name of Harvey Dent. But that was a name, he'd decided some time back, that only put one side of him on display. That was no longer sufficient. He had needed a moniker that captured his duality, so that when people were dealing with him, they'd know *all* aspects of the man they were doing business with.

The name had somehow come naturally to him.

"Counting on the winged avenger to deliver you from evil, old chum?" asked Two-Face. He clutched his coin more tightly. "*We* most certainly are."

Regrets poured through Tully's mind. All of them centered around the notion that if only he'd encountered Two-Face when he was young . . . if only he'd been facing the six thugs when he was young . . . all of it when he was young, instead of a scared old man with a lousy pension and a hearing aid which, at the moment, he would have given anything to be able to turn off. Disgusted by his weakness, he tried to keep his voice level as he asked, "You gonna kill me?"

Two-Face didn't seem to hear the question at first. He simply continued to stare out into space. But then, quick as a cobra, he was squatting next to the guard. He held the silver dollar under Tully's nose. The clean side winked at him.

"Maybe. And maybe not. You could say we're of two minds on the matter. Are you a gambling man? Suppose we flip for it?"

Tully said nothing.

It didn't matter. Two-Face was no longer listening. Instead he was speaking softly to himself, murmuring, "One man is born a hero, his brother a coward. Babies starve, politicians grow fat. Holy men perish, junkies become legion. And why is this? Why? Heredity? Environment? Fate? Karma? No, my friend. Luck. Blind, simple, idiot, doo-dah luck. The random toss of the great celestial coin is the only true justice. Triumph or tragedy, joy or sorrow, life or, dare I say—"

He turned the coin over, and there was the scarred face of the coin. ". . . death."

Two-Face looked to the left and the guard tried not to look away. He didn't succeed.

"Death," he repeated, and he flipped the coin.

It twirled in the air and landed directly in front of the guard's face. Tully didn't see what side came up and, to prolong the agony, Two-Face brought his foot down quickly on top of it. He winked down at the sweating guard, as if they were old buddies sharing a few laughs over a harmless game.

"What greater thrill? What greater agony? Like the touch of God." He put up a finger, waggling it slightly. "Wait. Wait. Wait. How will justice be served?"

He removed his foot from the coin and the guard forced himself to look at it.

The unblemished head looked back at him.

"Fortune smiles upon you, my friend," Two-Face said gently. "Another day of wine and roses, or in your case, beer and pizza."

The guard sobbed with relief, and hated himself all the more for the weakness.

Two-Face snapped his fingers, twice. The thugs converged on the guard. One lifted him up by his bound arms, another by his legs.

"You said you'd let me live."

"Too true. And so you shall. Nothing better than live bait to trap a bat."

Two-Face nodded to the two guards, who carried Tully away to fulfill his function in Two-Face's scheme. One of the thugs stepped forward and said with just a hint of annoyance, "Too many witnesses. We shoulda just killed him. . . ."

Two-Face appeared to give the matter a moment's

thought, and then he flipped the coin. This time he didn't let it fall, but snatched it out of the air and slapped it onto the back of his hand.

The scarred side was visible.

Before the thug even had time to register the significance of the decision, Two-Face roared. His hand shot out, pinning the thug's throat to the wall. He shoved his face into the thug's and snarled, "You stinking piece of virus-breeding rat droppings. Did you question our coin?"

"Boss . . . you're . . . you're hurting me . . ." he managed to get out.

"Oh, *are* we?" Two-Face thrust his face even closer, and the petrified thug felt his foul breath blowing at him. "Look at this face. Look closer! Do you think there's anything on earth we don't know about pain?"

And then he started slapping the thug across the face, each smack punctuating the next four words: ". . . Never . . . Argue . . . With . . . Us! *You got it?*" he bellowed.

He released his grip on the thug, who promptly sank to the floor. "Anything you say, Boss," he managed to get out between bleeding lips.

Two-Face nodded approvingly. "Exactly. Excellent response."

He walked away from the thug and stepped over toward the window, taking care not to present a target. Far below him, in the heart of Pan-Asia town, he could see the SWAT teams and police wagons, the spotlights that had been set up, everyone scurrying around as if any of their activities had the slightest meaning or importance to him.

All of it was irrelevant.

Only one being had anything to do with anything . . . and anything to do with him.

"You're all little bugs," he murmured. "We are waiting . . . for the big bug."

"How do you know he'll be here?" asked Chase Meridian.

Commissioner James Gordon, wishing like hell that his

bad heart hadn't forced him to give up smoking, chewed on a breadstick as he surveyed the heavens. The Bat-Signal continued, unblinking. "He will be."

"You don't know for sure," pressed Dr. Meridian. "He could be out of town, or sick. He could be dead. The man behind the mask might have suffered a nice, simple embolism and be lying on a slab somewhere with a tag on his toe. Being bigger than life doesn't guarantee a spectacular or heroic death. Look at Lawrence of Arabia."

"I don't get out to movies much," replied Gordon. He swiveled his gaze towards her. "Is there some point to this, *Doctor?*"

"I'm wondering why you have such unflappable confidence in him? Is it the cape? The mask? That emblem?"

"I don't appreciate the condescension, Doctor."

"My apologies," she said.

"You want to know why I have confidence in him?"

"Yes."

He pointed towards the Bat-Signal, which was suddenly blocked out by a swinging figure. "That's why," he said.

Batman dropped down, face-to-face with Dr. Chase Meridian.

The meeting had been a long time coming for her. She had built up a variety of no-nonsense, or various businesslike introductions to make.

"Hot entrance," she heard a voice that sounded remarkably like her own and, even more astonishingly, passing through her lips. Inside her there was an agonized *Oh my Godddd did you just say that?!*

For his part, Batman seemed to have lost interest in her. Actually, that might not have been the case; it was entirely possible that he hadn't any interest in her in the first place. All business, he turned to Gordon. "Two-Face?"

Gordon nodded. "Two guards down. He'd holding the third hostage. Didn't see this one coming."

"We should have, though," said Chase, trying to insert

herself back into the conversation. "The Second Bank of Gotham . . ."

"On the second anniversary of the day I captured him," said Batman. It was hard to tell whether he'd figured it out on the way over or had just realized it now.

Chase had never had any sort of lengthy intercourse with a man behind a mask, unless one counted that time she'd spent two weeks at hockey training camp dealing with a suicidal goalie. It was disconcerting. All the little things she sought to help her "read" people were utterly absent. It was like staring into a black hole. She pushed gamely forward, saying, "How could Two-Face resist? Uhm . . . Chase Meridian," she prompted, when Batman didn't shake her outstretched hand.

He still didn't, instead merely staring at her as if she were some new strain of bacteria, or perhaps a rare animal who'd popped up at a zoo one day.

It made her feel very odd. She never thought she would encounter a situation where a man dressed like a six-foot bat could make *her* feel unusual.

Gordon piped up, sounding slightly regretful, "I asked Dr. Meridian to consult on this case. She specializes in . . ."

". . . multiple personalities," Batman interrupted. "Abnormal psychology. I read your work. Insightful." He paused, then added, "Naive. But insightful."

"I'm flattered. Not every girl makes a super hero's night table."

Dr. Meridian was the expert, but for all Gordon knew, Batman had similar credentials in civilian life. So Gordon addressed the question to both of them: "Can we reason with him? There are innocent people in there."

Chase shook her head. "Won't do any good. He'll slaughter them without thinking twice." She didn't seem to be aware of the irony of her comment about "thinking twice."

If Batman noticed it, he chose not to say anything. "Agreed. A trauma powerful enough to create an alternate personality leaves the victim . . ."

"... in a world where normal rules of right and wrong no longer apply," Chase picked up.

"Exactly," agreed Batman.

"Like you."

Batman looked at her inscrutably. It was impossible for her to be sure, but it seemed—just for a moment—as if there was the slightest hint of a smile on his mouth. But if it had been there, it was gone just as quickly. Feeling the need to fill in the gap, Chase said, "Let's just say I could write a hell of a paper on a grown man who dresses like a flying rodent."

"Bats aren't rodents, Dr. Meridian. Same phylum, Chordata. Same class, Mammalia. Different order, though: Chiroptera, not Rodentia. No sharp front teeth for gnawing."

She inclined her head slightly at the correction. "I didn't know that. See? You are interesting. And call me Chase." She turned to look at a bustling group of SWAT members. "By the way, do you have a first name? Or do I just call you Bats?"

She looked back to see his reaction, but he was gone.

That was when she heard the crash. A crash that sounded as if the world were exploding.

The building shuddered under the impact, but Two-Face seemed unperturbed. Instead he raised his voice and shouted, as if addressing an audience in an ancient coliseum, "Let's start this party with a bang!"

From outside there was a grinding of motors, the whoosh of air, and this time when the wrecking ball struck the building, it didn't merely quiver. Instead the wall exploded inward, cement and plaster raining down and the massive ball swinging to within inches of Two-Face.

He didn't even glance at it, instead sanguinely checking his watch. He frowned. Could it be that Batman would let him down, and not be . . .

From the elevators nearby there was the amazingly ordinary sound of a chime, indicating that one of the cars had reached the floor.

Two-Face nodded approvingly. "Punctual. Even for his own funeral."

He whirled toward the elevators, his gang members leaping forward with machine guns under their arms. One of them tossed a gun to Two-Face, who caught it easily and aimed at the elevator doors. The entire maneuver, from the signal that alerted them to the clattering of machine guns, took no more than three seconds. Two-Face chided himself, even as he and his men opened fire. He would have far preferred it if they had trimmed it to two seconds.

Armor-piercing bullets punched through the heavy metal doors. They fired until the clips were empty, and then Two-Face put up a hand, indicating that they should move forward to see the results of their assault. They walked cautiously toward the elevators, slamming new clips into the weapons as they went.

The doors slid open.

The shaft was empty.

Two-Face gaped in confusion. He barely had time to wonder how in God's name Batman had managed to override the controls, forcing the doors open despite the absence of the elevators themselves . . .

Because the next thing he knew, he was under attack.

Batman swung down from the middle shaft, feetfirst, plowing into the thugs and sending them scattering.

He landed cleanly, his hands on his Utility Belt. He pulled two weapons, gripping one in either hand. In the right was a small projectile launcher. He squeezed the trigger and a pellet shot through the air, smacking onto the floor squarely in front of two of the thugs. When it landed it was with a soft, almost disgusting noise, like toothpaste ejected from the tube by having someone smash his fist on it. The crooks were on their feet, but—as it happened—so now were the contents of the pellet. It was a thick superadhesive. It soaked through their shoes, and into the skin of their feet. Before they even realized that their forward motion had been impeded, they'd been brought to a dead halt. They wavered and then pitched back, their arms pinwheeling but unable to stop them.

In Batman's left hand, meantime, was a bola. He hurled it with a casual sidearm toss that released its whirling cable. It snaked out and wrapped itself around the upper torso of a third thug, who went down struggling and struck his head so forcefully that he knocked himself cold.

A fourth thug was charging. Batman slugged him once in the stomach, doubling him over, and then twice more in the head. Immediately the thug lapsed into unconsciousness even as a fifth charged. Gripping him firmly by the shoulders, Batman spun him around so that his flying legs crashed into the onrushing thug, sending him sprawling.

A defiant howl of rage alerted Batman as another thug charged down the hall. He had two lethal spike-covered gloves, and he was barreling toward Batman, waving them viciously. The spikes might not have had tremendous impact on Batman's armor, but on the other hand, one good shot to his chin might take off the lower half of his face.

Batman stood his ground, fists poised, feinting, angling for position. The gloved felon came at him, lunging toward him and bolstering his own confidence with his bansheelike screams. He thrust his deadly appendages at Batman, who ducked under the charge. Overbalanced as he was, the thug wasn't able to halt his forward motion. He tripped over Batman's crouched form . . .

And fell down the elevator shaft.

Batman nodded to himself in satisfaction as he heard a thud from a distance below. The car that he'd ridden up the shaft (before leaving it to gain the high ground) wasn't all that far, so there was every chance that the thug had only sustained minor injuries.

Unless, of course, he had fallen headfirst, or on his own gloves.

Batman glanced down the shaft and saw the thug was, indeed, quite alive and moaning softly. Nevertheless, a faint chill struck Batman as he thought of the relative callousness with which he'd handled the guy. What if . . . ?

He turned just in time to see Two-Face disappearing down a hallway. Without hesitation, he gave chase.

Tully sat in the sizable vault area, rocking back and forth in hopes of somehow tipping the chair over, perhaps breaking it, and in that way managing to free his bound arms and legs. His gagged mouth was aching from the tape that was across it.

He heard footsteps and braced himself for the likelihood that Two-Face was coming back to kill him. Or perhaps instead to play that demented coin-tossing game of his again, and this time there was every likelihood that Tully wouldn't be quite so fortunate. For that matter Two-Face might just keep it up, again and again, tossing and tossing until he got the answer he wanted, and then Tully would be . . .

A caped figure stepped into the narrow entranceway to the vault.

Tully's eyes went wide. It was *him!* Dammit, *it was him!* Except it couldn't be him! It mustn't! Tully made frantic noises in his throat, trying in some way to warn him off.

Batman either wasn't listening or simply didn't understand. He moved quickly to Tully, free his hands, and tore the tape off Tully's mouth. Pain roared through Tully's face, but that didn't stop him from getting out the words, "It's a trap!"

It was a useful, if somewhat tardy, sentence.

The safe door slammed shut before Batman could even turn. Before the resounding clang of the heavy metal barrier had even begun to fade, Two-Face's voice issued from a speaker hidden somewhere within the vault.

"Good evening, Mr. Bat," he said in grave imitation of an old television series. "Your mission, should you choose to accept it—or not—is simple. Die!"

Batman and Tully were hurled to the floor as the safe

jerked forward, starting to move. There was the sound of chains outside dragging across the floor.

"We have a problem," said Batman.

By the time Gordon's people had gotten to the huge crane that had operated the wrecking ball, all they found was an empty cab.

The monstrous machine had done its work, and the operators—more of Two-Face's people, no doubt—had fled. Gordon banged a car hood in frustration, feeling helpless.

Then he heard something. It was the unmistakable sound of whirling helicopter blades. He looked up toward the twenty-second floor and moved from helplessness to utter shock.

A Blackhawk helicopter had moved into position, a giant winch dangling beneath it. It seemed to be drawing something through the huge hole that the wrecking ball had pounded in the side of the building. After a moment, Gordon was able to make out what it was.

It was the safe from within the bank, dangling hundreds of feet above the ground and being drawn slowly up into the helicopter's cargo hold.

"That Two-Faced son of a bitch," muttered Gordon. "I just hope to God that Batman and the hostage are safe."

Inside the safe, Batman was able to figure out, from the swaying of the vault and the pounding of the whirly blades outside, just exactly what the situation was.

"Why does he want to kill you?!" asked Tully apprehensively.

"I was his friend," replied Batman, scanning the interior of the vault in hopes of finding a way out.

"Do all your friends want to kill you?"

"Only the ones who get to know me." He hadn't spotted any convenient means of exit aside from the locked door. What he had spotted, which he didn't like one bit, were small spigots on the wall. What the hell did they have to do with anything?

Once again, Two-Face's voice came through the hidden speakers. "Two years ago tonight, you abandoned us to that madhouse! So . . . happy anniversary! And for your dying pleasure, we're serving the very same acid that made yours truly the men we are today."

The purpose of the spigots, which Batman had not been able to divine, was quickly made clear. Acid, with a reddish color that had long seared itself into his memory, started pouring out of them. Wherever the acid struck there was loud hissing and rising smoke. The acid wasn't strong enough to eat through steel, so the money—safely ensconced in steel drawers—would be unharmed. But Batman and Tully weren't in quite as fortunate a position.

"When we open this safe," crowed Two-Face, "we'll have all we ever wanted. Enough cash to open a mint. And you— Dead."

Ignoring Two-Face's prescription for a happy life wasn't too difficult. The acid, however, was more problematic. As the acid spread across the floor, Batman said with remarkable calm, as if he'd been in this particular jam any number of times, "Know the combination?"

"No," said Tully, trying to scramble up the cash drawers, seeking higher ground. "Don't you got a Bat-something in that belt to blow the door?"

"Acid's flammable. We'd be incinerated."

Batman steepled his legs, feet pressing on opposite sides of the wall in front of the safe door. It gave him some elevation, but not much. Acid started to burn at his cape.

He looked around, fighting down desperation, and suddenly his eyes lit on something useful. "I need to borrow this," he said and grabbed the guard's hearing aid. Holding it to the door, he used it to augment his own hearing and started working the combination.

He focused his concentration, not rushing his way through the soft clicks of the tumblers. It meant that he had to ignore the acid licking at the soles of the boots, the frantic urging from the guard, and the continued shouting of Two-Face.

"Once we were allies, bound by a passion to fight evil," Two-Face told him.

The guard, from his precarious perch, wiped the sweat from his face. He accidentally knocked off his glasses. They fell into the rising acid and turned molten in no time.

"Know what I've learned, Bat, old pal? Passion burns." And as the acid starting pumping in faster, Two-Face called out in demented joy, "Burn, Batty, burn."

The final tumbler clicked into place. Batman threw open the door, grabbed the doorjamb in one hand, the guard in the other, and swung out onto the safe's top just as the hissing acid streamed past below his feet.

The streets of Gotham City spread out far below them, and the wind was vicious as Batman saw that they were almost to the top of the bank tower. Tully was clutching desperately onto the chains from which the safe was dangling, whimpering deep in this throat. Batman held on with one hand, looking around and assessing the situation.

Then he pulled out his wirepoon and fired it into the bank wall. The hook embedded solidly, and Batman quickly attached the trailing end of the cable to the safe with another hook, snapping it into place.

Theoretically, the tensile strength of his cable was sufficient to dangle the Batmobile off the side of the Gotham Bridge. But he'd never had to test it in that manner, and furthermore, he wasn't sure how heavy the safe was. He suspected the cable was sufficient.

He had to, because he didn't have very many other options.

He palmed his Utility Belt, and a laser torch snapped into his glove. With his free hand, he reached up and grabbed the chain that was suspending the safe.

"Hang on!"

"What?" shouted the guard.

Batman gripped the chain and, using the torch, sliced at

the links just below his hand. The safe swung down and away, the cable line drawing taut. In a perfect arc, the safe swung back through the hole from which it had emerged mere moments ago. It slid across the floor, skidding with the sound of screeching metal, and slammed into the far wall. Tully sat there for a moment, stunned and confused. And then he had the good grace and intelligence to pass out.

Batman, in the meantime, was clambering up the chain toward the open cargo hatch. The yank upwards had been so quick, so violent, that it had knocked the blowtorch out of his hand. But losing a weapon wasn't going to deter him. He was going to rein in Harvey Dent, and nothing was going to stop him.

From within the cockpit, Two-Face stared down in pure fury. If his gaze could burn as fiercely as the acid had, Batman would have been a blackened corpse before getting halfway up.

He pulled out his twin Colt .45s and muttered, "Gonna punch some nice holes in him the fish can swim through."

But then he hesitated. This was a decision point, and he was honor bound to do right by the moment. He holstered one of his guns, pulled out his coin, and quickly flipped it. It came up clean. Reluctantly but briskly, he holstered the other gun. "On *second* thought, bullets are far too crude. The Bat wants to play? Fine. We'll play."

The pilot started to ask what it was that Two-Face wanted him to do, when Two-Face grabbed the controls away from him, yanked back on the throttle, and sent the chopper shooting straight up into the night sky like a rocket.

Batman held on, never losing his confidence or his nerve. He decided that he was far less of a target with all this maneuvering going on. He allowed the swinging back and forth to continue as he pulled himself up hand over hand.

The helicopter angled toward Gotham Harbor, where a giant sign read "WELCOME TO GOTHAM CITY."

Two-Face gunned the chopper's engines and angled toward the sign. He ignored the pilot's cries of terror that he was coming in too low.

Two-Face sent the helicopter roaring downward, the lower half and trailing chain smashing through the sign, ripping it to shreds. It had been a terrible risk; if any part of the chopper had gotten hung up on the sign, the vehicle could easily have been sent spiraling downward toward the choppy water of the harbor. But instead, under Two-Face's steady hand, the Blackhawk moved up toward the dark Gotham sky.

As if he'd totally forgotten about piloting the chopper, Two-Face moved away from the controls so that he could better see out the side. The pilot quickly grabbed control of the chopper as Two-Face made his way over to the cargo hatch. He peered down at the chain and saw exactly what he thought he'd see: nothing.

"Good-bye to that pointy-eared, steroid-eating, rubber-suited, cross-dressing, night rat . . ."

Then a shadow suddenly cast itself over him. The only source of light was through the windshield, and with a berserk yell Two-Face spun. Sure enough, covering the Plexiglas windshield was a familiar black cape.

Two-Face yanked out his guns and started firing. Bullets went everywhere: through the windshield, through the cape, and, unfortunately, through the pilot. Blood spattered the inside of the windshield. Two-Face didn't care. All that mattered to him was that the cape was gone. But he had no certainty that Batman had gone with it.

The pilot slumped forward on the stick, sending the chopper into a dive. Two-Face was hurled forward. He smashed into the windshield, which was already riddled with bullet holes. It cracked further under the impact and Two-Face scrambled back so that he wouldn't crash completely through it and be hurled down to the icy water below. He grabbed the pilot's corpse, wrested it from its position, and tossed it aside. Then he clambered into the vacated seat and regained control of the spiraling chopper.

That was when a fist smashed through the side window,

tagging Two-Face squarely in the jaw. His head snapped back, crashing into the cushioned wall behind him with enough impact to send stars exploding between his eyes.

Crouched on one of the struts on the outside of the speeding helicopter, Batman hung on with single-minded determination. "Harvey, you need help. Give it up."

A sneer crossed the distorted portion of his face. "*We* need help? Looked in the mirror recently?"

Suddenly he brought his feet up, slamming them squarely into Batman's face. "*Mano a Mano a Bato,*" called Two-Face as Batman lost his grip, sliding and having to grab on to the lower half of the strut. Batman took a breath, then hauled himself back up, ripping apart the last remains of the side door that were acting as a barrier to him. He grabbed Two-Face's foot, flipped him to the floor, and started dragging him out of the helicopter. Two-Face struggled back furiously.

"Dark Knight, huh? *Dead* Knight sounds more to my liking," Two-Face snarled contemptuously.

"Surrender," was Batman's only response.

Two-Face didn't even acknowledge the word as his hand fought for purchase against Batman, trying to push him away or strangle him or *something*. "Two years in Arkham Asylum planning your demise. There's only one way out of this waltz. One of us dies."

"I won't kill you, Harvey."

But Batman's actions were contradicting his words. His fingers found Two-Face's throat and clamped down, adrenaline pumping, instinct pushing him. There he was, looking deeply into the face of the promise he made that he hadn't been able to keep. The face that had once trusted him, even come to consider him a friend and ally. The face of the man he'd let down.

The face that was laughing at him.

"Batman doesn't kill? What's that homicidal gleam in your eyes? That lethal curl of your lip? Oh, too good to be

true. A Bat with a taste for blood. We're just the same."
Turning the screws, he said, "You're a killer too."

For the briefest of moments, Batman's concentration was thrown.

A second later, so was Batman, as Two-Face shoved him away and he vanished from sight beneath the chopper.

Harvey yanked himself back into the chopper and looked at the course in front of him.

There was the Lady Gotham statue, tall and proud and recently refurbished, standing proudly in the harbor.

Two-Face smiled as it all came together. "Hello, my lovely. Ready for your face-lift?" He reached under the seat and pulled out a large iron brace that he used to lock the controls into place, fixing the helicopter on its deadly course. "Let the world be made new . . . in our split image."

Clutching onto the underside support strut, Batman hauled himself up, up once more toward the open side of the helicopter. He paused there a moment, bracing himself so that he would be able to move quickly, because sure as hell Harvey would be there waiting for him.

With a thrust of his powerful legs, he shoved himself into the cockpit.

No sign of Harvey.

What he did see were two things: the iron bar holding the chopper steady, and Harvey Dent poised over the cargo hatch. It was as if he'd been waiting for Batman to show up.

"This time, have the good taste to die," he requested in a rather formal tone. And he leapt through the cargo hatch.

Batman moved quickly to the cargo hatch and stared in stunned disbelief as Harvey Dent plummeted toward the dark water below. Then there was a sudden flurry of expanding color, caught in Lady Gotham's lighthouse beam, and a parachute opened over Two-Face. In an additional bit of whimsy, it unfolded into a giant Yin and Yang.

A shadow loomed directly in front of the copter. Lady Gotham was staring in at him.

Batman grabbed at his Utility Belt to pull out his laser torch, in hopes of slicing through the iron bar and by some miracle managing to change the helicopter's course. He had exactly one second to realize that his laser torch was gone, dropped down the side of the bank building when he'd severed the chain.

And then there was no more time as the helicopter smashed into the left side of Lady Gotham's face. Batman was hurled through the cargo hatch as the Blackhawk erupted in a massive fireball, consuming part of the statue's visage and transforming it, in a matter of seconds, into a damaged ugly parody of itself.

Batman wasn't conscious to see it.

Instead he was falling. Eyes closed. Body limp.

Perhaps dead. That was . . . if he hadn't already been dead for quite some time . . .

And he saw them go down, bullets striking them with sickening thuds, twisting in a bizarre distortion of the alleyway . . . he saw them hit the ground, and their eyes, their eyes stared at him, and the accusation that was there . . .

. . . and there were the roses that his mother had been clutching, the roses his father had bought mere minutes before, the last purchase he would ever make . . .

. . . and he was running, running from the bodies lying in state at the wake . . .

. . . and there was the mud and the plunge, the plunge that he remembered, of course, but the details had been hazy for so long and the air was rushing past him . . .

. . . and the bat, the huge one, the one that had come after him . . . screeching at him . . . and something had dropped from Bruce's hands . . . what was it . . . what . . .

"You're a killer, too . . ."

The words ripped across his mind, forcing his mind awake, forcing his eyes open . . .

He had just enough time to curve his body into a diving form, and then he split the water. He had to hit it just perfectly. He wouldn't be much good to himself or anyone else with a broken back.

He vanished beneath the water's surface, and to any onlooker . . . had there been any . . . it would have seemed impossible that Batman would be resurfacing. Considering the impact with which he'd struck the water. Considering the height he'd plunged from. And his barely conscious condition. And the cold of the water, and its choppiness. And the length of time that he was under.

Impossible.

It was a word with which Batman had only a passing acquaintance.

He broke the surface, gasping for air, arms and legs moving desperately to keep himself above water. Within moments he'd steadied himself enough, and then he trod water and looked up at the ungodly illumination high above him.

Half of Lady Gotham's once-beautiful face was still flaming, a blazing mockery of all of Batman's efforts.

He slapped the water in frustration and then, with a sigh, he began the long, unpleasant swim to shore, as the burning lady Gotham lit the way.

CHAPTER 6

Someone was working late at Wayne Enterprises.

Edward Nygma hunched over his device, working at a fever pitch. The only addition to his cubicle was a large pot of coffee which, if he could have figured a way to run an IV line to his arm, he would have attached. His hands moved in a deft, almost-delicate manner. His concentration was complete, the only indication of its intensity being the sweat that beaded his forehead . . . and the steady stream of muttering.

" 'Too many questions. Too many question marks.' I'll show you, Bruce Wayne."

Then an officious voice, sounding like a cross between a foghorn and a Rottweiler, snapped from the entrance to his cubicle, "What the hell is going on here?"

Edward looked up at Stickley, his eyes not even fully focussing on him. "I told you your project is terminated," Stickley went on.

Nygma gave no response, but that was okay with Stickley. He wasn't looking for any. Instead he smiled nastily. "For that matter . . . I'm canceling you, Nygma. You deliberately disobeyed me. That was insubordination. But not only that, you roughed up Bruce Wayne and subjected him to your . . . fixations. That was just plain stupid." He leaned against the edge of the cubicle, interlaced his fingers. His tone changed and he sounded almost conciliatory. "It's pretty obvious what you were doing, Nygma. You tried a little power play. Thought you'd make an end run around the boss. And, y'know . . . that's understandable. It's even okay. Goes with the territory of corporations. But there's an old saying you didn't think about. And that old saying is, When you go up against the boss . . . you better win. You didn't win, Edward. You lost."

He waited for some reaction, but all he saw was the fevered intensity of Edward Nygma's gaze centered on him. It was as if everything else in Nygma's world at that moment had fallen away with the single exception of Stickley.

It was not a location that Stickley found particularly desirable. He turned away gruffly and said, "I'm calling security."

He got two feet before Edward brought the coffeepot crashing down on his head. Stickley went down without a sound.

"Caffeine'll kill you," Ed informed the unconscious body. Then he hesitated, wondering what the hell he should do now. He'd acted totally on impulse. . . .

Brain impulse . . . thought impulse . . .

He looked from Stickley to the machinery and back again. A wide grin split his face.

"When you least expect it . . . you're elected," he said.

When Stickley awoke, he wasn't sure where he was at first. He tried to piece together what had happened, tracing for himself the sequence of events that had resulted in his discovery that he was strapped to a rolling swivel chair. He felt a dull ache in his head and a further pain in his neck when he tried to look around.

Then he became aware that there was something balanced on his head. He nodded back and forth, trying to shake it off. It felt like a hat or . . .

There were wires trailing from whatever it was. Wires to a machine, and now enough of his confusion fell away so that he was able to perceive Edward Nygma wearing a similar rig on his own head, making what appeared to be some final adjustments. Nygma must have somehow sensed that Stickley had come to, because he didn't even bother to look over to his boss (or ex-boss) as he said, "This won't hurt a bit." Then he gave the matter a moment's more thought and added, "At least I don't think it will."

Nygma did turn to him then and flashed a brief, if slightly pained grin, as he reached over toward a toggle on the power source. Mustering his ire, Stickley bellowed, "Nygma, you press that button and—"

"And what? I'm fired?"

He flipped a switch.

The TV screen flared to life, and a green glow emanated from it. And hovering there, in the glow, was a holographic representation of Stickley reeling in a prize bass. Then the figures began to waver and tremble.

"Losing resolution," muttered Edward to himself. "More power."

He threw a second switch, and immediately warning lights flared to life. But the lead time between the warning and the opportunity to shut down was way, way too short. A white beam lanced out from the TV, into Stickley's headband. The systems, both in the circuitry and in Stickley's own neural pathways, overloaded, and the feedback smashed back into the machine and terminated in Edward's own headband.

If Stickley had been at all aware at this point of what was happening, he would have taken some small measure of rejoicing in the fact that Nygma was screaming as loudly as he was.

But he was not aware of what was happening. Indeed, one look at his glazed, slack expression made it quite clear that he was not aware of anything at all.

But a look into Nygma's eyes would have told the exact opposite. He looked invigorated, even reborn. The normal glimmer of twisted genius had been accelerated by somewhere around a factor of a hundred.

It was as if his brain had been blown in an infinite number of directions all at once, and was now hurriedly reassembling itself. And from that reassembly came different impulses, different thoughts, a scattergun of personalities and notions, people that Nygma and/or Stickley had met, or hated, or loved, or had made any impression on him at all—all of them bubbling to the surface, struggling for their moment, fighting for dominance.

Sounding much like the host of a game show Edward had enjoyed in his youth, he barked, "Ed Nygma, come on down. You're the next contestant on Brain Drain. I'll take what's inside thick skull number one. What have we got for him, Johnny?"

Then for a moment the emcee eased back and Edward's own personality . . . what there was of it, at any rate . . . came roaring back to the surface, speaking so quickly that it would have been impossible for anyone overhearing to understand a single thing he was saying. "Stickley, I've had a break-through! And a breakdown? Maybe. Nevertheless. I'm smarter. I'm a genius. No, several geniuses. A gaggle. A swarm. A flock of freaking Freuds." Then, switching to what he imagined to be an approximation of Freud's voice, he continued, "Unt I am experiencing a saturation of the cerebrum . . ."

His mind flared once more, and suddenly he was the short order cook at the greasy spoon Stickley occasionally stopped by for breakfast on the way to work. "Yo, Charlie. Gimmie an order of brain-fry. Extra well. Hold the neurons."

Too many question marks . . . Wayne's assessment and caution asserted itself.

Thinking of Wayne grounded him just slightly, and he looked at the slack-jawed Stickley. "Riddle me this, Fred. What is everything to someone and nothing to everyone else? Your mind, of course. And now mine pumps with the power of yours."

He flashed onto a movie musical that Stickley had fallen asleep watching three weeks ago and, to the tune of "Top Hat, White Tie and Tails," began to sing, "I'm sucking up your IQ . . . Vacuuming your cortex . . . Feeding off your brain . . ."

And when Stickley had woken up, a British comedy of manners was on . . .

In a clipped accent, he said, "Fred, I must confess you were a wonderful appetizer. Simply divine. But now I yearn for a meal of substance. The main course. A wide and varied palate. Ah, to taste the mind of a hero. A nobleman. A poet. Einstein in a Jungian sauce with a dash of Nietzsche on top."

He sensed that his mind was starting to peel away completely and, with what little control he had left, he reached over and shut off the machine. The light flickered and died and, with a sigh as if having just physically separated from a lover, Nygma murmured, "What a rush."

Then Stickley, for what might possible have been the first time in his life, actually did something . . . interesting.

He spoke.

The reason this was interesting was that Edward had had no clue that Stickley *would* be able to speak, or think, or make himself understood after the treatment. So being subjected to the device wasn't terminal. Clearly a best-case scenario.

"What the hell just happened?"

Nygma smiled gleefully. "A surprising side effect. While you were mesmerized by my 3-D TV, I utilized your neural energy to grow smarter. And yet, now that my beam is off, your intelligence—as it were—has returned to normal with no memory of my cerebral siphon." Boisterously he added, "I am a Columbus of the mind. Land Ho!"

It took Stickley a few moments to truly comprehend what it was that Edward Nygma was telling him. Nygma had been . . . what? Puttering around in his brain? Sucking away neural energy? It was . . . it was like some sort of mind rape.

Making no attempt to restrain his fury, Stickley roared, "Bruce Wayne was right, you demented, bizarre, unethical toad. It *is* mind manipulation! I'm reporting you to the FCC, the Human Experimentation Board, the AMA, the police, the federal government. You're going to court, to jail, and then to a mental institution for the rest of your twisted little life!

But first and foremost, Nygma, you are fired! Do you hear me? Fired!!!"

Cackling with the demented glee he'd once seen a comedian display in a movie, Nygma shot back, "I don't *think* so!"

He lashed out with a foot, kicking the chair to which Stickley was tied. The chair rolled back across the slick floor at high speed, Stickley yelling obscenities and totally unaware of his jeopardy until he smashed through the large round window at the end of the corridor.

Stickley shrieked . . . and stopped short.

The chair was teetering on the edge, glass plummeting down and away. Only one thing was keeping him from tumbling off the precipice, and that was the long wire attached to his headband.

Edward Nygma charged up to him, terror and concern on his face. Clearly he had not meant for this to happen, and the potential ramifications for the near fatality had . . .

Then he leaned in close, gripping the wired headband, and Stickley barely had time to realize that Nygma was concerned, not about him, but about his precious machine. With a twisted sneer of contempt he said, "Fred. Babe. You are fired. Or should I say: terminated."

He yanked the headband off Stickley, and his former boss's only means of support was gone. He barely had time to utter a screech before the chair tilted backwards and out, plummeting to the ground far below.

Edward didn't even bother to hang around to see the landing. By the time Stickley hit, Nygma was already back at his cubicle. He was not, however, engaged in a flurry of activity as one might expect after having just committed his very first murder. Instead he was busy staring intensely at the photos of Bruce Wayne all over the interior of his cubicle. "Question marks, Mr. Wayne? My work raises too many questions?"

With mind-blinding fury, he started ripping the pictures down from the walls. "Two years—3.5762 percent of my estimated life span—toiling for your greater glory and profit. Well, let me ask you some questions, Mr. Smarter Than Thou. Why are you so debonair? Successful? Richer than God. Why should you have it all and not me?"

He looked around at the smashed and shattered remains of what he'd torn down. And then slowly his gaze turned to focus on a surveillance camera up on the wall. It was not being monitored, Edward knew, but it had dutifully recorded everything that had happened.

He reached up for the lens as he muttered, "Yes, you're right, there are too many questions, Bruce Wayne. Here's a good one. Why hasn't anybody put you in your place? And it's time you came up with some answers. Starting right now."

CHAPTER 7

The images were flying toward him . . . his parents lying in state . . . the leaves . . . the ground giving way beneath him . . . and the object . . . small, leather, clutching tightly to him . . .

And the giant bat (if it was a bat, or something worse, something spit out from Hell) lurching toward him. And it screeched at him in a voice that, for the first time, had discernible words:

You're a killer, too . . .

Bruce Wayne lunged backwards and, in doing so, woke himself up.

He blinked against the intruding sunlight, which was pouring through the window thanks to Alfred's having just moved the curtains aside.

"Dreams, sir?" he asked, already knowing the answer.

"No time for dreams," he said, brusquely and falsely. "Status?"

Alfred didn't even bother to point out that most mortals said something along the lines of "Good morning" rather than "status." "The Batcomputer has been scanning the Emergency bands all night. No sign of Two-Face. He's disappeared."

"He'll be back. Did you get those file tapes from Arkham Asylum?"

"In the player, sir, and ready."

Bruce rose from the bed, bare-chested, and Alfred couldn't help but notice the bruises that decorated his torso. "What a marvelous shade of purple." He paused a moment and, when Bruce didn't respond, he spoke again and made no effort to keep the concern out of his voice. "Really, if you insist on trying to get yourself killed each night . . ."

Bruce, not wanting to get into it so early in the morning, walked away from Alfred, toward the TV and video player. He stepped over the ripped, dented, and punctured costume that lay on the floor. It wasn't that he was slovenly; it was that he had literally forgotten about it. An old costume was an old problem. He was already on to the next one.

Alfred picked up the battered uniform and continued, ". . . would it be a terrible imposition to ask you to at least take better care of your equipment?"

"Then you'd have nothing to complain about."

"Hardly a worry, sir."

Bruce turned on the TV and, as he loaded the tape in, said, "Speaking of equipment, I want to get back to work on the prototype."

Alfred shuddered. "Sir, the last time you tried to run it through a test—the relay overloads and short-circuiting almost . . ."

"I remember what happened last time, Alfred. I was wearing it, remember?"

"I doubt I could ever forget."

"It was just a test, Alfred," protested Bruce. "And it wasn't so bad . . ."

"Once the burns healed," Alfred sniffed.

"You're exaggerating. Besides, if I'd been wearing the prototype yesterday, things might have gone very differently."

"Indeed they might have. For one thing, they might be scraping your incinerated remains off the side of the Second National Bank building."

"Alfred . . ."

"With a spatula."

"All right, all right." He flipped on the TV and started up the videotape. There was the tortured face of Harvey Dent, staring in the camera and sneering at the off-camera doctor who was asking him questions. The date and time on the video track indicated that it was one of the last interviews . . . if not the last . . . before he'd made his break. He was methodically flipping his coin, reaching the same height with each toss.

"Come on, Harvey," Bruce said urgently. "What's on those twisted minds of yours? Where are you going to strike next?"

Harvey, of course, didn't hear him. Instead he was saying to the doctor, "Where would be the ideal place for a man like me, Doc? Ideal means imaginary. But to me, Doc, it's not imaginary. It's someplace that I'll find. I'll find a land where light is shadow and freaks are kings."

And then suddenly Harvey shifted his gaze . . . and was looking straight at Bruce Wayne as he said, "You're a killer too, Bruce."

Bruce's head turned quickly to see Alfred's reaction. But Alfred was merely standing there, calm, passive, holding the costume draped over one arm.

Quickly Bruce rewound the tape, ran it again. And again. Two-Face was saying, "Where light is shadow and freaks are kings." This time, though, he didn't turn and look at Bruce. Instead he just sat there, staring at the doctor.

The doctor said from offscreen, "And where would that be, Harvey?"

Dent studied him a moment and then said, "You're so smart. *You* figure it out." Then he leaned back and lapsed into silence and not all the doctor's probing could prompt another response out of him.

There were other times, other sessions on the tape, but a disconcerted Bruce Wayne decided now was not the time to hear them. Instead he shut off the VCR and brought the TV on line.

The station owner, a man with whom Bruce had had dinner several times and who considered Bruce Wayne to be one of the true treasures of Gotham City, was staring into the camera with the words "EDITORIAL" pasted across the upper right-hand side. "The city should charge Batman with felony landmarks destruction. His vigilantism is a plague on Gotham."

Bruce moved away from the TV, making a mental note not to pick up the dinner check next time, and stepped into a high-tech workout machine. His pressure on the footpads brought the machine to electronic life. "Good morning, Mr. Wayne. Select difficulty level."

"Bruce, please," he corrected, feeling that if he couldn't be informal with an electronic system of weights and pulleys, who *could* he let down his hair with? "Maximum resistance."

He began running through his regimen. Alfred, meantime, had come out of the bathroom, having begun to run Bruce's bath for him. The butler slowed and glanced appreciatively at the TV screen, and Bruce looked over to see what had caught Alfred's attention.

It was a file interview with Chase Meridian, as she dissected the mind-set of multiple personalities.

Bruce made an impatient noise. "You know what she said to Batman last night? She practically accused him of being crazy."

He waited for Alfred to concur loyally that such an assessment was completely out of bounds. Tacky, even. Instead, Alfred considered the matter and then said, "Sir . . . you are a good man. A brave man. But perhaps you are not the most sane man."

The comment stopped Bruce cold as he turned to look at Alfred. Any number of times, this man who had become like a substitute father to him had made oblique comments about Bruce's mind-set. Most of them had been cloaked in withering or drily sarcastic terms. But Alfred had never made such a flat, inflectionless . . . and even slightly frightening . . . assessment of his employer's mental state.

Alfred immediately became aware that perhaps he had

crossed the line that he should not have. Trying to angle the conversation into a more social, even jocular, direction, he suggested, "Perhaps the lady is just what the doctor ordered. She seems lovely . . ."

But Bruce wouldn't be put off. Instead he stared at Alfred as if he were dissecting him with his eyes in hopes of finding some sort of answer to long-standing questions.

"Alfred," he said slowly, "why did I become Batman?"

You're asking me? was the first thing to come to Alfred's mind. But he had the good grace not to say it. Instead he simply repeated what Bruce himself had said on occasion. "To avenge your dear parents. To protect the innocent."

But Bruce waved off the rationalizations as if they no longer interested him. "To fight crime, of course. But there's something else . . ."

He looked toward the window, blinking against the autumn sun. The day couldn't have been more unlike that hideous night. "What was I doing outside the night of my parents' wake? What sent me running into the storm?"

Alfred shrugged. From a distance of many years, he was able to look back at himself, running around like a madman and shouting Bruce's name into the storm. At the time that very question had flamed in Alfred's mind. *Where could the boy have gone? What could have driven him out? Why the bloody hell wasn't I watching him?*

"I don't know," Alfred admitted. He thought of Bruce's parents for the first time in . . . oh . . . a day or two. "Such a tragic loss. Rain fell like tears that night."

He wasn't sure if Bruce had entirely heard him. Instead he was running that night through his mind, trying to reconstruct events. "I remember racing through the fields. Falling into the cave," and he started ticking off the moments on his fingers, "the bat chasing me . . . those fangs . . . that breath." Then he paused. "But there was something else. Something I was running from. I just can't remember."

The phone rang, and to Bruce it seemed as loud as a cannon barrage. He started slightly as Alfred picked up the phone.

"Wayne Manor." He listened for a moment, and then turned to Bruce and said, "It's Commissioner Gordon, sir. There's been an accident at Wayne Enterprises."

Suddenly the exercise machine shut down automatically. The device had been monitoring his breathing and respiration, and apparently hadn't liked what it found. "Routine terminated. Recommend rest. You need a vacation . . . Bruce."

Bruce and Alfred looked at each other. Clearly it was shaping up to be one of those days.

Edward Nygma leaned against the outside of his cubicle, sobbing profusely onto the shoulder of the head of personnel. She was patting him awkwardly, not quite sure what to make of this display of grief.

"Why? Oh, why?" he moaned inconsolably. "I can't believe it. Two years. Working in the same office. Shoulder to shoulder, cheek to cheek . . ." Then he stopped crying for just long enough to clarify, "We're talking face, by the way." Then he went right back into his histrionics. ". . . and then this."

"This," as it happened, was a note (with a few tear stains on it) that Nygma was thrusting into the confused woman's hands. "I found it in my cubicle. You'll find handwriting and sentence structure match his exactly . . ." he added in a perfectly rational voice before breaking down once more. "I couldn't possibly continue here. The memories. I'll get my things."

He ducked quickly into his cubicle, where he'd already boxed up his invention. The woman in personnel used the opportunity to slip away, which was fine by Edward. He, likewise, was going to be using the opportunity to slip away.

He heard voices. One of them was Bruce Wayne's. Another was older, gruff. Sounded extremely . . . coplike. There were a few other knickknacks still scattered around Edward's cubicle, but nothing important and certainly nothing he couldn't live without. He took one final glance around, as if to imprint on his mind a final image of what he was leaving behind. That way he could carry it with him mentally as he progressed toward a greater and far more glorious future—a future that would not be realized by being detained for more questioning. He knew he was at a delicate stage right now. He wasn't absolutely sure that he could contain the buzzing in his brain. He wanted to crow his achievements, boast about his prowess. Perhaps even chatter about Stickley's gloriously ludicrous expression as his chair had toppled backwards to oblivion.

That would not be good.

Instead, he took the opportunity to bolt out a side door, so that by the time Bruce Wayne and Commissioner Gordon walked past, he was barreling down the steps of the emergency stairway. If covering one's involvement in a homicide couldn't be considered an emergency, then what could?

Wayne and Gordon stood in front of the security console, studying the tape from the previous night. Stickley was clearly visible writing a note which they could safely assume was the suicide note that had been turned in to the head of personnel. Upon finishing, Stickley laid the note down carefully. Then he took a chair, gripped it firmly, and . . . using it as a battering ram . . . charged toward the large window at the end of the corridor. He smashed through it, clutching the chair, and vanished from sight.

"That all jibes," said Gordon. "What we found on the ground . . . well, there wasn't really enough to tell much of anything. Both your man and the chair, shattered to . . ." He paused. "Sorry, Bruce. I didn't mean to upset you."

Bruce nodded in acknowledgment.

"In any event, this looks pretty cut-and-dried. Definitely suicide. Thanks for the help, Bruce. We'll be in touch."

Bruce shook hands briskly, and then turned away from Gordon.

He walked through the electronics division, stopping to

whisper a few words to shaken employees, telling them to take a couple of days if they so desired, with pay of course.

He paused momentarily at Edward Nygma's cubicle, thinking about the intensity he'd seen in the man's eyes the other day. Nygma's ideas might have been a bit odd, but that sort of passion—if properly channeled—could accomplish miracles. That was something Bruce Wayne certainly knew better than anyone else. Perhaps *after* this fiasco was the time to take Nygma aside under less-pressured circumstances. Start again . . .

But the cubicle was almost empty. Nygma's personal items, and that odd-looking device of his, were gone.

Bruce stared at the vacant cubicle for a time. And then he headed to his office.

Moments later Margaret was following him in, scribbling notes furiously. "Make sure Stickley's family is taken care of. Full benefits."

"He wasn't on our corporate life insurance policy."

"He is now," said Bruce, and repeated, "Full benefits."

She nodded. There was no point in arguing, and besides, she had no intention of trying to act the heavy in this instance. Taking the opportunity to attend to unfinished business, she flipped to a different page in her notebooks and said, "Gossip Gerty and the society columnists have called a record thirty-two times. I think if they don't know soon who you plan to take to the charity circus, the world is surely going to end."

Bruce was about to answer when he noticed something on his desk. It was an envelope. "What's this?"

She was genuinely puzzled. "I don't know. I didn't see anyone."

He flipped it over and scrutinized it. "No postmark. No stamp." He pulled it open and read off, " 'If you look at the numbers upon my face, you won't find 13 anyplace.' "

Margaret wasn't sure what she'd been expecting inside the envelope, but it certainly hadn't been that. "Say what?"

He turned the paper over, but there was no signature. He

looked back at the message. "It's a riddle. Numbers upon my face. One through twelve. No thirteen. . . ." He shrugged at the obviousness of it. "A clock."

She scratched her head. "Who would send you riddles?"

He turned to her and said, "Maggie, *that's* the riddle."

The run-down tenement building was notable only for its unique decoration. It had once been directly across the street from an outfit called Criss Cross Cleaners, and consequently, a large ad for the dry cleaners consisting of an immense crossword puzzle adorned the exterior. The wall painting was the only reminder that the cleaner had ever been in business there. The paint was peeling and, to make matters worse, graffiti artists had filled in a few of the empty "puzzle spots" with letters that spelled out obscenities.

All of this was irrelevant to at least one of the building's tenants, a man who had never viewed the place as anything other than a brief rest stop on his determined drive along the superhighway to success.

The problem was that the tenant had always assumed that Bruce Wayne would present him with the opportunity needed to get that final, extra mile. But it was patently clear to Edward Nygma that Bruce Wayne was too self-absorbed, self-important, and self . . . well . . . self-ish, to give a damn about Edward Nygma and his plans.

Indeed, as he worked in his cluttered apartment, putting the finishing touch on his second riddle, he had finally begun to grasp just what had happened. Years ago, when he had looked into the eyes of young Bruce Wayne, he'd seen a peer. But when the adult Bruce Wayne had come face-to-face with Edward Nygma, Wayne had seen only a rival. That was it, of course. It was painfully, even agonizingly, obvious.

"Guess what, Bruce Wayne," he muttered. "Now I'm the guy with all the answers."

He turned and looked lovingly at his modified brain scan equipment.

The box.

It sparkled and sputtered slightly, running self-tests and di-agnostics. It was almost ready. Almost ready.

He rose and went to the window, resting a hand gently on the Box's gleaming surface. He looked out over the ugliness of his neighborhood, toward the gleaming spires of the up-town sections of Gotham. And beyond that, up in the hills . . . the residence where Bruce Wayne sat on high, like great Zeus, looking down at the puny mortals and rendering judgments. This person shall be raised up, this other one cast down.

Who gave him the right? Who gave him the goddamn right? Well . . . ultimately, It didn't matter. Because Edward Nygma was going to take it away from him.

"There are seven million brains in the Naked City. And they'll all be mine."

Later that night, cloaked in darkness, Bruce Wayne sat in the depths of the Batcave. He felt as if he were standing on the edge of a diving board, and it would only take the slight-est nudge to send him plummeting, headfirst, into . . . what? Bottomless depths? An empty pool?

His entire life was a riddle . . . and was now being further aggravated by some weirdo who had dropped off a riddle in his office.

He was used to weirdness in his life as Batman. But did it have to intrude into his life as Bruce Wayne?

Who had sent him the riddle?

Unbeknownst to Bruce, the answer to that question had slipped a second riddle into the mailbox near the great front gate and was scurrying away as fast as his bicycle would take him. . . .

CHAPTER 8

When Alfred did not find Bruce in his bedroom, he felt that same little jump of concern he always felt at such moments. Had Bruce decided to don his caped leisure suit and make an evening of it? Was he lying in an alleyway somewhere, dead or dying? And, as always in such moments when Alfred's fancy turned to morbidity, he started asking himself what he could have done to prevent it.

All this tumbled through his mind as he descended to the Batcave to check. And there, seated in a high-backed chair, was Bruce Wayne. His fingers were steepled and he was staring off into space.

"Mister Wayne?" Alfred said rather formally.

"Alfred," replied Wayne.

"Have you been to sleep, sir?"

"On and off. A few minutes here and there."

Alfred couldn't think of what to say. Wayne's voice was so distant . . . and so unspeakably sad. And perhaps it held something else that Alfred couldn't recall hearing since Bruce was a young boy. Perhaps he sounded just a little bit afraid.

"Can I get you anything, sir?" he asked finally.

"Yes." Bruce nodded slowly. "You can get me an appointment with Dr. Meridian. I think . . . I could use a sounding board for some . . . things . . . going through my head lately." He looked up at Alfred. "I hope you aren't insulted?"

"You mean because, for once, you've chosen not to make me the sole beneficiary of your . . . odd confidences?" He smiled ever so slightly. "I shall manage to live with the devastating humiliation."

By the time he'd gotten upstairs, however, Alfred had brought in the mail . . . and discovered the second riddle. Which meant that, all of a sudden, Bruce Wayne's reason for going to see Dr. Meridian had changed.

Bruce Wayne drove his gleaming red Jag into the municipal police complex, the guard recognizing him and waving him through immediately. He pulled into a spot, made a mental note of a car parked illegally in a handicap slot, and then made his way upstairs.

Dr. Meridian was a fairly new arrival to Gotham City, and Gordon had rather graciously afforded her office space at the police complex. In return she made herself available several days a week to consult with Gordon and other police officers on various investigations. Her private practice was just starting up but—knowing what a major supporter of the police the Wayne Foundation had always been—she had agreed to make time for him.

Bruce walked briskly down the hallway, needing to ask directions to her office only three times and getting lost only twice. But as he approached the office, he heard grunts and the sounds of combat from within. Quickly he tried the doorknob, but it was locked tight.

He heard Dr. Meridian cry out, and there was the sound of a vicious punch being landed.

He put two and two together, and got . . . Two-Face.

Without hesitation or regard to his secret identity, Bruce Wayne kicked open the door. The lock and knob flew off, clattering to the floor, and the door banged inward. Bruce leapt in, fists cocked . . .

And realized he'd slipped up.

Chase's hair was a bit matted and hanging down. Her fists were taped up and poised in front of the punching bag that she had been whaling into until Bruce had charged into her office.

Bruce froze where he was, as did she.

The air should have been rife with embarrassment, or shock. Or shouting, "Get out!" or "Oh my God, I'm so sorry!" or something.

Instead there was a long moment of tension that didn't seem to arise from stress but from something else entirely. . . .

Act casual, buzzed a voice in Bruce's head. He tried to do so, leaning slightly against the doorframe and saying, "I guess I'm early. I have an appointment. I'm Bruce Wayne."

"The billionaire. Oh, good. Then you can afford to buy me a new door."

Bruce stared at what little she was wearing and, clearing his throat, said, "I can come back . . ."

"Oh, absolutely," she said wryly. "Maybe you'll catch me in the shower next time."

He glanced around. "There's a shower here?"

She sighed and gestured, "Turn around."

Bruce obediently turned in a 360-degree circle, and then held out his hands as if to say, "Ta daa."

She pursed her lips, clearly unamused (or, at least, trying to pretend that she was unamused.) This time Bruce obeyed the spirit of the request in addition to the letter, and turned his back. To make some use of the time, he worked on closing the door. Without benefit of the lock it seemed inclined to swing open, and he finally settled on propping it shut with a chair.

From behind him Chase said, "Okay."

He turned back to her and, except for the fact that she was busy untaping her hands, she could have been another woman entirely. She was wearing a dark brown wraparound skirt and a cream-colored blouse. Bruce gestured with some chagrin to the door. "I'm sorry. I thought you were in trouble."

She indicated the bag with a nod of her head. "It's therapeutic." Then she looked back to Wayne and actually smiled.

She had the smile of someone who didn't smile quite enough. "I guess I should be grateful. You risked danger for someone you haven't even met."

She waited for a modest "It was nothing," or perhaps even an endeavor to parlay his heroism into some sort of pass. Perhaps. But instead he just shrugged and kept a level gaze on her.

"Somehow, I thought you'd be older," she said after a moment. "Well . . . how can I help you, Mr. Wayne?"

He reached into his vest pocket and pulled out the two riddles, tossing them onto her desk. "Somebody's been sending me love letters. One at my office, one at home. Commissioner Gordon thought you might give me your expert opinion."

She read them both quickly. "A clock," she said. Deciphering the first one almost as quickly as Wayne had. "But . . . this second one: 'Tear one off and scratch my head. What once was red is black instead?' " She shrugged. "A newspaper?"

"No, that's black and white and read all over." He indicated the riddle. "The answer to this is a match."

She nodded absently and continued to study the riddles— looking for some further clue or indicator of the author's mind-set. The first one seemed as if it had been done hurriedly, but the second was far more elaborate. Letters were trimmed out of newspaper and magazine headlines, and there was also bizarre calligraphy around the edges. Question marks snaking in and out of everywhere. And, most disturbing, a border composed of dripping daggers.

"Didn't exactly pick up this stationery at a Hallmark store," she observed. Then she noticed that Bruce Wayne was drumming his fingers absently on the chair arm. "Psychiatrists make you nervous?"

"Just beautiful ones."

"The infamous Wayne charm," and she sat back slightly in the chair. "Does it ever shut off?"

He smiled thinly. "You should see me at night."

She took it as a come-on and brushed it off. Then she held up one letter in either hand. "My opinion: This letter writer is a total wacko."

"Wacko?" He seemed amused. "Is that a technical term?"

"Patient may suffer from obsessional syndrome with potential homicidal inclinations. Work better for you?"

"So what you're saying is that this guy's a total wacko, right?"

She smiled just slightly. "Exactly." She couldn't help but find his reaction fascinating. "I can't help but observe, Mr. Wayne: Most people, if informed that they were being harassed by someone who was quite likely off his rocker, would show some degree of concern or fear. But you seem . . . more amused than anything. Then again, I guess someone like you encounters more than his share of nutcases, eh?"

He looked at her levelly. "You'd be amazed." Then he saw, over her head and to the right, a framed print of a bat on the wall. This struck him as rather odd. It wasn't the sort of thing one ordinarily would stumble over in an office, particularly a shrink's. But there indeed it was, black and with its wings spread wide. He pointed at it and said, "You have a thing for bats?"

From her expression it was clear that she hadn't a clue as to what he was talking about. She turned to see where he was pointing, and when she looked back at him it was with that unmistakable air of clinical interest in her eyes. "That's a Rorschach, Mr. Wayne. An ink blot. People see what they want."

Bruce started to say, "Oh, come now, I know an ink blot when I see it . . ." but didn't get any further than a simple, "Oh." Because when he looked back at the print he saw that it was, indeed, a Rorschach ink blot. Oh, there were the vague outlines of what could be a bat, certainly. But it could also have been a butterfly. Or two faces in profile. Or . . .

A bat. Dammit, it looked like a bat, ready to flap its way off the paper . . .

Dr. Meridian watched Bruce Wayne's face carefully as he

stared at the ink blot. There was something going on. Something in the conversation, some subtext, that she was missing. She could sense it, almost taste it. With a raised eyebrow, she said, "I think the question would be, do *you* have a thing for bats?" she asked.

It was an inquiry that he clearly had no interest in answering and every interest in avoiding. He reached over and tapped the papers. "So, this . . . Riddler, for want of a better name . . . is dangerous?"

She pursed her lips in thought, letting the topic drift. "What do you know about obsession? Seriously, Mr. Wayne."

"Seriously?" He hesitated. "A little."

There it was again. That same tone of voice which she'd heard in his comment about seeing him at night. A tone that she'd at first dismissed, but now was starting to notice recurring at key points in the conversation. She made a mental note to watch when such vocal shifts occurred again. "Obsessions are born of fear. Recall a moment of great terror. Say you associate that moment with . . ." She paused and then thought of the blot. ". . . a bat. Over time, the bat's image penetrates the mind, invades every aspect of your daily life. Can you imagine something like that?"

"It's a stretch but I'll manage."

Damn! There it was again! That same tone of voice, practically sending off flares screaming into the night, saying, *Look here! Right here! More than meets the eye, right over here!*

She gave no clue to what was going through her mind. "The letter writer is obsessed with you. His only escape may be to . . ."

"To purge the fixation. To kill me."

"You understand obsession better than you let on."

He nodded slightly as he picked up a small wicker totem doll from the table. "Still play with dolls, Doctor?"

"She's a Malaysian dream warden. Some cultures believe

she stands sentry while you sleep and guards your dreams. Silly to you I'm sure—"

But Bruce's expression stopped her short. Somewhere within her, her little inner psychiatrist cried *Bingo! Paydirt! You got him! There's something there, just reel him in now . . . start asking questions, probe, find out what's bothering him . . .*

"You look so sad. Do you need one?"

"Me?" He laughed easily. He was clearly rather practiced at masking his feelings. "No. Why would I?"

She made a thrust forward, a probing question. "You're not exactly what you seem, are you, Bruce Wayne? What is it you really came here for?"

He wanted to answer her. That much she could easily see. But instead he coolly looked at his watch and said, "Oops. Time's up."

"That's usually my line."

"Look, I'd love to keep chatting . . ."

"Would you?" She looked at him, so appraisingly that if he'd been an automobile, she'd be kicking his tires. "I'm not so sure."

"You misunderstand, Doctor. That wasn't an open, 'Gee it might be nice in the indeterminate future' type comment. And if you didn't have the annoying psychiatrist habit of interrupting people with questions . . ."

"Now when have I—?" But then she caught herself and smiled sheepishly. "I'm sorry. Go ahead."

"I was simply going to say that I would love to keep chatting, but I'm going to have to get you out of those clothes."

She felt lost. "Excuse me?"

"And into a black dress." Once her confusion was utter bafflement, he said, "Tell me, Doctor, do you like the circus?"

CHAPTER 9

Dick Grayson rummaged through his costume box. Although he was already dressed in the red-and-green tights that he and the rest of his family would be wearing tonight, he was still looking for some other sort of accoutrements that would spiff up the old outfit a little. He was always trying to convince his folks to jazz up the look, and was forever modelling masks, flared boots, capes . . . whatever occurred to him. But he always had trouble convincing his father. John always argued for simplicity, and naturally mom went along with him. Wherever John Grayson stood, Mary Grayson was right there with him. It was kind of comforting in a way, but it was also as annoying as hell.

The door to the trailer that he shared with his brother Chris slammed open. The sounds of the crowds and the organ music were that much louder as Chris entered quickly and grabbed Dick by his shoulder. "Fer cryin' out loud, Dick. Will you come on? We're going on in five minutes!"

"Chris, how about if we add a—"

Chris didn't want to hear it. Instead he pulled Dick to his feet and said, "Look, you want to go into clothing design? So leave the act and become a fashion designer, okay? Until then, will ya come on!"

"I'm the only one in the family with vision, Chris," he said as he allowed himself to be pushed out the door by his older brother. "When the rest of you are so old and decrepit that

108

you fall off swings at playgrounds, I'm going to be living in a mansion and driving the bitchingest car in town. Just wait and see."

"I should live so long," said Chris Grayson.

It wasn't a black dress.

It was dark maroon, crushed velvet. Still, it had been more than sufficient when Bruce had picked Chase up at her rented town house. Bruce was in his tux, and the two of them were third row center at the Gotham Charity Circus, being held in the midst of the vast Gotham Hippodrome. From all over, gossip columnists were peering at Bruce's date. Chase noticed it, and Bruce noticed Chase noticing.

"They're trying to determine who you are and what our relationship is," he told her.

"Don't you find that intrusive?"

"You get used to it. Besides, don't worry about it. What they don't know, they can easily make up." He regarded her thoughtfully. "It wouldn't bother you if, a week from now, it's reported that you're pregnant with a space alien's baby, would it?"

"Depends."

He wrinkled his nose and stuck out his tongue at her.

Damn . . . even when he makes a hideous face, he's gorgeous, she thought bleakly.

From the center ring, the ringmaster was calling, "Ladies and gentlemen. Seventy feet above the ground, performing feats of aerial skill without a net, the Flying Graysons!"

The name "Grayson" immediately rang a bell with Chase, and she looked up at the family of aerialists, already embarking on their trapeze act to the accompaniment of pounding drums. There were four of them . . . it shouldn't be too hard to pick out . . .

She pointed. "Some guy was making off with my purse the other day, and that boy—that one there," and she pointed as Dick hurtled across the open air into the waiting hands of his father, who was dangling upside down from his knees.

"He stopped him. His father was with him. Richard and John, those were their names. Richard and John Grayson. The boy was incredibly brave, and now I understand why. Look what he does for a living."

Bruce nodded as Chase bit her lower lip thoughtfully. "They ran off before I really had a chance to talk with them. I'm not sure why. A pity, too; it would have been fascinating to investigate the kind of psyche that would not only risk death on a regular basis, but subject one's own children to the same sort of danger."

"Did they 'run off' right after you told them you were a psychiatrist?"

"Hmm? Uhm . . . yes. Why?"

"Nothing. No reason."

She jostled his arm. "What are you implying?"

"Me? Nothing. Nothing at all."

Before she could ask him anything further, they suddenly found themselves with a spotlight shining directly on them. And the ringmaster was announcing, "Tonight's charity benefit has raised $375,000 for Gotham Children's Hospital. Let's thank our largest single donor: Bruce Wayne."

Bruce shrugged to Chase in a "Whattaya gonna do?" manner and stood, taking a quick bow before quickly regaining his seat.

"And now," continued the ringmaster, "Richard, the youngest Flying Grayson, will perform the awe-inspiring Death Drop."

Chase watched raptly, as did Bruce.

Dick Grayson stood on the highest platform. Grabbing the trapeze bar, he swung out high into the air above the crowd. Sometimes it seemed to him that this was the only time when he was happy: when he was in flight, when he felt the wind rushing past him and heard the gasps of the crowd over his stunts.

And he would always look down at those poor, earth-bound creatures, each of whom was undoubtedly wondering,

How? How could he risk death day after day, just to experience the momentary thrill of flight?

To which Dick could only wonder, How could they *not*?

And then as he soared above the center of the arena, Dick released the trapeze. He fell, somersaulting in midair, over and over again. The crowd was a blur around him and then suddenly his downward plunge was halted by a pair of strong hands that he knew, beyond question, would always be there for him.

"Fly, robin, fly," his father intoned to him.

They swung toward the platform, then back again toward the center as the acclamation from the crowd below swept over them. Mary was on the opposite platform and, with practiced skill, sent the other, empty trapeze arcing toward them. John Grayson released his son as Dick twirled in midair and snagged the other trapeze. It was a move that was so simple to him, so routine, that the applause it got was as odd as if a little girl had gotten a standing ovation for successfully skipping rope.

Then again, he wasn't about to knock it.

He landed on the platform next to his mother, and together they waved down to the crowd. On the opposite side Chris waved too as he hauled his father in. Chris hadn't done anything on this particular maneuver, but heck . . . the hurrahs were for all of them, weren't they?

"Life doesn't get better than this, does it, Dad," Chris said.

To which John could only reply, "Never."

As the ringmaster watched the proceedings, something suddenly caught his eye. It was a gloved hand, poking from between some curtains offstage. A finger was waggling, trying to get the ringmaster's attention.

He glanced upward at the Graysons. He knew the act; he wouldn't have to make another announcement for sixty seconds as they climbed down the guy wires, at which point he would give their final salutation, they'd take their bows, and get offstage.

Besides, who the hell was sneaking around backstage? If someone hurt themselves back there, the insurance claims and civil suits could wipe out everything they'd accomplished this evening.

He headed toward the curtains to see what was what.

"Look, I'm rock-climbing Sunday," Bruce Wayne said to Chase Meridian. "How about coming along?"

"I'd like to, actually. I love climbing. I really do . . ."

He supplied the next, obvious word for her. "But . . ."

"I guess I've met someone."

"Fast work. You just moved here."

She gave him a sad look. "You know, much to my surprise, you really are terrific. But . . . you could say he kind of dropped out of the sky and . . . bang. I think he felt it too."

Oh my God . . .

"Bruce?" She seemed concerned.

*Not again. Not **again**. This one is fixated on Batman too?*

"Bruce?" She shook his arm.

What was it, anyway? The mask? The cape? The codpiece? Sure, that had to be it.

"Bruce," and this time her voice was firm, yanking him out of his reverie. "Has anyone ever told you that you can act rather strangely?"

"Not to my face," he said. "So, uhm . . . you think he felt it, too. Well, of course he did."

"What?"

He looked at her with a vast depth of sadness. "Who wouldn't?"

In the center ring of the circus, a tiny car—horn honking away—roared into the middle. Clowns began tumbling out, one over the other. As that happened, the Graysons descended on the guy wires.

Chase smiled at the crazed activity. "A land of light and shadow where beasts dance and freaks are king."

He was so startled by the comment, and recently so accustomed to confusion between what he perceived and what was reality, that he asked her to repeat it. She did, puzzled, word for word. "It's a description of the circus. From a fairy tale my mother used to read called 'The Tale of the Twin—'"

That was all he needed to hear. He took her quickly by the hand and said, "We've got to get out of here. Now."

Suddenly the voice of the ringmaster pulled his full attention back to the center ring.

"Ladies and gentlemen, please forget all good American, wholesome fun," the ringmaster called out, his face obscured by a hanging barker's mike. "We are here to bring you absolute chaos and true justice which, my darling ignorant friends, are no more or less than two sides of the same coin. Tonight, a new act for your amusement. We call it Massacre Under the Big Top."

The newly arrived clowns immediately shed their garments, yanking massive guns out of the oversized clown clothes. Some people in the crowd were still laughing uncertainly until a couple of the thugs fired random shots into the air. The unmistakable chatter of the machine guns was the confirmation—for any who still needed it—that the evening had taken a deadly turn.

There was panic and screaming, and the ringmaster stepped out from behind the microphone. His hideous split face was now apparent for all to see. "People, people. Show some grace under pressure. A little decorum, please," cautioned Two-Face. And then added, *"Shut up or die!"*

The deadly admonition, backed up by the armed thugs, had the desired effect. There was still the occasional whimpering, but largely the crowd was silent.

Two-Face nodded approvingly. "If we may direct your attention . . ."

A couple of thugs rolled a round object into the ring. They attached the sphere to ropes hanging from the rafters.

"Inside that harmless-looking orb," continued Two-Face, "two hundred sticks of TNT. In our hand: a radio detonator." Calmly he pushed a button on the box.

The bomb promptly beeped in response, and continued to do so, one beep per second.

"You have two minutes," he informed them with no more concern in his voice than if he'd been hawking red hots.

An angry voice spoke up from the crowd. "What the hell do you want?"

Bruce turned to see the origin of the speaker and, of course, recognized him immediately. It was the mayor. Chase, meantime, was clutching Bruce's arm. Under other circumstances, the pressure might have been pleasurable.

"Want, Mr. Mayor?" Two-Face called. "Just one little thing: Batman. Bruised. Broken. Bleeding. In a word: dead." He gestured to the collective crowd. "Who do we have assembled before us? Gotham's finest. Rich, influential. One of you must know who Batman is. Hell, odds are one of you *is* Batman. So, unless the Bat is surrendered to us posthaste . . . we're off on a proverbial killing spree. Citywide mayhem and murder. Cries of agony and bloody streets, with all you folks as our very first corpses-to-be. You have two . . ." and then he nodded toward the bomb, "well, just under two minutes."

Bruce watched helplessly as the bomb, attached to wires, was hoisted high into the air, toward the upper structural supports of the tent. It made sense, of course. It would make for the most spectacular blast from the furthest distance. If there was one thing that Two-Face lived for, it was high-profile mayhem.

Wayne rose to his feet, for no secret . . . not even his . . . was worth innocent lives. Chase, not understanding what he was about to do, tried to pull him back down.

He started to shake her off, to shout out Harvey's name. Get his attention and repeat to him things said at their first meeting on that rooftop so long ago.

That was when people started to shout and point. He looked up toward the rafters, and gaped.

The Flying Graysons were scaling the scaffolding, heading for the bomb.

*   *   *

"Boys! Move, move, move!" bellowed Two-Face, furious.

Several thugs started climbing the guy wires. It quickly became obvious to the Graysons that Two-Face had not come unprepared; the thugs doing the climbing were obviously trained gymnasts.

Chris prodded Dick upward. "Go! We'll hold them off!"

John, Mary, and Chris swung from trapeze to guy wire to platform, setting up a barrier of human bodies to try to delay the thugs. They kicked, they shoved, they blocked egress. And the thugs, needing both hands to climb, weren't in a position to pull guns and start shooting.

In a daring display that made his earlier theatrics tame in comparison, Dick launched himself from trapeze to trapeze, bounced off the high wire, and just managed to snag an overhead catwalk. He hoisted himself up onto the catwalk.

One of the thugs grabbed John's leg. John Grayson kicked him away and jumped to another trapeze.

Momentarily distracted by her husband's danger, Mary Grayson was unaware of her own. From underneath the platform she was crouched on, one of Two-Face's thugs swung up and slammed into her. Mary Grayson's arms flailed as she tried desperately to regain her balance. But then gravity seized her and pulled her downward.

As one, the audience screamed.

At the last instant, Mary snagged a wildly swinging trapeze with her leg. It jolted her to a halt, but it was too sudden a stop and she started to slide off. But her other leg, dangling wide, wrapped itself around a trailing rope. She hung precariously high above the ground.

Dick was clambering toward the bomb and was able to see what several of the other thugs were now pointing at: the time clock. As he watched, it ticked down to 43, and he had the sick feeling that it didn't signify minutes.

The thugs, not having signed on for a suicide mission, started sliding down the ropes and guy wires to put distance between themselves and the bomb.

John Grayson, meantime, was moving to help his wife. He didn't panic, didn't even come close. They'd been in tighter spots than this, and the threat of falling didn't paralyze the Graysons the way that it might others. But he couldn't do it alone. *"Chris!"* he shouted, and, as if by magic, Chris was there by his side. He'd already been on his way, having seen his mother's predicament. Quickly they clambered out onto a trapeze, John anchoring Chris.

"Just like a thousand times before, Chris," said John calmly. "Same old same old. Not a problem." The mark of his bravery was that it was impossible to tell whether he believed this to be as routine as he was putting across. John set the trapeze swinging, building up momentum.

Mary saw them coming. She reached out, stretching her fingers desperately. The trapeze twisted and tilted under her leg and she felt herself slipping off. The ankle of her other leg throbbed; the rope twined around it provided her major source of support.

It was all laid out beneath Dick Grayson. And yet, remarkably, he wasn't concerned about them. His father was on the case, his brother was helping, and his mother was the most resourceful of the bunch. Dick, meantime, had his own problems, as he worked quickly to unlash the bomb from the rafters. He made a point of not looking at the timer counting down, because he couldn't possibly work any faster than he was . . . and knowing precisely how much time he had, or didn't have, wasn't going to do him any good.

He heard the chatter of machine-gun fire and prayed that it wasn't aimed up at him.

Then the bomb came free in his hands, and, God help him, he almost dropped the damned thing. It bobbled momentarily, but then he recovered it and inadvertently caught a glimpse of the amount of time he had left.

Thirteen seconds . . .

Two-Face's thugs were firing over the heads of the crowd, trying to cause panic, to drive the people back, keep them in their places. Meantime the thugs were inching back toward the trapdoor through which they'd made their entrance. The moment the bomb went, so would they.

But as the crowd panicked, falling one over the other, it was Bruce Wayne's chance. A sea of people came between him and Chase, and he used the opportunity to slide between the rails. Within seconds he had closed in on one of the guards who blocked the way to Two-Face. The guard spotted him at the last moment and swung his gun up, but he was too slow. Bruce slugged him and he went down without another sound.

He afforded himself a glance upward, and saw that the daring young man from the flying trapeze had gotten his hands on the bomb and was clambering through a roof hatch. Presuming the kid could dispose of the explosive fast enough, the people were going to be okay. Bruce prayed that the boy—Richard, Chase had said his name was—would be up to it.

Then his gaze shifted to the rest of the Graysons, high above the ground. The father was swinging the son toward the mother, still twisting between the trapeze and rope. They were swinging back now, toward the far end of their arc, and now they angled back and up toward the trapped woman.

The boy's hands closed on his mother's. They had her. With the additional support, it would be a matter of moments for her to disentangle her leg, free herself, and swing safely with her son and husband to the opposite platform.

And then he saw Two-Face. Two-Face, and one thug between Bruce and the maniac who had turned a charity evening into a hellish disaster.

Bruce charged.

This thug was faster, however. Faster, bigger, and far more formidable. He was holding a machine pistol and squeezed off a few shots. Bruce dropped to the ground, bullets cutting the air above his head. He rolled and came up, slamming his feet into the thug's face. The thug staggered but didn't go down. Bruce grabbed the machine pistol, but the thug wasn't inclined to let go. The two of them struggled against each other, angling for position.

And that's when Bruce saw the coin glittering in the air.

Two-Face had to admire them. A gutsy trapeze family, acrobats, performers. They had decided to try to be heroes.

And they were worthy of the same chance that Two-Face afforded other heroes.

"Day in, day out, time passes, fate has her fancies," he intoned, speaking to an audience only he could hear. "God stands absent, daydreaming, and the universe asks the same old question. Life . . ."

The coin spun in the air and landed at his feet. "Or death."

He looked down at the scarred head and smiled a twisted smile. "Our kinda day," he said.

He pulled out his guns and aimed high.

Bruce slammed his head into the thug's face. It was the kind of maneuver he far preferred to do when wearing his reinforced mask. Nevertheless it did the job. The thug staggered, and Bruce dealt the thug another vicious shot in the head. It sent him down to the ground and Bruce grabbed up the machine pistol.

He swung it up and aimed it squarely at Two-Face. He had him dead in his sights.

Dead . . .

You're a killer, too . . .

He leapt toward Two-Face, and just as he did a thug came in out of nowhere, taking him to the ground. *Noooo!* screeched through his mind. And then, even as he went down, refusing to acknowledge that time had run out, he hurled the machine pistol.

It scissored through the air, spinning like a boomerang, and it crashed squarely into Two-Face's head . . .

. . . but only after Two-Face had squeezed off two shots.

The first bullet sliced through one of the trapeze supports that were suspending John and Chris Grayson. The support snapped, and John Grayson skidded off, still clutching onto his son's legs. Chris was still holding onto Mary, and he screamed. His mind hadn't fully registered what happened. He only knew that suddenly he felt as if he were being torn in half.

Mary shrieked as well, because two seconds ago she'd been on the verge of being rescued. And now, instead, with the crack of a bullet, she was the only thing keeping her son and husband from plunging to the ground. Her frantic hands wrapped around Chris's wrists as he howled *"Don't drop me don't drop me Maaaaaaa . . ."*

And John knew that he was dead. That he was about to let go of his son's leg and plummet to the ground because then maybe, just maybe, Mary could hold on and they would survive.

His life flashed before him and, to his utter surprise, there was nothing he would have done differently.

For the three flying Graysons, the agony seemed to last an eternity. But it was, in fact, no longer than it took for Two-Face to squeeze the trigger a second time.

The second bullet sliced through the rope supporting Mary Grayson.

Dick Grayson scrambled across the roof of the Hippodrome, the bomb ticking under his arm. With a prayer, and all the strength in his young arms, he hurled the bomb down, down into the water. He uttered a prayer, begging that it wouldn't explode in midair. For one thing, he was completely without protection atop the roof, and the flying shrapnel would cut him to pieces.

And for another, he really hated loud noises.

Apparently God decided to be merciful, for the bomb made it all the way to the water and even sank beneath it. Seconds later there was a muffled explosion and the water erupted upward about fifty feet, sending a geyser and mist through the air before settling back down.

"I did it," he whispered in amazement. "I saved 'em. This is great . . . *this is great!!*"

He scampered back up the roof, his mind racing. He was going to be a hero. No . . . not just him. His whole family were going to be heroes. The Flying Graysons, the daredevils who saved the Hippodrome. They'd be everywhere. Newspapers, magazines, talk shows. They'd be able to write their own tickets. They were set for life.

His joy lasted until he regained the catwalk and looked down . . . and saw the broken bodies of his family lying on the ground.

Then he heard a loud, piercing, gut-wrenching scream of agony that seemed to go on and on, and somewhere along the way he realized it was his own voice. . . .

"The greatest show on earth!" crowed Two-Face a split instant before the machine pistol hit him. It struck him on the scarred side of his face, so it wasn't as if the damage was going to be noticeable. Nevertheless it hurt like hell as he went down. He fired wildly in all directions, unaware of precisely where the weapon had come from, and unknowingly forcing Bruce Wayne to dive for cover.

Then Two-Face dived for the trapdoor through which he'd come, slamming it behind him. A split second later Bruce was there, clawing at it, trying to pry it open. But he'd heard the bolt slam shut beneath, and nothing short of an explosive or a blowtorch was going to get through it. Both of those would have been at his disposal had he been in costume, of course, but he was not. Instead the only option left to him would be to run like hell, try to find where the tunnels came out that ran beneath the Hippodrome, and track down Two-Face.

It was not a workable notion.

That was when he heard the shriek, the shriek from on high. He recognized it immediately; it was his own voice.

Except it wasn't. It was another voice, but with the same

grief and agony that Bruce recalled from himself so many years ago.

It was the boy. The boy who had done everything he could do, and was—to the other still frantic people within the Hippodrome—a hero.

None of which mattered one bit.

Bruce and Chase stood outside the Hippodrome, watching the ambulances roll away as more and more police cars seemed to materialize. Bruce felt a certain amount of impatience. What was the purpose of all this? Two-Face was gone. The thugs who had been captured wouldn't be able to tell the police anything useful. Wayne was certain that they were all hired goons, brought in especially for this particular job. Harvey was too canny to risk the loss of people who might betray him.

Chase drew his arm closer. "Where did you go running off to?"

"Nowhere," he said. "I got separated from you by other people, and spent the rest of the time trying to find you."

Even as he spoke with her, he didn't hear his own words. Instead he was running that moment, *the* moment, back through his mind.

He had sworn not to use guns. A gun was what had cut down his parents, and the very concept of wielding such a weapon was anathema to him. He had hurled himself into the midst of the criminal element in order to combat it, and he was fearful of staring too closely into the abyss, lest it stare back at him. To use a gun, to shoot at people, was to draw it dangerously close to becoming that which he opposed.

Yet there he had been, holding the machine pistol in his hands, finger curled around the trigger. A quick squeeze and Two-Face would have been dead. And . . . perhaps . . . the Graysons would be alive. It was hard to be certain, for everything had happened so quickly. Perhaps, and then again, perhaps not.

What was certain was that he'd had Two-Face in his sights ... and Two-Face in his head, taunting him, defying him.

And Bruce's reflexes had kicked in. The revulsion over guns, the haunting sneers of Two-Face ... it had all compelled him to throw the gun instead of fire it.

Gently, Chase said to Bruce, "Do you want to talk about it?"

He looked down at her and shook his head. "There's nothing to talk about," he said.

Then he saw Dick Grayson from a distance away. He had a blanket draped over him, covering his red-and-green leotard. His head was lowered, his face ashen.

"Incredible," said Chase. "Incredible how things turn out. First that boy saves my pocketbook ... and then he saves my life ... and look what happens. He deserved so much better. I wonder if he has any other family."

"No," Bruce told her. "Gordon said no. It was just his parents and ..." He paused and then amended, "Just him."

"It's just so unfair."

"What happens to him now?" asked Bruce.

"Now? Now he gets pumped into the system, I guess."

He thought about the system. The overcrowded, underfinanced system ...

"The hell he does," said Bruce Wayne.

CHAPTER 10

It was the next afternoon when the police cruiser pulled up in front of Wayne Manor. Dick Grayson, pack on his back, came riding up behind it on his motorcycle. It was a small, modest little vehicle, but his folks had scrimped and saved to get it for him and it meant the world to him. The day that he'd gotten it and unwrapped it, he was sure that he would never again see anything nearly as impressive as the shining red little 'cycle.

And he hadn't.

Until he'd pulled up into the main drive of Wayne Manor. Then he stared at the house, and continued to stare at it. As Bruce Wayne emerged from the house, Commissioner Gordon stepped out of the back of the cruiser and headed toward Bruce to speak with him. On the way he paused next to Dick in order to push his mouth shut.

"It's good of you to take him in," said Gordon with no preamble. "He's been filling out forms all day. He hasn't slept or eaten."

"Oh, well," said Wayne, gesturing for Dick to come forward. "I'm sure we'll be able to scrape together something in the fridge."

Dick walked past Gordon, still awestruck by what he was seeing. Gordon began to say good-bye, but quickly became aware that he wasn't remotely a part of the boy's reality at that moment. He shrugged, shook Bruce's hand, gave his thanks once more, and then headed for the cruiser.

In the foyer of Wayne Manor, Dick was looking around in undisguised amazement. Bruce stood in the open doorway, still a little bit unsure of what to say. Should he speak gently, or firmly? Was the boy looking for a friend, or an older brother, or just someone to talk to . . . or perhaps none of the above?

He knew one thing for sure. The boy was going to be in mourning. He would likely be somber and serious, and prone to unexpected crying jags at the wrong words. And in his state of mind, any words could be the wrong ones. Best to proceed on eggshells until he had the situation sorted out.

From the other direction came Bruce Wayne's trusted butler. "Welcome, Master Grayson. I'm Alfred."

Dick looked at him in confusion. "*Master* Grayson?"

"A standard honorific," said Bruce.

"Huh." And then, to Bruce's astonishment, Dick elbowed Alfred in the ribs. "So . . . how ya doin', Al?"

He stepped away from Alfred as the butler looked in barely contained amazement at Bruce and mouthed, "Al?"

Bruce shrugged and turned to Dick. "We prepared a room for you upstairs. But maybe you'd like to eat first."

The last statement didn't even seem to register. So instead, Alfred and Bruce stood patiently and waited for Dick to guide the situation.

Dick, for his part, was watching out the window until the police cruiser carrying Gordon was safely out of sight. Then he turned to them and said, "Okay. I'm outta here."

Bruce hadn't been precisely sure what to expect, but this definitely wasn't it. Chase Meridian had offered to be there to try to smooth things along, but he had confidently said that he could handle it. Now he was starting to regret that decision. "Excuse me?"

Dick shifted the weight of his pack slightly on his back. "I figure telling that cop I'd stay here saved me a truckload of social service interviews and goodwill. So no offense but see ya. Thanks."

Bruce made a subtle gesture to Alfred, and then matched Dick's stride as they both headed outside.

"Where will you go? The circus is halfway to Metropolis by now."

"I'm going to get a fix on Two-Face," said Dick matter-of-factly. "Then I'm going to kill him."

Wayne endeavored to take the flat pronouncement in stride. "Killing Two-Face won't take the pain away. In fact, it'll make it worse."

Dick looked at him with open skepticism. Bruce could practically read his mind: *You're a rich guy who lives in a mansion the size of Rhode Island, with more money than most people have in a lifetime. What the hell do you know about pain.* "Look, spare me the sermons, okay? I don't need your advice. Or your charity."

Bruce didn't seem to be paying attention. Instead he was looking ahead to Dick's motorcycle. "Nice bike."

He looked Bruce up and down skeptically. "You a big motorcycle fan, Bruce?" He lowered his voice derisively. "Hang at a lot of biker bars?"

"I know a little about bikes," Bruce replied easily.

As Dick began to mount the motorcycle, he waited for the protestations or angry orders from Wayne. Instead, Wayne stood a couple of feet away and said serenely, "Well, good luck." He started to turn away and then, struck by an afterthought, said, "Oh, you might want to fill up in our garage. No gas stations for miles."

Dick stared at him for a moment, and then figured, "What the hell? Why not?"

He rolled the bike toward the garage, Bruce leading the way. Wayne wasn't even trying to make pointless small talk, and Dick even felt reluctantly grateful for that. Couldn't fault the guy for trying. It's just that he was trying to help someone who cared about only one thing in . . .

The garage door rolled up to reveal five vintage automobiles, each serenely parked in its individual and customized parking spaces. A Rolls. A Bentley. A Spider. And two . . . good lord, *two* Turners.

"Oh, man!" was all he was able to get out.

As if unaware of the boy's excitement, Wayne said, "Pump's this way."

Dick followed him, unable to tear his gaze away from the cars. Unable, that was, until he saw another array of vintage crafts lined up.

Motorcycles.

This time Dick made no pretense of disinterest or even high-handedness. He started pointing, "That's a BMW 950. A Kawasaki Razor. And that's a Harley Mongoose. I think they only made ten."

"Seven, actually. She's our pride and joy." He sighed sadly. "Doesn't run though."

"Probably the gearbox," Dick said with authority. "They were touchy. And sometimes the fuel caps carbonize."

Bruce gave the matter some thought, and then mused, "I've been looking for someone to restore these. Hell, someone gets these going, he could take any bike he wanted as a fee. Plus room and board while he worked on them." He looked at Dick blandly. "Too bad you're not staying around. Anyway, have a good trip."

At that moment Alfred walked into the garage, carrying a tray stacked with London broil, baby potatoes, and fresh greens. Even Bruce, who had eaten barely an hour ago, felt his mouth starting to salivate. So he could only imagine what it was like for the hungry Dick Grayson.

"Oh, is the young master leaving?" Alfred asked, the picture of unwitting ignorance. "Pity. I'll just toss this away then. Perhaps the dogs are hungry—" He turned and headed back into the house.

It was at that precise moment that Dick Grayson knew that he was utterly overmatched. He wasn't sure precisely why Wayne was going to this much trouble to extend hospitality. It was almost as if he felt guilty over something. It sure couldn't have been because they had something in common, since they had, in fact, *nothing* in common.

Still . . .

"Maybe just a couple days," Dick said, trying not to lick his lips as the aroma of the meat hung in the air around him. "Get these babies purring." He started after Alfred, calling, "Yo, Al, hold up . . ."

In the Wayne Manor library, Bruce Wayne touched a vase of fresh roses while the rays of the setting sun filtered through the window. Next to the roses were photographs of Thomas and Martha Wayne, laughing into the camera, their arms draped around their young son, Bruce.

He heard the two gunshots.

The room became abruptly darker and he turned to see two coffins, a room filled with mourners. It was as if all the events of several days were being compressed into one hideous day.

He was standing next to a desk as people filed by, shaking their heads at his parents, clucking sympathetically at him. He stepped back, trying to get away from them, and his hands rested upon a leather bound book atop the desk. He pulled his fingers away from the book as if it had scalded him.

The front door of the library blew open, a fierce and somehow evil wind whipping through the house. Bruce tried to lunge for the book, to prevent it from being blown away. Instead the cover blew open, pages flipping wildly back and forth as if his entire life, past, present, and future, was dancing past him.

The window smashed open, exploding, glass shattering, and out of the darkness flew a huge, evil creature.

The monster wrapped its massive leather wings around itself, and it spoke with Bruce Wayne's amazed, understanding voice. . . .

"A bat . . . I shall become a bat . . ."

"Master Bruce . . . ?"

Bruce was jolted awake. He looked around in confusion, for his dream surroundings had been identical to his genuine whereabouts. Minus, of course, the coffins, the mourners, and the gargantuan bat. . . .

Although maybe the bat was actually there, albeit it only in spirit.

He was holding a rose which he had pulled from a vase of fresh ones. "It's exactly the same as with my parents, Alfred. It's happening again, except this time to that poor boy. The precise same scenario: A monster comes out of the night. There's a scream. Two gunshots." He took a deep breath and said, "I killed them."

Alfred, who was by and large unflappable, nevertheless was unable to help gaping at his employer. "What did you say?"

Bruce looked up, confused at Alfred's reaction. "He killed them," he said, not comprehending why Alfred seemed so disconcerted by such a self-evident statement. "Two-Face. He slaughtered that boy's parents."

"No. You said *I*. 'I killed them.' Who, Mr. Wayne?"

Before Bruce could answer, a light through the window illuminated their faces. Immediately Bruce was on his feet. He turned to Alfred and said, "Take care of the kid." And he was out the door before the butler could say anything further.

Alfred could never remember a time when he'd been genuinely pleased to see that hyperactive flashlight burning in the sky. But he was hard-pressed to remember a time when he was *less* pleased to see it.

In Dick Grayson's room—one that he had picked out after Alfred had offered him a plethora of choices—he was staring out the window at the gleaming Bat-Signal in the night sky.

He'd heard about Batman, of course. Even people on the road heard about genuine phenoms like Batman.

So where the hell had the renowned crime fighter been when the Flying Graysons needed him?

There was a knock at the door. Dick grunted a semisyllable that passed for telling someone to come in.

Alfred took the noise as it was meant and stepped into the room. "Can I help you settle in, young sir?"

"No . . . thanks. I won't be here long."

Alfred's foot bumped up against Dick's motorcycle helmet. A typical teenage boy. Why put anything on a shelf or a cabinet when there was always a convenient floor on which to drop it? Alfred picked it up. On the back of it, curiously, was a decal of a common red-breasted bird.

"A robin?" he said.

Dick shrugged as if it were nothing of consequence. "My brother's wire broke during a show. I swung out, caught him. Afterwards my father called me his hero, said I flew like a robin." He paused at the memory, which had always been so pleasant for him. No longer, though.

Because his brother, whom he had saved, was gone.

Because his father, who had praised him, was gone.

Because his mother, whom he had loved, was gone.

"Some hero I turned out to be."

It was rather remarkable for Alfred. He had seen that same air of frustration hanging over Bruce Wayne mere minutes before, hovering like a dark cloud. It gave him some hope for what Dick Grayson might become. It also gave him some fear.

He settled for saying, "Ah, but your father was right, young man. You are a hero. I can tell. Broken wings mend in time. Perhaps one day Robin will fly again."

Dick said nothing, made it rather apparent that . . . as far as he was concerned . . . the conversation was over. Alfred waited a moment more, and then turned and walked out of the room.

As soon as he was gone, Dick cracked open his knapsack. He pulled out a newspaper, opened it, and smoothed out the headline which read, TWO-FACE SLAYS 3 AT CIRCUS.

He upended the knapsack, and other clippings about Two-

Face spilled out. He stared at them, his rage growing and roiling within him.

He had no clear idea to what end he was going to turn his fury. He wasn't sure where he would look for Two-Face, or how he could ever find him, or just precisely how he would destroy him when they did finally meet.

But he knew they would. He knew it beyond any doubt.

And the outcome was never in doubt, either.

CHAPTER 11

The Batmobile glided to a halt several blocks away from police headquarters. It sat there for a moment as if contemplating the darkness, and then the cockpit slid open. Batman eased himself out, then stepped away from the vehicle. "Shields," he said and moved away without glancing back as the heavy-duty shields slammed into place, locking down the Batmobile.

He walked to the base of a building, pulled out his grappling hook, and fired it skyward. Seconds later he heard the satisfying clack of metal that indicated the hook had a grip on something. He pulled on it twice to make certain that it was firmly anchored, and then pressed the retractor. Instantly he was hoisted skyward, joining the shadows of the city's sky-high spires.

He made his way across the roofs toward the roof of police headquarters. If someone had been watching for him with both eyes peeled and the aid of infrared night goggles, then maybe they might have had a shot at spotting him. Other than that, there was no chance.

He got within one rooftop of the signal. It appeared to be deserted. That was odd. Odd immediately sharpened his senses.

He stayed to the shadows and studied the rooftop carefully.

Then he spotted it. Someone was standing on the other

131

side of the spotlight itself, staring toward the sky. He couldn't quite make it out from where he was, but whoever was over there was taller and slimmer than Gordon.

And, for all he knew, armed.

He leapt over to the roof of police headquarters, landing so silently that the unauthorized individual was utterly unaware of it. He moved slowly through the shadows. The rooftop had plenty of gravel on it. It made no sound under his feet.

He heard a low sigh from the waiting individual, and knew it immediately.

He allowed the shadows to part from him and said in a slightly ironic tone, "Commissioner Gordon?"

Dr. Chase Meridian turned with a start, her hand to her bosom. Her breath came out in mist through the chill night air. "He's at home. I sent the signal."

"What's wrong?"

"Last night at the circus. I noticed something about Dent. His coin. He's obsessed with justice. It's his Achilles' heel. It can be exploited."

He couldn't believe it. She was telling him nothing new. Hell, she had to *know* it was nothing new. It was in the case files.

She had only a small amount of time, and apparently zero interest, in dealing with him as Bruce Wayne. And yet she was willing to go to any lengths, no matter how preposterous . . . no matter how transparent . . . to garner Batman's attention.

He stepped in close to her, his voice rough, his manner intimidating. "You called me here for this? The Bat-Signal is not a beeper."

She didn't back off. Instead she took a breath and said, in a rush, "I wish I could say my interest in you was purely professional . . ."

He paused a moment, contemplating the best way to handle the situation. She wanted dark . . . mysterious . . . all the elements that terrified criminals, that froze thugs in their tracks . . . these were what attracted her.

He thought of Dick Grayson, the teenager. Even in his grief, he was effortlessly able to summon up the facade of a swaggering smart-ass. The antithesis of Batman's somber, mysterious persona.

No harm in throwing her off the track. Who knew? Maybe it might divert her back into Bruce Wayne's train station.

He stood in a slightly relaxed position, one knee bent, and pitched his voice slightly higher. "Are you trying to get under my cape, Doctor?"

"A girl cannot live by psychoses alone," she replied.

Which was not exactly the response he'd hoped for. Nonetheless he pressed on. "It's the car, right? Chicks love the car."

Chase, true to her name, pursued him. "What is it about the wrong kind of man?" she asked wistfully. "In grade school it was guys with earrings. College, motorcycles and leather jackets." She pressed up against him. "Now black rubber."

"Try a fireman. Less to take off."

"I don't mind the work. Pity I can't see behind the mask."

"We all wear masks."

"*My* life's an open book. You read?"

He looked at her eyes, at the amusement there, and he dropped the attitude. His tone becoming darker, he said, "Where do you think this is going to go?"

"Depends. Where are you going to take me?"

He took her rather ungently by the wrists. "Am I just another specimen, another lab animal for your maze? Or perhaps you thought of bringing me home to meet the folks. In case you haven't noticed, I'm not the kind of guy who blends in at a family picnic."

"We could give it a try. I'll bring the wine, you bring your scarred psyche."

"You are direct, aren't you?"

He squeezed her wrists more tightly. She didn't flinch, but her voice was more defiant. He was stripping away the banter, cutting to the core of her interest in him. "You like strong women," she said. "I've done my homework. Or do I need skintight vinyl and a whip?" she added sarcastically.

"I haven't had much luck with women. . . ."

"Maybe you just haven't met the right woman."

He wasn't entirely certain how their mouths had drawn as close as they had. But he was suddenly very aware of their proximity . . . and of her warm breath against him. . . .

"I saw the beacon. What's going on?"

Batman's head snapped around as he saw Commissioner Gordon standing by the roof entrance. His trenchcoat, flapping in the breeze, couldn't completely conceal the fact that he'd yanked on his pants over pajamas, his flannel pajama shirt peering out.

Gordon looked from one to the other, puzzlement slowly turning into suspicion.

"Nothing," Batman told him, turning away from Chase. "False alarm."

"Are you sure?" asked Chase.

He didn't even glance back at her as he leapt onto the adjoining roof, the shadows welcoming him back within their embrace. Chase Meridian watched him go and then heard a stern "harrummph" behind her. She turned and met Gordon's hard gaze.

"You have some explanation for this?" he demanded.

She shrugged. "I needed to bring him up to speed on some thoughts of mine."

"Then you do it through me," said Gordon. He cocked his head slightly. "Or, in this case, did you feel that three would have been a crowd?"

In what she hoped was her most disarming manner, she smiled.

The Batmobile streaked along the aqueducts extending through the cityscape of Gotham. Flared arches supported one roadway over another . . .

. . . and behind one set of arches, Two-Face lay in wait.

"Public calls for help cut two ways," Two-Face said to no

one in particular as he sat within his sleek armored car. "We've seen the general direction you come from enough times, Bat, to know where the optimum points for ambush are. And all we had to do was wait for some fine night that your services were requested. Apparently, this is the night. Your night . . . and ours . . . and we dance the final dance."

On an underpass just below, the Batmobile shot past. Two-Face spoke into a microphone, alerting the other cars. "Gentlemen . . . start your engines."

And two cars roared from side entrances. Each was painted red and black. They moved so quickly that their undercarriages scraped along the asphalt, sending up sparks, as the cars tore after the Batmobile.

Batman looked off to the left. He was passing by the site of his first meeting with Harvey Dent. The combination of himself and Dent, working both sides of the fence, had seemed a legitimate, beneficial way to go. Everything had seemed so filled with potential back then, so brimming with promise.

Well . . . promise had been the problem, hadn't it? The promise that he hadn't kept.

Should he have known better at the time? Or was it that he was so brimming with confidence that he had overreached himself? How much could he be expected to accomplish and then be able to lean back and say, "I did it. Good day's work."

How much would ever be enough? Would there never be rest? Would there never be an end to it?

Then an internal warning system began to beep at him. One or more vehicles had been detected as moving too quickly, and too directly toward him, to be considered mere "other traffic."

"Tactical."

Flashing graphics of the Batmobile and the pursuit cars winked into life on the windscreen. Suddenly two more snapped into the picture as well.

Cars pursuing him in a two-by-two formation. Cars that were determined to provide Batman with the rest he craved. Unfortunately, it was a rest from which, if they had their way, there would be no awakening.

"He needs another hobby," Batman muttered.

Up ahead of him was traffic. Innocent people, going on about their lives. Driving home to the family, or out on a date, minding their own business and not caught up in an existence that sent every lunatic in Gotham howling for their heads.

He thought about his early escapades, and the previous Penguin fiasco, and suddenly he had very little desire to give the residents of Gotham more reason to fear the sight of the Batmobile. But he knew that Two-Face would have very little trepidation about smashing through whatever cars might stand between himself and his target.

Which meant his target had to make himself scarce.

It began on the rooftops. Perhaps it would end there.

He cut hard to the left, skittering across two lanes to an off ramp. And then, in a maneuver that most routine observers would have termed completely insane, the Batmobile veered off and plowed straight through the guardrails that stood between the off ramp and the city. Like a missile, the Batmobile shot through the air, tires spinning, engine roaring.

It landed on the rooftop with two distinct *thuds*, back and then front. An instant later the car roared past chimneys, across the rooftops so close to one another that it was as flat and easy as driving on the Salt Flats. Except these flats were made of tar paper.

With any luck, this getaway would put a quick end to the pursuit.

Unfortunately he couldn't remember the last time he had had any serious luck. And this occasion was not about to start a trend. His tactical display informed him that a car was in pursuit. The chances that it was a Gotham City black-and-white, pulling him over to ticket him for reckless driving, seemed fairly slim.

Sure enough, a moment later he heard the familiar clattering of bullets ricocheting off the Batmobile's armored hide. He wasn't particularly concerned about his own welfare. Nothing short of a surface-to-surface missile was going to put a dent in the Batmobile, although Batman wasn't willing to disallow the notion that Two-Face might have one stashed away for just such an occasion.

But the flying bullets might blast through a window somewhere. He didn't need some sleeping three-year-old getting a bullet in the brain that had bounced off the impregnable Batmobile.

The situation was quickly in danger of becoming moot, however.

After all the roofs that stayed tightly one upon the other, he was finally approaching an area where there was a gap. It was a fairly significant one. He was coming up on it too quickly to slow down in time.

He slammed his foot on the gas, kicked in the afterburner, and hurtled towards the abyss. He gunned more speed out of the vehicle, and the Batmobile hit the gap, soaring through the air. It looked like nothing so much as, naturally, a massive bat.

The Batmobile thudded down to the roof on the far side and kept on going.

There were two thugs in the car. The passenger looked at the driver with a face like rancid oatmeal. And the driver, the picture of calm, said smugly, "Not a problem."

He revved the engine to maximum and sent the car leaping into the air. . . and down.

Batman glanced at the tactical display once more, expecting to see no more cars. Instead there was another one. Looking at his surroundings, he saw that it must have come in from another angle, down the side of a nearby apartment complex.

Ahead of him was a chasm, but a much narrower one. This time what was beyond the chasm posed the problem. It was a steep, angling roof, which Batman immediately recognized as belonging to the Gotham Insurance Building.

Still . . . this might not be a problem.

"Suction," he said, as the car propelled itself across the gap.

Instantly, hundreds of miniature suction cups blossomed on the Batmobile's tires. The car hit the roofside squarely and kept on going, up at a forty-five-degree angle.

Not realizing that the Batmobile had an edge, the pursuit car made the jump as well. It landed on the roofside with no effort, and the driver slammed the stick forward.

Unfortunately, this did not begin to compare with the tendency of the car to slide backwards. Which it did, skidding smoothly down the roof and, a second later, dropping off.

The buildings seemed to be converging, the rooftops becoming narrower. The Batmobile streaked down it as if running a gauntlet. Directly behind him raced three cars: Two red-and-black pursuit vehicles, and Two-Face's own armored car.

And Batman was running not only out of luck, but out of options. Directly ahead was a big fat dead end. A huge mural on the side of a giant building.

"He probably always wanted to make a big splash on the art scene," said Two-Face. And then, into the microphone, he snapped, "Cook him."

From the pursuit cars emerged oddly-shaped cannons which, instants later, discharged their payload. Massive fireballs blossomed forth like lethal flowers. They roared toward the Batmobile.

Within the cockpit, Batman rapidly ran through his options and narrowed them to two . . . unless he ruled out dying, in which event he was down to one. He took it, and hit a button on the dash.

A tiny hood-hatch blew off, shooting a Bat-grapple high into the air. The grapple grabbed the wing of a giant stone gargoyle atop the roof of the mural building. A powerful hood-winch was activated, gripping a powerful cable in the car's front, and the Batmobile was jerked vertical. He drove the powerful car straight up the side of the building.

The two foremost cars slammed into the side of the mural, arriving just seconds after the fireballs they had launched. A second later the ruptured gas tanks fed the fireballs, inflating them to massive proportions. The drivers were thrown clear.

Two-Face's armored vehicle skidded to a halt barely inches away from the mural. He stepped out and, surrounded by licking flames, screamed his rage into the night. The image of the bat symbol burned into his mind, and in his imagination it was surrounded with flames.

And as the Batmobile vanished over the elevated cityscape, Two-Face knew that he was going to live to bring that image to fruition. Nothing was going to prevent it. Nothing.

CHAPTER 12

In the stone bowels of an ancient support arch near the Gotham Bridge, Two-Face stewed in his hideout.

The decor of the place was suitably unique. It was split right down the middle. On the left half, the decor was one extreme—cheerful, upbeat, with a look and style that seemed straight out of a 1950s sitcom. Simple mahogany furniture, pleasant orange shag carpeting, cheerful wallpaper with little flowers on it.

On the right-hand side, it was a stroll down memory lane, if one's memories happened to be those of a porn star or sexual deviant. Everything, everywhere, was black. Black leather, stretched over black metal. Chains hung down, and there was a thick stench of something unpleasant burning. Whips, hooks, and studded collars decorated the walls and harsh lighting flickered overhead.

On each side of the room there was a woman preparing a meal. They were dressed according to the theme and mood of the respective rooms.

Two-Face wasn't paying them much mind. Instead he was staring into space, murmuring, "The Bat's stubborn refusal to expire is driving us insane."

He stuck a cigarette in the left side of his mouth. A delicate hand offered flame from a silver lighter. It belonged to the woman from the cheerier side of the room. She was dressed in a lacy outfit that displayed her to her best advantage. Next to her was a rolling cloth-covered table bearing a closed silver service and white, hand-tapered candles.

Two-Face then shoved a cigar into the right side of his mouth. A small blowtorch flared, lighting it up. The torch was wielded by another woman, her blonde hair spiky and moussed as compared to the around-the-shoulders, gentle look of her counterpart. And whereas the other's outfit was airy lace, this one was clad in black leather and spike heels. She likewise had a rolling table with food, but it was of butcher block, with a pit of coals searing a twitching lobster.

The former was Sugar.

The latter was Spice.

"I've prepared your favorite, *mon cher*," cooed Sugar. "Quail eggs and aspic."

Two-Face rose and stepped over to her cart, examining it . . . and her . . . approvingly. "Light to shine as your beauty does. Foie gras. Excellent."

With a disdainful sniff, Spice called over, "Liver. Don't make me puke."

Interest piqued, he stepped over to the other side, moving with Spice toward her rolling cart. His mood with her altered completely. Rather than flowery compliments, he simply said, "Trollop."

"Scold me again."

"No."

She licked her lips. "Sadist."

He lifted a flagon from her rolling table, gulped back some liquid. Some of the liquor spilled into the fire pit and burst into flame. It was like Happy Hour in Hell.

The girls nodded toward each other, the little game following its usual course. They moved the two tables together, and Harvey sat at the head.

And a voice from the dark said, "I hope you made extra."

Two-Face was on his feet immediately, shoving the table away and pulling out his twin Colts. He aimed them squarely at the mysterious silhouette that had materialized in the darkness at the far end of the room. The figure made no effort to get out of the way, but the fact that he had the intruder squarely targeted only slightly mollified him. "Who the hell—"

"Just a friend. But you can call me . . ."

The figure stepped out into the light, slowly so as not to spook the man who had two guns trained on him. Two-Face squinted in confusion. Up until now, he'd had a lock on being the oddest-looking guy in the room. But that was quickly being challenged.

He was faced by a gangling individual clad in a lime green leotard covered with question marks, and a similarly patterned green jacket over it. He wore a green eye mask, a bizarre derby perched on his head, and he was leaning on a cane with a large question mark for a handle.

". . . The Riddler," he said after a suitably dramatic pause.

Two-Face tossed the girls his guns, and then stepped forward and grabbed the Riddler, slamming him hard into the wall.

"We'll call you dead, more like it. How'd you find us? Talk."

"Ah, I think not, my twinned pals. For then what would keep you from slaying me?"

Two-Face was in no mood for games . . . unless, of course, he was making the rules. "You got sixty seconds to spill how you tracked us here. After that, you'll beg for bullets."

The Riddler giggled a high-pitched laugh. It was hard to tell whether it was from nervousness or simple glee over Two-Face's ire. "Has anyone ever told you you have a serious impulse control problem? All right, all right, I'll talk," he added, sounding like Edward G. Robinson.

Deftly he slipped downward, leaving the frustrated Two-Face clutching his jacket. The Riddler walked in a circle, studying the lair. "I simply love what you've done with this place. Heavy Metal with just a touch of Home and Garden. It's so dark and Gothic and disgustingly decadent! Yet so bright and chipper and conservative!" He looked to the left and then right, saying respectively, "It's so you . . . and yet so you!" He sauntered back to Two-Face and touched the fabric on his bisected suit. "Very few people are both a summer and a winter. But you pull it off nicely."

The Riddler was curious, in a clinical way, with just how far he could push Two-Face. He found out quickly as Two-Face grabbed his guns and shoved one into each of the Riddler's nostrils. "Show's over. Let's see if you bleed green."

In a distinctly nasal tone, the Riddler said amiably, "All right. Go ahead. Fire away. But before you do, one question. Is it really me you want to kill?"

The Riddler brought his hands up in front of an exposed light bulb, interlacing his fingers and making an up-and-down, flapping motion. Despite his fury, Two-Face looked away long enough to see what the Riddler was up to. And what he saw, on the wall, was a shadow puppet of a bat.

"Do you know about hate, my dual-visaged friend?" asked the Riddler in a tone that was both conversational and yet somehow seductive. "Slow, burning hate that keeps you sleepless until late in the night, that wakes you before dawn. Do you know that kind of hate? I do."

As he spoke, Two-Face slowly lowered the guns, listening to what the Riddler had to say. The Riddler, for his part, wove a spell of words. "Kill him? Seems like a good enough idea. But have you thought it through? A few bullets, a quick spray of blood, a fast, thrilling rush, and then what? Wet hands and post-coital depression. Is it really enough? Why not ruin him first? Expose his frailty. And then, when he is at his weakest, crush him in your hand."

The Riddler then moved quickly. The moment he had entered, he had seen the twin TVs on either side of the room. One was playing "Leave It to Beaver." The other was airing "Exit to Eden."

"Have you seen the latest program?" he directed the comment to Sugar and Spice. Automatically they both glanced at the TVs, and as they did so, he pressed a stud on the head of his cane.

Instantaneously an invisible signal fed from a Box that he

had hidden within his jacket. The television sets glowed green, the pictures vanishing, and white beams arced out of the sets, spearing straight through Sugar's and Spice's heads.

Two-Face stared at them, not understanding what he was seeing. If he'd truly cared anything for them, of course, he would have shouted in protest, yanked them out of the way. Tried, in some way, to spare them whatever it was they were going through. Such was not the case, and instead he merely watched, transfixed.

The Riddler reached for his jacket and removed a receiver from it. He held it out invitingly. "This is how I found you. Take a hit and see. It makes you smarter."

He considered it a moment, still wary of a trap. But the temptation was too great. He brought the receiver up to his head experimentally . . .

. . . and the world was suddenly open to him.

As if it were an utterly trivial string of deductions, Two-Face said, "You correlated all dualities in the city, orders of half-and-half pizzas, wine splits, two-toned clothing, cross-referenced all addresses with multiples of two, crunched the probabilities by bicoastal, bizonal location leading you . . . here . . . holy shit!"

The Riddler winced at the coarseness of it, and then shrugged it off. "So not everyone can be a poet," he philosophized. "Still, I respect the sentiment." He pointed at Sugar and Spice, who were still mesmerized, and then at Harvey. "This is your brain on The Box," he said to the former, "This is your brain on their brain." Then he pulled the receiver away from Two-Face, who gasped at the separation. He put the receiver to his own brain, soaking in the rush of accelerated neural pathways . . . not to mention the sensual awareness of the women. "This is my brain on their brains after your brain. Does anybody else feel like a fried egg?"

Slowly Two-Face's eyes refocussed. He grabbed for the receiver, but the Riddler easily kept it out of his reach.

"More . . . " he said in a strangled voice.

The Riddler waggled a finger at him. "Oh there's more.

But only the first one's free. Here's the concept, counselor. Crime: My IQ, your AK-47. This is the bargain: you will help me gather production capital so I can produce enough of these . . ." He held up the Box, which was so far miniaturized from its original prototype as to be almost unrecognizable. It was in the shape of a stylized question mark, with a glowing light in the bottom dot.

". . . enough of these to build an empire that will eclipse Bruce Wayne's forever. And, in return, I will help you solve the greatest riddle of all. Who is Batman? Then we'll find him and kill him."

Two-Face eyed the Riddler, interest dawning.

"You are a very strange person, a distinction we do not level lightly. You barge in here unarmed when it is clearly suicidal to do so. You speak to us as if we were old friends, which we are not. Still, an intriguing proposition." He pulled out his coin. "Clean side: We take your offer."

And then he placed the barrel of one of the guns against the Riddler's temple. "Scarred side: We blow your god-damned head off."

The Riddler licked his lips, suddenly dry. This wasn't supposed to happen. He'd forgotten to take Two-Face's madness into account. He cursed bitterly to himself. All the potential that was riding on this new identity, this new business venture . . . and it depended on the toss of a coin.

And as the coin arced through the air, he said what might very well have been his last words: "Don't rule out the concept of two out of three."

CHAPTER 13

In the Gotham Jewelry Exchange, Two-Face's thugs were hurriedly scooping out handfuls of gems from glass cases and shoving them into bags. Nearby, the Riddler and Two-Face stood over a pallet of black jeweler's felt, which was littered with bright, sparkling diamonds. The Riddler dropped a third riddle, then slipped on a magnifying monocle and lifted a gem to study it more closely.

Two-Face grabbed the rest of the pallet and upended it, pouring the diamonds into a loot bag. The Riddler looked at the rather uneven distribution of wealth. "One for me . . . one hundred for you." But then he saw Two-Face's glare and, rather than risk another toss of that damned coin, simply shrugged. "Sounds fair to me."

As the Bat-Signal flared in the sky, the party moved across town.

In the Gotham Casino, the guards were struggling with Two-Face's thugs, but they were sorely outnumbered. Two-Face strode over to them, surveying them thoughtfully, and then he gestured to the Riddler. Curious, the Riddler joined him, while the rest of the thugs relieved the patrons of their jewels and cash.

"You wanted to get into crime," said Two-Face. "Time to get seriously into it." He held up his hand. "Close your fist. Reach back."

Then he swung suddenly, smashing one of the guards in

the face. The guard went down, unconscious. Two-Face then turned to the Riddler, who looked a little pale. "Get it?"

The Riddler nodded uncertainly and then stepped up to the next guard. He closed his fist, cocked it, and slammed it into the guard's face with all the power and destructive force of a bag of rice cakes.

His two-toned partner looked at him in disgust. "Riddler . . . you punch like a girl. Put some heart into it." Feeling that a further demonstration was in order, he punched out the third guard, knocking him cold.

This time the Riddler put everything he had into it, and managed to rock the fourth guard back an entire inch.

"My God," said Two-Face, shaking his head and walking away. The Riddler turned back to the relieved guard apologetically. "I'm actually not a violent person. So I need the practice." He raised his cane. "Batter up."

As Two-Face idly spun the roulette wheel, the Riddler kept darting in close to the guard, smashing him with the cane, then dancing away and back in again. He moved elegantly, weaving back in and clubbing the helpless guard once more before cavorting away again.

Moments later, Two-Face's car was speeding away. With Two-Face at the wheel, the Riddler had slid open a hidden panel on his cane. There was a small array of buttons displayed within.

"You better be right about this," said Two-Face.

"Oh, I am," the Riddler said confidently. "Been tracking all the bands for weeks now. I'm absolutely, one hundred percent positive that I've tapped into the 'private' band Gordon has reserved for Batboy. His priority channel. His e-mail. The Batphone, if you will. All electronic . . . and if it's electronic"—and he tapped the buttons with malicious glee—"then it's mine."

Two-Face nodded. "So where are you sending him?"

With a smile, the Riddler said playfully, "I think the Bat needs a new 'do.'"

*   *   *

Batman's eyes narrowed as the flashing sign "Crime in Progress" flashed on his tactical screen. His own position was marked on the map and he was drawing closer with every passing second.

It was an upscale neighborhood . . . exactly the type of place that Two-Face and his bizarre new cohort were likely to strike.

Still . . . something seemed a little off. But he couldn't take the time to figure out precisely what it was. He had the feed from police headquarters, and that was all he needed.

The Batmobile rolled up to the service entrance of the building where the crime was reported. Batman wasted no time, charging up the stairs and smashing in through the door.

There was a collective shriek from within.

Batman stood in the middle of the "Curl Up and Dye" beauty salon, which was open late night since it was Friday. He looked around for the source of the disturbance. Unfortunately the only one who fit that description was him. The women didn't seem particularly upset, though. After their initial astonishment, both beauticians and customers started babbling excitedly, crowding in around Batman, laughing and flirting.

Behind his mask, Batman fumed.

He wasn't certain which annoyed him more: that he had not gotten his hands on his target, or the kind of field day that the media was going to have with this.

". . . with millions in diamonds, cash and personal effects stolen," said the newscaster, "while, bizarrely, Batman chose to make an appearance in a crosstown beauty parlor."

With the late morning sun flooding in through his window, Bruce Wayne adjusted his tie while the morning news aired. He shook his head as the newscaster continued, "Witnesses clearly identified Two-Face as the perpetrator and mastermind behind the robbery. However, this station has learned exclusively that Two-Face has a new partner, who phoned earlier with the following message."

A graphic of a question mark appeared on the screen as the Riddler's voice crowed, "Blame Two-Face? I demand equal acclaim for my offenses. Recognition for my wrongdoings. Credit for my crimes. Gotham has a new bad boy in town and his name is the Riddler!"

The newscaster came back on, adding, "The caller then described several pieces taken in the heist that police confirmed were on a list not released to the public. At this stage, therefore, it would seem that Two-Face has now decided, appropriately, that two heads are better than one."

Alfred entered Bruce's bedroom, carrying coffee and the morning mail. Bruce turned to him and said, "I knew scrambling the downlink to misdirect me to that beauty salon was too sophisticated for Harvey alone."

Alfred shook his head. "A madman calling himself the Riddler. Riddles delivered to Bruce Wayne. Apparently, you and Batman have a common enemy, sir."

He handed Bruce an envelope, the style of which he'd come to recognize. This one, however, had postmarks on it. Unfortunately, it was postmarked Romania, and Sioux City, Iowa.

"He's getting more ambitious," said Bruce. "Either that or he's just getting stranger and stranger."

Alfred nodded deferentially. "I bow to your expertise on that, sir."

Bruce glanced suspiciously at the butler, whose face remained unreadable. He then tore open the envelope, only listening with half an ear as the newscaster continued, "In other news, entrepreneur Edward Nygma has signed a lease for Claw Island. Nygma says he plans to break ground on an electronics plant . . ."

And there was Nygma, holding up sketches of what his fully refurbished Claw Island would look like. It was a bizarre blending of art deco styling with tall sleek factory chimneys, all intertwined with twisted piping. Furthermore it was elevated, mounted high above the water on a central pole which, presumably, contained elevators.

Bruce Wayne barely gave it a glance, Edward Nygma at that moment was the furthest thing from his mind.

And also, as it happened, the closest.

In the combination garage and gym in Wayne Manor's west wing, Bruce Wayne entered to find Dick Grayson pummeling a straw-filled action dummy. Immediately he noticed the modifications that Dick had made to the dummy. He had drawn in a face on the dummy's head, a smiley face. But there was a vertical line bisecting it. The left half of the face was smiling, while the right half was sneering, with a grossly distorted eye, mouth, and fangs.

Dick paused, clearly waiting for Bruce to make some comment. This, of course, Bruce didn't do. Instead he turned to Dick and said approvingly, in reference to the motorcycle that the teen had been working on, "I just started the Black Knight. She sounds great. Why don't you grab the Harley and we'll take a ride?"

With a sigh, Dick lowered his arms from the cocked and punching position. He didn't sound angry or arrogant . . . merely resigned, and even sad. "Look, man, I appreciate the gig, but let's leave it at that. We're not gonna be buddies, okay? You don't even know me."

In a very mild tone, Bruce said, "I know the pain that's with you every day. The shame. Feeling somehow you should have saved them. I don't know you," he agreed. "But I'm like you."

Dick shrugged in that way that only teenagers could and started pounding on the dummy again. It shuddered slightly under each thrust. Bruce watched him and then said, "Have you thought about your future? The Wayne Foundation has an excellent scholarship fund. Once the bikes are finished . . ."

With an impatient noise, Dick grabbed a copy of the *Gotham Times* that he'd tossed on the floor. He thrust the paper into Bruce's face, and Two-Face's image glowered back at him from the cover.

"*He's* my future."

Bruce shook his head sadly. "Don't let your love, your passion for your family, twist into hatred of Two-Face. It's too easy."

"Look, no offense, man. But I don't think you've got a lot to teach me."

Bruce raised an eyebrow, and then stepped in front of the dummy. His two left hooks rattled the dummy with ear-shattering impact. His right took off the dummy's head. Dick gaped at the two-faced stuffed head lying on the ground, rolling gently from side to side.

"Don't be so sure," Bruce informed him.

CHAPTER 14

"What are you going to do about him, Mr. Wayne?"

Bruce sat behind his desk, staring at one of Wayne Enterprises' top lawyers, Stu "The Exterminator" Schoenfeld. Schoenfeld was an intense young man with intense black hair.

"Do?" he asked, going through a variety of documents. Off to the side, Margaret, as always, was manning the phone back. "You mean about Nygma?"

"Yes, sir," said Schoenfeld in exasperation. He waved documentation and memos around. "As near as I can determine, this 'Box' he's planning to market . . . it's from a device that he was creating while he was in our employ."

"This is the mind control thing, right?" asked Bruce.

"With all due respect, Mr. Wayne, that's a grotesque over-simplification." He rose and crossed over to the far wall, inserting a CD file that he'd been composing. "I've been keeping track of his activities over the past weeks, sir. As you'll see, I find the entire business most upsetting."

Bruce sat back and watched a time-lapse sequence of Claw Island under construction. One had to credit Nygma and whoever his backers were. Things were getting done damn quickly. Mere weeks ago the place had looked about as promising as a crater on the moon. Yet there Nygma now was, standing in front of the main building, with a huge sign that read "NYGMATECH" being raised into place by a crane. A sort of final crowning glory.

"Now you can be part of the show!" Nygma was proclaiming to the press and onlookers. "Nygmatech brings the joy of 3-D entertainment into your own home. Ladies and gentlemen. Let me tell you my vision. 'The Box' in every home in America. And one day the world. I've seen the future and it is me!"

Schoenfeld froze the screen on Nygma's chortling expression, and he turned to Wayne. "We've been doing some preliminary market research of our own, sir. If this Box can really do what Nygma claims it can . . . cheap, easy to watch, 3-D holographic entertainment in the home . . . sir, we're talking billions. Billions that Nygma will be raking in for a device that he researched while in our employ."

"You mean the device that Fred Stickley canceled research for."

"Only one day before his suicide. It never came to you for finalization, sir. We could argue diminished capacity on Stickley's part. With the company resources that Nygma made use of, sir, we have a very solid case . . ."

Bruce was staring into the gaze of Edward Nygma on the screen. At the time he had considered holding out some sort of olive branch to the rather intense employee, but Nygma's abrupt departure from Wayne Enterprises had precluded that. Now, as he looked at the intense desperation of nearly fanatic glee, he couldn't help but feel that his having missed connecting with Nygma was a blessing in disguise.

"Drop it, okay, Stu?" Wayne said.

Schoenfeld's face practically slid off his head. "*Drop it? Sir, the money . . .* "

He turned to Schoenfeld and said, "I don't doubt you're right, Stu. And we might very well be able to take a big bite out of the Box. But I don't need the money, Stu. And you know what I suspect I need even less? Extended dealings with, or grief from, one Edward Nygma."

"But . . ."

Margaret turned from the switchboard and said, "Mr. Wayne . . ."

He immediately shook his head. "Margaret, I said don't put anyone through, remember?"

"You said anyone except Dr. Meridian."

"Yes, I know, so please don't tell me about calls that . . ." He stopped, concentrating on what she was saying. "Oh."

"Line two," she said.

He waved off Stu, who sighed and walked out, shaking his head. Then Bruce picked up the phone and hoped it wasn't another prime minister. "Chase. Good to hear from you."

"I just wanted to know how Dick is doing? And, for that matter, how you're doing."

Dick? Oh, he's spent the past weeks pounding dummies, punching bags, walls . . . anything he can until his knuckles start to bleed, and then he starts kicking it. And he's starting to poke around the mansion. Alfred said Dick was staring at him when he came out of the study the other day, as if he suspected something was "going on." He might stumble over the hidden entrance to the Batcave. Oh, and the Riddler and Two-Face are all over, and by the way, reality and fantasy continue to blur for me as time goes by and pressures mount . . .

"Fine," he said. "Everything's fine. We're getting along great."

"You're lying."

"I'm lying," he agreed. "You'd think I'd get better with practice." He paused. "I miss you. I'd really like our schedules to hook up. Unless, of course things have become more serious with you and the . . . other fellow."

The line was silent for a moment.

"Chase?" he prompted.

"I don't know if 'serious' is the right word. 'Strange' might be more appropriate. Last time we met I behaved rather unprofessionally. I don't know if we'll be seeing each other again. I don't know if we won't. My life is kind of . . . complicated."

"I can certainly relate to that."

She hesitated and then said, "Let me do some schedule juggling and get back to you."

"Sounds great," he said.

As he hung up, Margaret took the opportunity to bring over a stack of papers and drop them on his desk.

On top was a *leather-bound book covered with mud and dirt. He clutched the book to his chest, and the young man held it desperately as* . . .

"What the—?" said Bruce.

Margaret leaned forward to see what had caused such a reaction from her boss. All she saw was a stack of papers. And Bruce, upon looking again, saw only that as well. He rubbed his temples, smiled gamely, and waved Margaret off.

And the screaming of the young man in torment echoed in his head.

Ten miles southeast of Gotham, on Claw Island, Edward Nygma stood over the production process that had just begun to swing into high gear. It was fully automated, robot arms assembling the boxes, descending claws and high-speed machines loading them into boxes to be shipped to waiting customers.

In Nygma's control room, Two-Face was busy taking a hit on the neural stimulator. Nygma had it timed for a ninety-second session, but Two-Face was so blissed out from it that it would feel like ninety minutes.

Soon . . . soon they would be out there. In droves. In tons. And people all over Gotham would be buying them, using them, staring at the dancing holographic images and letting their neural waves be sucked in through the receiver/transmitters in the Box. And these, in turn, would be beamed through dazzling white light to the pulsing spider antenna, jutting from the dome tip of Nygmatech that was already powered up and ready for business.

And all into Edward Nygma, the Riddler. Ever since he could remember, dealing with the mundanities of the world had been a drain on his genius and ability. But finally, finally, finally, he was going to turn it around. He was going to drain them, get back what they had taken from him. He would sit on his great electronic throne, a giant diode delivering pulses of glowing neural energy into his brain.

The great gestalt of the city's mind would be laid bare to him, and he would skim through it, take what he wanted, leave the rest behind.

And as the crates with the Boxes were loaded out to waiting airlifts, Nygma looked down upon it all, spread wide his arms, and shouted in glorious celebration, "Ssssssomebody stop me!"

But no one did.

CHAPTER 15

In the depths of the Batcave, Bruce stood over the assorted riddles that he had received. Riddles sent to Bruce, and also—at the scenes of various crimes—to Batman. It was likely the first time in the history of criminology that the same man was "carboned" with evidence.

Could it be that this "Riddler" was aware that Batman and Bruce Wayne were the same? It seemed unlikely. He could see a puzzle-maker like the Riddler transforming such a situation into a massive game, but his partner, Two-Face? Two-Face wasn't exactly subtle. If Harvey Dent knew who Batman was, he'd have stormed the place with guns blazing weeks ago. No, the more he thought about it, the more he was certain that his secret was safe.

Still . . . it made no sense.

Alfred, in the meantime, was looking at a computer simulation of a screaming bat . . . part of the programming tied in with the project that Bruce and Alfred had simply come to refer to as "the Prototype."

"I see you've apparently gotten the new radar modification running," said Alfred. He stood and straightened his jacket. "I still doubt it will work."

"That's what you said about the Batmobile." He studied the forensic evidence the computer was giving him on the screen. He fingered the riddle as he said, "Same obscure paper stock. No prints. Definitely the same author." He

157

looked at the riddle again and read, " 'The eight of us go forth, not back, to protect our king from a foe's attack.' Pawns."

"I couldn't agree more, sir. We are all just pawns in these madmen's . . ."

"No, Alfred. That's the answer to the riddle," said Bruce with a slight smile. "Chess pawns . . ." Then he started to tick off the other answers on his fingers. "A clock. A match. Pawns. All physical objects. Man-made . . ."

"Small in size. Light in weight."

"Time. Fire. Battle strategy." He shook his head, the stream of consciousness not getting him anywhere. "What's the connection?"

"With all due respect, sir, I think that's why they call him the Riddler."

Bruce sighed. "No success with the riddles. No success with the Prototype." He reached into a drawer and pulled out a newly purchased Box. With all of Edward Nygma's talk of brain manipulation, he was curious to see whether this so-called toy, which was selling briskly everywhere in Gotham, was more than it seemed. "Let's engage in some child's play, shall we?"

He got out several tools and proceeded to dissect the Box. He got about thirty seconds into the project, and then there was a hiss and a trail of smoke. He pulled his hands away quickly as the sides of the Box fell open to reveal that the inner circuitry had completely vaporized.

"Three for three, sir?" suggested Alfred.

The phone that connected to the upstairs number rang next to Alfred. He picked it up and said, "Wayne Residence." He paused and then, covering the receiver with his hand, said to Bruce, "Dr. Meridian, sir."

Bruce stretched out a hand and Alfred handed him the phone. "Yes, Chase."

"Guess what. I can squeeze you in tonight."

"That sounds great."

"How about over here?"

A pleasant thought, visiting Chase at her home. "Good idea. It'd be fairly awkward discussing Dick with him around."

"I'm at 249 Robinson Road, Apt. 2C. Let's say 7:00 P.M.?"

"Sounds good to me."

"Oh, and Bruce . . ."

"Yes?"

He could almost see her smiling over the phone. "I look forward to seeing you." And she hung up.

Bruce put the phone down and looked up at Alfred. "That woman is in my mind," he told him.

Alfred sniffed. "At least one of you is," he said, and walked away.

CHAPTER 16

Chase Meridian's apartment was cramped and cluttered. Bruce had wedged himself through the boxes after Chase let him in, having to take a deep breath now and then to fit past. Chase had already gone back to the kitchen, skillfully maneuvering the obstacle course. "It must be difficult to live out of half-empty boxes," he said.

Looking into a pot of boiling macaroni, she replied, "Now that's psychologically intriguing. Why don't you call them 'half-full' boxes?"

"Because from an unpacking point of view, it's more depressing that way."

She considered that. "Okay. I'll give you that one. I just try not to think about it at all."

"I could have guessed that," he said.

"Find a spot and clear it off. I'll have food up in five minutes. I'll have you know spaghetti is my specialty," she said archly.

"How did that get to be your specialty?" he asked.

"Because I can't cook anything else."

Dick knew there was something going on. But he didn't know what.

He wandered the mansion, encountering rooms that he hadn't stumbled over even in all the weeks he'd been there. On the basis of the house's immensity, it wasn't unreasonable that Bruce and Alfred would occasionally vanish into it, sometimes for hours at a time, it seemed.

And yet . . .

And yet . . .

There was something going on.

Dick wandered into the study. The place was as huge and intimidating as anywhere else in the joint. And the design was . . . eclectic. Sky-high bookshelves, but with a grand-father clock, of all things, sandwiched between two of them. Tropical fish. Trophies. Pictures.

Pictures, over on the mantel. That, in fact, did catch Dick's interest. He walked over and stared at the photos.

There was a kid who he guessed was Brucie as a boy. Bru-cie Wayne. Now there was a strange case. At first he'd been prepared to write Wayne off as just some do-gooder rich man, taking pity on the kid who'd been rude enough to be-come an orphan in his presence. An airhead, trying to pre-tend that he was Dick's pal without the faintest idea of what was going through the kid's mind.

But his opinion had shifted. He just wasn't certain what it had shifted to. It was clear that there was something going on in Wayne's head, but damned if he could tell what it was.

There was a photograph of a couple of other people who Dick knew were Bruce's parents. He was aware they had died a while back, because he'd made a joke about Bruce "losing his parents" somewhere in the endless corridors of Wayne Manor. Bruce had grimaced slightly, and Alfred had taken Dick aside and told him simply that Bruce's parents were indeed deceased some years back. It was apparently a sore subject and, in one of his few moments of sincerity, Dick promised not to bring it up again.

He looked around the study and confirmed what he'd sus-pected. There was no other exit from the place. This struck him as particularly odd, because the other day he'd been looking around the empty study. He'd walked out, but hadn't gotten twenty feet when he'd heard a faint "clanging" of some sort from within the study. He'd turned back and been stunned to see Alfred emerge from the room. But he hadn't been there less than a minute ago. Alfred had returned the puzzled stare, smiling gamely and saying, "Can I help you, sir?" Dick had shaken his head and walked away, scratching his head. . . .

Clanging . . .

Suddenly his head snapped around and he stared once more at the grandfather clock . . . stared, in particular, at the pendulum. The pendulum would have made that exact noise if knocked around.

But why would it have been knocked around? Obviously, only if someone had been moving it.

Clock moves, Alfred appears . . .

Dick walked quickly over to the clock, looking it over. He pulled on it, but it seemed set into place. He opened the case, moved the pendulum. Yup, same sound. He closed it up, then looked at the clockface.

"That's how *I* would do it," he murmured.

He opened up the glass cover and started moving the clock hands, pushing them backwards since—he reasoned—clockwise was the normal motion. "What'cha got back here, Bruce?" he murmured. "A secret office? A vault with the Wayne billions? What's—"

He pushed the hands backwards to midnight, on a hunch . . . and then jumped back as the clock slid smoothly and noiselessly outward. Behind it was a black, darkened entrance into . . . what?

"Thanks again for dinner," said Bruce as he helped Chase clear off the dishes. He couldn't get over how much she changed from incarnation to incarnation. This evening she'd been wearing tight jeans and an off-the-shoulder angora sweater, bearing no resemblance whatsoever to the slip-clad bag puncher, the no-nonsense shrink, or even the glamorous woman who'd sat next to him at the circus. "Also, I appreciate your advice on Dick. Can I buy you a hospital wing or something?"

She laughed lightly and moved toward the stove. "Instant coffee okay?"

He nodded.

She glanced behind the coffeepot and snapped her fingers. "Oh, that's right. I forgot."

"Forgot—?"

She pulled out a small, gift-wrapped box and handed it to him. He turned it over curiously. "What's this?"

All she did in response was smile enigmatically. So, with a shrug, Bruce opened it. Inside was a small wicker doll. A dream doll.

"Call it clinical intuition," she said. "I thought your dreams might need changing."

"That would be nice."

She turned to face him. "Tell me . . . what do you find more frightening? Dreaming about things that have no basis in reality . . . or dreaming about things that did happen?"

"No contest. The second."

He hesitated, staring out the window. He almost hoped for the Bat-Signal to shine so that he'd have an excuse to call it an early evening, fabricate a meeting . . . something so that he could bolt out the door.

If he told her what was on his mind . . . if he shared part of himself, split himself off . . . would what was left over be half-empty? Or half-full?

Before he could decide—because he knew that *if* he decided, he would decide against it—he said, "My parents were murdered. In front of me. I was just a kid."

Chase nodded. She leaned back against the counter, her face carefully composed and neutral.

"I can't remember exactly what happened. I get flashes, in my dreams. I'd gotten . . . used to them. But now there's a new element, one that I don't understand. A book. Leather . . ."

He paused, and Chase guessed to keep him talking. "There's something else?"

He nodded. "The dreams have started coming when I'm awake."

She took all that in, considering her next words carefully. "Bruce, you're describing repressed memories. Images of some forgotten pain trying to surface. It . . ."

The phone rang. "Damn," she said. "Almost nobody has this number, and the few people who do . . ."

"Would be upset if you didn't answer. Go. I'm not going anywhere."

She moved quickly into the living room. Her desk was a rolltop and the phone was jangling inside. She shoved up the rolltop and papers piled up inside cascaded to the floor. She grabbed at the phone as Bruce, in a sense of chivalry, went over to help pick the stuff up.

"Yes, Mr. Greenberger . . . yes, I know I gave you this number, to be used in case of an emergency . . . no, I'm sorry, aliens taking over your mind is not an emergency . . ."

Bruce wasn't listening. That was because the first two files he picked up off the floor were about Batman. As were the next five. Articles, newsphotos, clippings. He glanced up and, to his shock, the interior of the desk was lined with stuff—all of it, regarding Batman. Every bit of printed material known to mankind about his costumed alter ego was adorning the desk of Dr. Chase Meridian.

It gave him an uncomfortable flashback to Edward Nygma's wall of adoration to Bruce Wayne. Damn it. *Damn it.* Why couldn't he have the right people obsessed with the right aspects of his life? Nygma adored Wayne, Chase was hung up on Batman. Perhaps Edward and Chase should get together and move to a house in Cape Cod, and leave Bruce alone with his empty house, his business, and his spiralling-out-of-control delusions.

"There is *no* white light coming out of your television. Mr. Greenberger. I assure you. Yes. We'll discuss this tomorrow during session." She sighed, hung up, and looked at Bruce, trying to turn matters back to business. "Is it possible there's an aspect of your parents' death you haven't faced? You were so young."

But she saw that he wasn't listening, and then she turned and saw what he was staring at.

"Is that the 'other man,' Doctor?" he asked stiffly.

"Please, Bruce, don't change the subject. I want to help."

"I'd say all this goes a little beyond taking your work home."

"All right," she sighed in frustration. "He's fascinating. Clinically. Why does a man do"—and she put her fingers up at the sides of her head, imitating the bat ears—"this?" Then she studied Bruce a moment and said, "Okay, look . . . if you're no longer interested in discussing yourself . . . you want to help me try and dissect Batman? It'll be challenging. You may even find out something about yourself."

"Now, that would be a treat," deadpanned Bruce Wayne. "And maybe you'll find out something, too."

Bruce Wayne is Batman . . .

Dick had figured it out in no time flat. If the computers, the equipment, and the entire incredible setup weren't enough, certainly the cape that Bruce had left draped over a chair was sufficient tip-off.

From one of the caverns up ahead, he heard a clanking, like tools being set down and picked up. With the cape draped over his arm, he made his way forward and soon saw that that was exactly it.

It was the Batmobile. The hood was up, the motor humming softly, as Alfred was bent over the mighty black car making some sort of minor adjustments to the engine.

Never had Dick Grayson moved more silently than he did at that point. The cowling on the cockpit was open and he eased himself in. He had no sure idea what he was doing or what his plan was, or even if he *had* a plan. All he knew was that there was a great likelihood he'd never get this opportunity again. So he was going to milk it for all it was worth.

He studied the dashboard. Everything was clear, easy to

find. Made sense. If he was in a fight, he didn't want to have to start fumbling around to find weaponry.

Alfred slammed the hood, wiping his hands on a white rag he had dangling from his belt. He moved toward the cockpit at just the precise moment that Dick Grayson located the button that would slide the cowling shut.

As the butler started to reach in for the purpose of shutting off the engine, the cowling quickly began to slide forward into its locking groove. With a startled yelp Alfred yanked his arm clear and then, to his horror, caught a glimpse of Dick Grayson's grinning face.

"Don't wait up, Al!" he called as the cowling clicked into place.

"No!" shouted Alfred.

Dick slammed his foot on the gas. The Batmobile lurched forward so quickly that for a moment Dick lost his nerve and slammed on the brakes. Dick was tossed forward, slamming his head on the steering wheel.

"Master Grayson, no! Get out of there!" But by that point it was too late. Dick Grayson had recaptured his nerve. With a screech of tires, the Batmobile hurtled away, picking up speed with every second.

And for just a moment, the polished British butler vanished, to be replaced by a very unpolished, and very frantic, Alfred Pennyworth.

"Oh bugger!" exclaimed Alfred.

We'll screen some news footage first," said Chase, keying up a CD ROM file on her computer.

"Of what?"

"Of Batman in combat."

"Batman fighting." Bruce made a production of yawning. "Been there. Done that."

Ignoring his comments Chase brought the first footage up on the screen. Bruce watched and, more precisely, watched her watching.

"Look at the abuse he's taking," Chase observed. "He's

not just fighting crime. It's as if he's paying some great penance. What crime could he have committed to deserve a life of nightly torture?"

Bruce hit a key, blanking the screen. "So, Batman just had a lousy childhood. Is that your diagnosis, Doctor?"

He started to turn away and she grabbed his hand as if grasping a life preserver. "Why do you throw up that superficial mask? I want to be close but you won't let me near. What are you protecting me from?"

He moved toward her and she backed up slightly. In a dark, even morbid way, he found that amusing. He'd made a similar movement towards her once as Batman, and she'd stood her ground. But Bruce Wayne was capable of intimidating her. "You want to know me, Doctor? We're all two people. This side we show daylight. That we keep in shadow."

She continued to back up and bumped against a wall. "Rage . . . violence . . . passion," she whispered, and for a moment he felt himself drawing her into him . . . or perhaps it was the other way around . . .

His watch beeped at him. With a slightly strangled grunt, he stepped back and raised the watch to his face. "Screen," he said, and the holographic watch face was replaced by the frowning face of Alfred.

Chase looked at it with interest. "Oooh. Dick Tracy. Do you have a flying platform, too?"

"Not with me," he said. "Yes, Alfred?"

Aware of Chase's presence, Alfred chose his words carefully. "Sorry to bother you, sir. I have some rather distressing news about Master Dick."

"Is he all right?"

"I'm afraid Mr. Dick has . . . gone traveling."

"He ran away?"

"Actually, he took the car."

"He boosted the Jag?" Bruce felt relief sweep over him. An A.P.B. to the cops would have the Jag located in no time, and the driver with it. "Is that all?"

"Not the Jaguar. The other car."

"The Bentley?" He was surprised. The Bentley was more upscale, but the Jag was cooler.

Alfred looked ready to reach through the watch and shake his employer. "*No*, sir, *the* other *car!*"

Then it clicked.

Bruce closed his eyes in pain.

"What's the problem?" asked Chase

With a soft moan, he simply replied, "Car trouble."

CHAPTER 17

In an alley off Arkham Square, the young girl ran, with several young toughs in pursuit. She cried out for help, but no one was willing to buck the odds to come to her assistance. One guy ran off to call the cops, but the chances were that they would never get there is time.

She dashed down the alley, crying out, and then the gang caught up with her. One of them knocked her to the ground, and she cried out in supplication to the God that she was certain wasn't listening.

And then blinding headlights framed them in the alleyway. They looked up in shock as the Batmobile rolled down the alley toward them.

There were six of the young punks in all, and every single one of them was quaking.

The Batmobile skidded to a halt, the right front fender bumping up inelegantly against the wall. Then the cowling slid back and there was deathly silence as a caped figure emerged from the cockpit.

He leaped down from the cockpit as the punks shrank back, the cape fluttering around him.

Everyone froze.

Something seemed off.

For one thing, Batman wasn't wearing a mask. He was just holding his cape in front of his face, like Bela Lugosi. And for another thing . . .

One of the gang kids leaned forward to the leader and whispered, "I thought he'd be taller in person."

"Shut up!" said the leader, slugging the other kid in the chest. He glared at the intruder and growled, "Who the hell are you?"

Trying to sound ominous, Dick Grayson rumbled, "I'm Batman." He took a step towards them but the cape was too long and he stepped on one of the scalloped edges, yanking it partway off his shoulders. It revealed his less-than-intimidating sweater and jeans.

"Damn, did I forget to dress again?"

They closed on him then, one of the gang members taking the lead while another swung a length of chain.

Dick Grayson faced death.

Old news.

"Chains. You don't seem the type," said Dick. His hand shot out quickly and he grabbed the chain. He slammed his open palm into the face of its wielder, who went down with a cry. Then he whipped the chain into the gut of the other punk who was coming at him. Swinging the chain in a parabola to drive the others back, he crowed, "The Dark Knight strikes again!"

Dick swung the chain upward, catching the low rung of a fire escape ladder just as another of the punks rushed him. He yanked himself into the air, swinging on the chain and slamming a kick into his face, knocking him flat. "Another victory for the Dark Knight . . . so Dark nighty-night."

He turned to face the remaining punks and said confidently, "Is your will up-to-date?" It was enough to break whatever spirit they had left, and with a collective yell they dashed off down the alleyway.

He watched them go, drawing the cape around himself and grinning broadly. "I could definitely get behind this super-hero gig."

He tossed a salute to the awestruck girl and started toward the car "Wait," she called. "You forgot the part where you kiss the girl."

He smiled, happy to oblige. . . .

And then he heard a series of shouts and screams that did not bode particularly well. Both he and the girl turned and saw several dozen bats coming their way.

Unfortunately they were the wooden type, being wielded by about thirty punks belonging to the same gang as the kids whom Dick had just put down for the count.

Dick and the girl dashed toward the other end of the alley, which was barred by a chainlink fence. Dick wasted no time and, with his own natural strength and a healthy dose of adrenaline, he practically tossed the girl over the fence. "Run!" he shouted.

"Call me!" she shouted back to him as she rabbited. It wouldn't be until she was a mile away that she suddenly realized she hadn't exactly been in a position to give her fast-moving savior her phone number.

Dick, meantime, went with the instinctive move: He sought safety in height. He leaped for the chain dangling from the fire escape. Within seconds he was clambering up the rickety metal platform, making for the safety of a nearby rooftop.

It was a fairly good plan up until the point where more of the gang came pouring over the rooftop. Dick couldn't believe it. Did *everybody* in the damned neighborhood belong to this gang? He spun and looked back down again. They had dragged down the ladder and were coming up after him.

He did the only thing he could. He leapt off the balcony, snagging a clothesline as he went to brake his descent somewhat. The fact that there were so many of them was the only thing that Dick had going for him, because it meant they were tightly packed into the alleyway. Dick used the opportunity to land on their shoulders and start leapfrogging across them to try to get to the Batmobile and safety.

To his credit, he almost made it. But one of them managed to grab his foot and pull him down into the midst of the pounding mass of flesh that was operating with a single thought: Tear the Batboy to pieces. Dick fought back valiantly, but he was hopelessly outnumbered. The darkness of the alleyway had helped him marginally in that no one had seen his face clearly. Ultimately it probably wasn't going to matter, because the chances were that, by morning, his face wasn't going to bear any resemblance to what it had been the day before.

And that was when a dark, caped figure descended from on high.

He zeroed in immediately on where Dick had gone down under the bruising fists. Within seconds he had pulled several of the gang members off Dick, tossing them around as if they weighed nothing.

"Smoke!" he called out.

Responding instantly to the preencoded voice message of its creator, the Batmobile ejected smoke grenades out from its front launcher. Wasting no time, Batman slung his young charge under his arm and carried him to the Batmobile, shoving him in as the punks coughed and gagged, running into each other blindly in the midst of the fog. By the time it cleared, and by the time their chests had stopped burning, the Batmobile was long gone.

The Batmobile hurtled down the deserted side street.

Dick Grayson had just managed to blink the last of the gas out of his eyes, and he stared at Batman, who was concentrating on the road ahead.

"Bastard," whispered Dick, his rage bubbling over.

Batman started to reply, but he didn't get the chance, because Dick Grayson slugged him in the head. *"Your fault!"*

The Batmobile lurched wildly as Batman, unable to defend himself, reeled from the blow. *"You killed them!"* howled Dick, and he didn't care about the danger he was putting them in, didn't care about Two-Face, and most of all, he didn't care about himself. *"You killed them!"* and he pounded again on Batman's head and chest.

Batman momentarily lost control of the Batmobile. The car went out of control. *"Autopilot!"* shouted Batman, as

Dick kept pounding on him, calling him a murderer, spitting out profanities.

Unable to discern the instruction above the noise in the car, the computer voice requested, "Please repeat instruction."

Too late. Batman slammed on the brakes, but the crash was unavoidable. The Batmobile skidded to the right and slammed into a fire hydrant. The hydrant went flying and the water pipe burst open, sending water geysering high into the air.

Dick continued to slam away at Batman, and at this point Batman did nothing to ward it off. The armor absorbed the impact, although not all the armor in the world could prevent the irate youth's words from cutting him to ribbons.

He hit him and kept hitting him until the breath was ragged in his lungs, until his fists were ripped and bleeding, and still he kept going until his arms felt like lead weights, and there was no more strength. And still he accused, "You killed them! You killed them! If you'd made Two-Face see who you are at the circus, they'd still be—!"

"Alive," said Batman flatly.

Slowly Dick's punches stopped, his arms going limp at his sides.

"It's all your fault," he whispered.

And then, finally, for all the loss and pain that he had carried with him . . . for all the agony he'd kept wrapped within him . . . Dick Grayson started to sob, and then cry, his chest heaving, his body shaking.

And Bruce Wayne's casual, tossed-off words to Chase Meridian earlier that evening rang in Batman's head.

Been there . . . done that . . .

Long into the night they were there in the Batcave. Bruce considered it a small triumph that Dick had apologized on his own to Alfred without any prompting from Bruce. But the interpersonal dynamics between the two "crime fighters" were somewhat more strained, and continued far past the point where an exhausted Alfred had retired for evening.

"I tried to tell Two-Face who I was, Dick," Bruce said, choosing to keep to himself his further doubts about shooting down the poor, lost district attorney once known as Harvey Dent. Enough that he was already openly admitting to his responsibility over the situation. No need to heap on top of that, *And not only do I feel guilty about your family's death for this reason, but there's also this other reason.* Matters were problematic enough. "I wish with all my heart there was something I could do to change things—"

To Bruce's surprise, Dick said, "There is." He paused and then said, "Let me be part of this."

"What?"

Dick rose to his feet and started to pace. "It's all I think about. Every second of the day. Getting Two-Face. He took . . . my whole life. But when I was out there tonight, I imagined it was him I was fighting, and all the hurt went away. Understand?"

"Too well." It was the kind of statement that Bruce had made earlier; the kind that Dick had previously considered to be patronizing. Now, though, he understood. Too well.

"So how do we find him?" said Dick, as if Bruce had already acceded to his request. "And when we do, you gotta let me be the one to kill him."

Bruce wanted to grab him and shake sense into him. "Listen to me, Dick. Killing damns you. I know. All this isn't about revenge."

Dick glanced at a framed headline over Bruce's desk. It carried the story of the murder of Bruce's parents . . . a story that, obviously now, Dick had been brought up to speed on. "Right."

Bruce stroked his chin tiredly, feeling the start of five o'clock shadow. Where had the night gone? "It's an addiction. You fight night after night, trying to fill the emptiness, but the pain's back in the morning. Somewhere along the way it stops being a choice."

"Save the speeches about how great you want my life to be, okay, Bruce? You want to help me? Train me. Let me be your partner . . ."

"No."

Dick eyed Bruce with anger born of pain. "You said we're the same. Well, you were right. I'm going to be part of this. Whether you want me or not."

He stormed out and Bruce watched him go, feeling a lot older.

CHAPTER 18

Bruce decided to take the day off. With everything that was going on in his life, he figured he would do more harm than good. They might ask him a simple question and he'd wind up selling the entire Tokyo office. So he called in to Margaret, who ran down a few quick outstanding questions that had to be attended to.

"Oh, and Gossip Gerty and her sisters of scandal are all over us," she concluded. "They want to know if you're bringing Dr. Meridian to the Nygmatech 'do' tonight."

"The what?"

"I've only mentioned it to you seven times, sir," she said, trying not to sound as if she were scolding him.

"Eight's the charm. Run it past me again."

"Big brouhaha at the Ritz Gotham Hotel, celebrating a new model of that silly little Box thing. Naturally a new model is required since they sold their first million."

"That was fast. And you sound disapproving."

"He was a creepy little man, Mr. Wayne," said Margaret, which was fairly strong language for her because Margaret was the most diplomatic person in his employ. "I don't like seeing creeps become successful. Makes you wonder if there's any justice in the world."

"I don't wonder about such things."

"If you ask me, I think he's nuts."

"Well, Maggie, no offense . . . but I don't think I'll ask

you." He thought a moment. "On the other hand . . . I know someone who I *can* ask. A close-up and personal opinion might not hurt at that. Maggie . . . call back the gossip ladies and tell them that I will indeed be taking Dr. Meridian with me to the Nygmatech soirée tonight."

"All right, Mr. Wayne."

"Then call Dr. Meridian and ask her not to make a liar out of me."

The red carpet had been rolled out that night at the Ritz Gotham Hotel. The Ritz was one of the older hotels in Gotham. In fact, directly across the street another hotel was going up that threatened to dwarf the Ritz, once the showcase of Gotham.

For now, though, the Ritz Gotham was still a hive of activity. A banner was draped across the front that read "NYGMATECH—IMAGINE THE FUTURE." At the curb, finely dressed folks poured from luxury cars. A battalion of valets scurried about.

Bruce Wayne's Bentley, driven by Alfred and carrying Bruce, Dick, and Chase, pulled up to the curb. Bruce stepped out and assisted Chase. Dick vaulted over the back of the car.

The party was in the rooftop ballroom. The place was packed with people sipping cocktails, munching hors d'oeuvres. A band was playing and couples were dancing on an elaborately decorated dance floor.

Lining the walls were curtained show booths. Partygoers were being invited to step in and sample the "new Box." People were emerging from the booths, giggling as if they were drunk.

Bruce, Chase, and Dick headed down a large staircase to the center of the ballroom. "Gotham high society," said Dick, unenthusiastic. "I'm excited."

"You needed to get out of Wayne Manor for a while. Too many . . . distractions," he said significantly.

"Oh, right. Whatever you say, Ba . . . Ba . . ." and several times he stammered, almost saying "Batman" until Chase finally turned to look at him, at which point he said casually, "Bruce."

Bruce fired him a look that, to Dick, seemed to say, "Please, Dick. Don't make me have to kill you."

For one quick instant, Dick wasn't sure whether Bruce was kidding. Bruce satisfied himself with that moment of uncertainty on Dick's part. And Dick, opting for the better part of valor, allowed his attention to be drawn away by a showgirl.

Bruce and Chase paused at a landing. He helped Chase off with her cloak. She was in a tight-fitting black dress, with a string of pearls, and she looked ravishing.

"About last night," Bruce started, "I want you to know . . ."

"It's important to me we stay friends," she said, overlapping.

"Yes. Definitely. Me too."

She smiled. "Then it's settled. Friends."

Yet neither of them looked, or felt, particularly pleased with the accord.

Edward Nygma laughed a little too loud and a little too long. Once upon a time, such behavior would have gotten him annoyed looks and the backs of people's heads.

Now it got him imitated. Reporters pressed in closer, snapping pictures and tossing questions.

"Edward, you sweet, bold, dashing darling," said Gossip Gerty. "How does it feel to be the city's newest, most eligible bachelor? Gotham *must* know." Suddenly she spotted a new arrival and called his name. "Oh! There's Bruce Wayne! Brucie!"

Edward stiffened slightly, but then relaxed. He had nothing to fear. Nothing to be angry about. He was Wayne's peer now . . . no. Not peer. Wayne's superior.

He was about to continue his performance for the crowd when abruptly the crowd evaporated. They surged toward Wayne.

No. No, it wasn't supposed to happen that way. A fury of

red, and then a blinding green of envy, flashed before Edward's eyes. He'd gone to all this time, this effort, this agony, built everything up from *nothing*, and Wayne was capable of pulling away his audience with his mere presence.

And on top of everything, they were wearing the exact same suit.

Edward's date for the evening, Sugar, sidled up to him. He waited for her to say something comforting.

"Ow. Wayne's too cute. Eddie"—she looked him up and down—"how come your suit doesn't hang like that?"

He wanted to pop her one. Instead he managed to say, "Shut up. You're here to work." Then, rather forcefully, he grabbed her by the elbow, plastered a smile on his face, and headed over toward Wayne.

He heard the bansheelike tones of Gossip Gerty asking Wayne in a sprightly manner, "Nygmatech stock is outselling Wayne Enterprises two to one. Edward Nygma's charitable contributions threaten to dwarf yours. Are you yesterday's news, Bruce?"

Before Wayne could get a word out, Edward had draped himself around Bruce's shoulder. "Yes, Bruce old man! The press was just wondering what it feels like to be outsold, outclassed, outcoiffed, outcoutured, and generally outdone in every way?"

He waited eagerly for the desired reaction. He wanted Bruce to shout, or tell him off, or throw some sort of tantrum that would look absolutely scrumptious in tomorrow's headlines.

But Bruce Wayne merely smiled. Could he really be that self-confident, that unconcerned? No . . . no, it had to be that he was doing it out of spite. That was it.

"Congratulations, Edward. Great party. Nice suit . . ."

Edward's fist clenched, flexing, wishing he had his cane. But then he spotted . . . *her*.

"And what light through yonder window breaks? 'Tis the east. And you are . . . ?"

"Chase," she said.

"Ah!" His voice, and hopes, soared. "And what a grand pursuit you must be."

Endeavoring to return the small talk, Bruce turned to the stunning woman standing next to Edward. "Miss . . . ?" he prompted.

She ran a finger along the curve of his ear. "You can call me anything you want."

"Bruce," said Edward, managing a voice that was both *entre nous* and, at the same time, playing to the press, "how humiliating my success must be for you. There you were, a real genius, and yet you couldn't recognize my own. Come. Let me show you what could have been ours together."

Visions of lawsuits danced in Bruce's head. Edward was admitting, in front of witnesses, that he'd worked on the Box during his employ at Wayne Enterprises. But as he'd told his lawyer, he didn't need the money. Sure, there was the principle of the thing. And, granted, he wouldn't mind wiping that smug look off Nygma's face. But he brushed off the notion, even as Nygma propelled Wayne and the rest of the group through the party. Now, more than ever, it would seem like envy or revenge rather than a justified suit. Bruce had an obligation to the image of Wayne Enterprises and its stockholders' concerns. Having the company's namesake look like a bad sport would help neither.

"Ladies and gentlemen," gloated Nygma. "The future!"

A woman was just stepping inside the first booth. Noticing that she suddenly had an audience, she waved gamely, like an astronaut climbing into the capsule. She moved into the booth, but everyone was able to watch her on a monitor, where she was turning and looking down in amazement. She was covered in glittering jewels.

"My new, improved Box offers fully interactive holographic fantasies."

"Edward, you're dashing *and* a genius," burbled Gossip Gerty. "How do you create the images, hon'?"

He waggled a finger. "That, my dear, is my little secret."

"Fully interactive holographs," said Wayne, thinking out

loud. "Only a high-frequency carrier wave beamed directly into the brain could—"

Nygma laughed loudly and nervously. "Enough shop talk! Behold!"

In a second booth, a bald man was entering and discovering, as the monitor indicated, that he had a beard and full head of hair. To his astonishment he was even able to finger it. It was solid . . . real . . .

"It's real because they believe it to be real," Nygma said. "An end to mundanity. Out of the darkness, Nygmatech brings you a life better than life itself!"

"Of course," Wayne was observing. "The Box's zombielike effects must result from an electroneural link with the viewer's brain."

Nygma's entire body quivered with what looked like rage. "Zombies! Worse than nonsense!" he sputtered.

Gossip Gerty was scowling disapprovingly at Wayne. "That's what they said about the first TVs," she sniffed.

"Yes, and they're still saying it," Bruce remarked amiably. "Except now the term is 'couch potatoes' instead of zombies."

But Gerty wasn't listening. She already had her angle, and a comment that pertained to common sense didn't fit in. "Wayne Whines Sour Grapes," she scribbled.

"Yes, Brucie," said Edward, quickly feeling back in control of the situation. "Don't be such a sore loser."

Screw it. Maybe he *should* sue the little creep.

Edward was gesturing toward the booth. "Go ahead, Brucie. Try it. Step on through to the other side."

Bruce glanced at another monitor where a man was enjoying a Hawaiian fantasy. "Edward," he said slowly, "if you can introduce images into the mind, what keeps you from drawing images *out* of the mind?"

Once again panic clawed at Nygma, but this time he didn't succumb to it. Instead he sneered and said, "Too timid to try my machine? Say so!" He smiled graciously at Chase. "If such cowardice before so fair a lady doesn't embarrass you. Shall we dance?"

Chase was about to say no, but then she noticed that Bruce, with a subtle nod of his head, was indicating that she should. Immediately she understood why. Bruce was still concerned about Nygma's behavior and just how obsessive it might be, or might become, and he was very interested in her assessment of him. Now would be the ideal time to gather some data. So when Nygma scooped her up in his arms, she did nothing to resist . . . although she couldn't help asking him, "Have you ever considered therapy?"

The crowd of reporters had seemed to dissipate, giving Bruce Wayne the distinct feeling of being old news. He didn't mind overmuch; garnering headlines as Bruce Wayne—or even as Batman—was never a top priority for him.

But now the girl with whom Edward had been was pulling at Wayne's arm. He looked down at her politely, curious if she was going to ask him to dance.

Instead she indicated a booth and whispered, "Come try one with me. You can't imagine what we can do in there."

He could, actually. Furthermore, he certainly didn't need having his fantasies displayed on a monitor for everyone to see. If that happened, he would likely move quickly from the gossip columns to the front page. He smiled and shook his head.

"Your loss," said Sugar, although her expression made it clear that she considered it hers as well. She disappeared into the crowd.

But Bruce now felt his curiosity piqued. His conversation with Edward, and Nygma's tensing up at certain points during it, indicated to Bruce that he'd been fairly on target about some of his observations. And if that were the case, there were potential ramifications that simply had to be dealt with. It didn't matter to Wayne at that point if people did claim that he was out to harass Nygma. If there was a question of public safety, or of potential tampering with people's minds, Wayne was going to have to take action.

He couldn't be sure, however. Nor could he make himself sure until he'd had the opportunity to look over the equipment. The smaller version of the Box had already proved less than cooperative. Perhaps the new and improved model might be more so.

He moved to an empty booth and pulled aside the curtain. It was empty, except for a faint green glow.

At that moment the attractive young woman was at his side again. "Naughty naughty," she said scoldingly. "Looking for something?"

"How to turn it off, actually."

She looked left and right, then put a finger to her lips in a "shhh" manner. Then she pressed a button on the small panel just outside. A power pack ejected into her hand. The booth went dark completely. Still suspicious, Bruce opened his palm. Without hesitation, Sugar dropped the power pack into his hand.

"Thank you," he said.

"My pleasure. And if you change your mind and want some company in there," and she ran her tongue along her upper teeth, "then we can both use our imaginations."

Bruce stepped into the booth.

Out on the dance floor, Edward tossed off random answers to Chase's series of questions. To him it was all a game.

He spotted Bruce Wayne entering the booth, and quickly spun Chase around so that her back was squarely to Wayne. Edward exchanged a glance with Sugar and then, once he was satisfied that Wayne was in position, he nodded to her.

Sugar promptly reached into her bodice, pulled out an identical power pack, and slammed it into the circuit panel. The booth hummed to life.

Bruce was looking over the interior of the booth, trying to locate the circuitry. Did it line the walls, or was it consolidated into small projectionlike devices?

He looked up toward the top of the booth, and suddenly

discovered that he was staring at a tropical bird. The bird screeched down at him and lifted off, accompanied by a flock.

Bruce spun and discovered that all around him was a lush jungle. Immediately he understood what was happening. He looked for a way out, but the door had vanished.

It was incredible. It wasn't just some sort of visual show. He felt the heat of the jungle, and the air wafted to him the scent of an ocean not far off. He could even hear it now, the waves lapping gently against the shore.

There was a slight rustling of the brushes and he turned to see a sultry showgirl emerging. She smiled dazzlingly. "Hi. My name is Holly and I'll be your holographic guide. I am computer-generated and *totally* interactive."

She took Bruce's hand and led him into the tropical wilds.

And as Bruce Wayne stood mesmerized in the booth, surrounded by a green glow with a tiny white light focused on his eyes . . .

. . . in a control booth on Claw Island, yet another holofile was created, added to the hundreds that had already been assembled this busy, busy night. This one was labelled "Bruce Wayne." A miniature schematic of the human brain appeared on a screen, and the new and improved Box began its guided tour through the graphic landscape of Bruce Wayne's mind.

Dick Grayson looked contemptuously down the array of booths, with people going in and out like cuckoos into clocks. He smoothed his hair and cast a smile toward the showgirl, who blew him a kiss and walked back downstairs.

"Fake reality. It'll never beat the real thing."

Then he saw all the booths go dark at once, and only had a second to wonder why before gunfire clattered across the room.

And bile rose in his throat as he saw Two-Face swagger into the middle of the floor. His thugs were converging from every direction. There was a black-clad masked woman at his side.

Two-Face bellowed, "All right, folks, this is an old-fashioned, low-tech stickup. We're interested in the basics; jewelry, cash, cellular phones. Hand 'em over nice and no one gets hurt." Then he paused and added in his gravelly, less-pleasant voice, "On second thought . . . put up a fight."

Bruce Wayne staggered out of the booth, disoriented, operating completely on instinct. The tendency of the other guests had been to freeze the moment they'd heard bullets being fired. For Wayne it was the other way around. He moved immediately toward a service entrance and shoved the door open. He did it with considerable force, and he even happened to get a small piece of luck. The thug assigned to cover the door had arrived just a couple of seconds late. Ordinarily this would not have been a problem. But Bruce thrust the door open with such force that it smashed into the thug's face just as he was about to reach the door. Two-Face's man staggered, never having the chance to see who it was that slammed a fist into the thug's face an instant later. All the thug knew was that everything suddenly went profoundly black.

Bruce tore down the emergency stairs as quickly as he could. He was moving so fast that he seemed a blur. Anyone else trying to imitate it would have stumbled and taken a header down several flights, but Bruce was surefooted as a mountain climber.

The moment he got outside he located the Bentley and ducked into it. Alfred twisted in the seat and saw the expression on Wayne's face. Immediately he knew.

"Emergency, Alfred," he said, but the butler was already pressing a hidden button that flipped open a secret panel in the back. A Batsuit was hidden within.

Dick Grayson bolted into the service kitchen. He heard the pounding of feet from both directions, the unmistakable clacking of bolts being shot home. He looked around desperately . . . and spotted a laundry chute. He wasn't sure where it led, but anywhere had to be better than this. He dived through it just as two thugs converged on the area that he'd vacated.

CHAPTER 19

Edward Nygma shoved his way toward Two-Face. Gossip Gerty grabbed him by the arm and bellowed, "No, Edward! He's a monster! Stay away from him!"

"I have to do something, Gerty," he said in a basso profundo, he-man voice. "Perhaps I can reason with that . . . that two-toned terror!" He shook loose of Gerty and made it over to Two-Face.

"Two-toned terror," said Two-Face thoughtfully. "We like it."

In a harsh whisper Edward said, "You're ruining my big party! Are you insane?" He stared into Two-Face's mad eyes and amended, "Actually, considering your present behavior, I withdraw the question."

"We're sick of waiting for you to deliver Batman, Riddle-boy. We're tired of your little games and your misdirections. The point is to nail the Bat . . . not send him flapping off in other directions. We're starting to wonder, in fact, how much of that was our idea and how much of it we only *thought* was our idea."

Edward began to sweat. "Patience, oh bifurcated one."

"Screw patience. We want him dead. And nothing brings out the Bat like a little mayhem and murder."

"Oh well, in *that* case," said Nygma sarcastically as if it made sense. "Look, if you were going to rob me, you could have at least let me in on the caper. We could have *organized* this, *planned* it, presold the movie rights . . ."

At that moment, a window exploded inward. Guests ducked back, glass flying over them, as Batman swung in. Glass crunched beneath his feet when he landed, and he wasted no time at all. Three thugs had been standing by the window when he entered; a quick blur of fists later, none were.

Nygma turned to Two-Face and said, with a tinge of regret in his voice, "Harv, babe, I gotta be honest. Your entrance was good. His was better. What's the difference? Showmanship!"

Two-Face shoved Edward out of the way, yanking out his gun and looking for a clean shot. He fired several times but only managed to destroy an ice sculpture and some liquor bottles. The screaming did his heart good, but the misses took some of the edge off it.

Dick Grayson shoved his face into the Bentley. Alfred gasped as he saw the thick red stain on Dick's chest. "Good lord, you've been shot!"

Dick looked confused, and then glanced down. "Ketchup stain. Laundry chute. I'll tell you about it later. Give it to me."

Alfred knew precisely what the "it" was. It had seemed a harmless enough indulgence when Dick had slipped the package to him surreptitiously before they'd started out for the party. What sort of problem could possibly arise that would necessitate its use, Alfred had figured.

Well, he'd found out.

He pulled the package out and handed it to Dick, muttering, "I'm sure to be fired for this. Perhaps I could find a position at Buckingham. Always liked the Queen . . ."

One thug charged Batman, but the crimefighter heaved him overhead, throwing him into a display of stacked Boxes that crashed down all around him. Then he moved toward a thug who was trying to rip Chase's pearls from around her neck. "Excuse me," he growled as he head-butted the thug, knocking him cold.

"My place . . . midnight," Chase whispered to him.

Batman spun, raced across the tops of chair backs, and engaged another group of thugs. He saw other guests starting to rally, pulling their courage together and trying to go up against Two-Face's thugs. However none of them were wearing armor or had trained for years in various forms of martial arts combat or battle strategy. Consequently, someone was going to get killed. He had to do something—fast.

He yanked gas pellets from his belt and hurled them. They exploded at the feet of several thugs, and immediately those went down from the fumes. But more of Two-Face's endless supply of such goons leapt to replace them.

And that was when the distant sounds of police sirens began to fill the room.

Upon hearing them, Two-Face holstered his guns. "Okay, boys. Phase two."

As Batman continued to battle, Two-Face and the nearest thugs dashed for the service elevator. The doors closed behind them . . . shutting out Sugar and Spice, who arrived seconds too late.

"We gotta vacate," said Spice.

"What's this 'we' stuff?" retorted Sugar. "I'm here legit."

Spice fired her a look. "Babe, if my sorry ass gets hauled in, I'm not going down alone. Read me?"

"We gotta vacate," Sugar immediately said. "And fast. Where's the stairs?"

"Thirty stories? In these heels?" Spice said incredulously. She flipped open a portable phone. "I know a guy with a helicopter."

Batman pulled several small cuffs from his belt and threw them toward the thugs who were advancing on him. The cuffs homed in on them, whipping through the air, securing themselves around the thugs' ankles. They went down hard.

Batman ran in the direction that he'd seen Two-Face go. He skidded to a halt in front of the elevator and watched the electronic readout reach the first floor. Could be they'd gone down to the lobby to escape. On the other hand, maybe they'd gotten off somewhere along the way. Second floor, perhaps.

He dashed out onto the balcony, looked out over it and yes, sure enough, Two-Face had indeed gone to ground. He and his thugs were just vanishing into an open manhole in the midst of the construction site across the street.

"We've got a gopher," muttered Batman. He threw his arms wide. Glider rods snapped up, drawing his cape taut and into place. He stepped up onto the railing of the balcony and leapt off, hurtling down toward the manhole at top speed.

The Gotham subway museum was planned to be an ancillary part of the new hotel, which was built atop a subway station that had fallen out of use thanks to cutbacks on service. The enterprising hotel builders were also funding an underground museum that gave an overview of Gotham's history of transportation. Plans called for a genuine old-style train to be rolled into place on permanent display, refurbished along with the rest of the station. Workers would be dressed in uniforms of the period.

It would be marvelous. And profitable.

And doomed.

Work on the station had already begun. Half of the station had been washed down, repainted, and retiled. The other half was still dank, dirty, and disgusting.

Crouching on the tracks below, Two-Face felt right at home. And what better way to make someplace a home . . . than with company?

"Boys, welcome our guest."

Upon the command, the thugs hoisted translucent red plastic industrial air-conditioning tubing, its maw matching precisely the diameter of the open manhole.

Not wanting to lose any time, Batman folded his "wings" just as he arrived at the manhole, plummeting straight in, feetfirst. He only had a split-second warning that something was wrong, and in this case it wasn't enough. Not even for the Batman.

He plunged into the red vinyl connector, skidding into the darkness, out of control.

The world spun around him. He tried to slow himself down, to find purchase, but there was none. He grabbed at his belt, about to draw a grappling hook that he would slam down right into the plastic to stop his descent.

By that point, though, it was too late. His amusement park–like ride had ended, and ended abruptly. He hurtled out of the tube into a blackened tunnel filled with scaffolding and supports from the work under way, and smashed squarely into a wall.

Staring into the darkness of the tunnel from the far end, Two-Face grabbed an aging valve wheel set into the crumbling wall. "Nothing worse than a bad case of gas." He spun it enthusiastically, and was rewarded with—in the distance—the sound of gas pouring into the tunnel.

There was no motion from within. Perhaps Batman was unconscious. Perhaps he was floundering around. Perhaps he was already dead. As one of Two-Face's thugs handed him a grenade launcher, he mused that it didn't matter. Whatever Batman's present status . . . his future status was now finally assured.

He aimed the launcher into the tunnel and said, "The Bat hath flown. Now shall be done a deed of dreadful note." He paused a moment, waiting for his thugs to remark on the quote. "Macbeth? Shakespeare?" He sighed. "Never mind. Fire in the hole, gentlemen."

The thugs scrambled to get out of the way as Two-Face fired the launcher. The grenade slammed into the gas main, and a flaming white fireball erupted, spiralling down the blackened tunnel and searing everything in its path.

Two-Face watched with rapt attention as the far end of the tunnel turned into an inferno. There were more explosions, and the glorious sounds of debris falling. It kept on going for several moments, the tunnel thick with smoke, residual flame burning here and there.

And no movement.

"Finally," whispered Two-Face. And then he raised his voice in song. "We are the champions, my friend. We'll keep on fighting to the—"

Then his smirk vanished.

Rubble was being shoved aside and, phoenixlike, a caped figure was rising from it. It was completely enveloped in its dark cloak. There were a few minor flames here and there, but they were quickly sputtering out, unable to do any damage to the fireproof material.

Slowly Batman lowered his cloak and began to move forward.

Consumed with rage, Two-Face started firing wildly at the scaffolding supporting the ceiling and walls. "Why don't you just die?" he shrieked, making what seemed to him to be a perfectly reasonable request.

And someone up there, or perhaps down there, apparently decided to oblige him.

The scaffolding cracked and fell, and the already overburdened structures of the tunnel gave way. Rock and sand collapsed inward on Batman, knocking him to his knees, pouring in from everywhere. He was driven back from Harvey by a storm of wreckage. It was as if the tunnel had come to life and decided to celebrate that miraculous event by committing suicide . . . and taking Batman with it.

Plaster and rubble fell around Two-Face as well. He didn't seem to notice it, so riveted was his attention on Batman. His henchman started pulling nervously at his jacket, but he shook them off. "Now the air is hushed save where the weak-ey'd Bat, with shrill short shrieks . . . dies."

And he continued to watch, unmoving, unblinking, as the ground beneath Batman sucked him down into a quickly filling pit of sand. He managed to yank his grappling gun free from his belt and fired a cable into the air. For a moment Two-Face held his breath, but then the grappling hook clattered back down, nothing above for it to grip onto. Sand continued to fall, entombing Batman, covering his mouth, his eyes . . . and finally, in a moment of transcendent glee for Two-Face . . . the tippy tops of Batman's pointed ears.

Hell took him back thought Two-Face, and then he noticed that the ground directly in front of him was starting to develop cracks of its own. Sensing this would be a good time to depart, he called out cheerfully, "Boys, let's go have us a party. Anybody else feel like donuts? Maybe the chocolate kind with the little sprinkles . . ."

Buried alive . . .

The screeching filled his ears and the blackness filled his soul. From down below him, although he couldn't see them . . . because he couldn't see anything . . . he sensed his parents' hands reaching up for him. Desiccated, skeletal, clawing at his feet, pulling him down with them into the grave that he had once stood in front of and sworn that he would dedicate his life to . . .

To what?

To fighting crime? He could do that through the Wayne Foundation. To vengeance? Why did killing grate against his soul, then? Why not an eye for an eye

(eyes filled with sand)

tooth for a tooth

(mouth spitting out dirt)

To bring them back? Nothing could. To make them rest easier? They were dead.

To join them?

Yes, of course . . . that was it . . . it wasn't about anything so noble as doing right and seeking justice . . . this whole thing was just a massive death wish, suicide on a spectacular scale. He'd worked for it. He deserved it. And now all he had to do was lean back and enjoy it.

The only problem was that, although it made so much sense to his mind, his instincts, his damned instincts, were still fighting, still battling. Screeches filled his ears, and they were his own except that he couldn't speak, and he thrust a hand upward, his air running out, his life running out, like sands trickling through an overturned hourglass . . . his hand clutched at something and it was air, but air was notoriously difficult to find a handhold in, and in his darkening mind he could see that hourglass, see the last grains of sand running through it. A few more grains and that would be it, finished, done . . .

A hand gripped his.

It was a strong, unwavering grip. The grip of someone who was not accustomed to letting go of whoever or whatever it was holding.

It provided him with all the support he needed. Although the sand continued to slide under him, he was nevertheless able to dig in the toes of his boots, drive himself upward, up and out. His head broke the surface, sand pouring out of his mask and giving him back visibility.

He was able to make out the hand that was holding his. It was green-gloved. Trembling slightly from the strain now, but still unyielding. He looked up.

Dick was dressed in his Flying Grayson costume. A black mask covered his features. His legs were hooked around some scaffolding that had fallen in such a way that it was wedged solidly.

"Don't worry," said Dick through gritted teeth. "Just think of it as a day at the beach. A really . . . *bad* . . . day at the beach."

In the depths of the Batcave, Alfred was busy bandaging up Bruce as Dick paced.

Bruce's reaction had been far less than what Dick considered the acceptable one, which would be at the very least a heartfelt "thank you."

"What the hell did you think you were doing?"

"You have a real gratitude problem." Dick stopped, struck by the vision of himself at Batman's side. "You know what, Bruce? I need a name. Batboy? The Dark Earl? Nightwing? What's a good sidekick name?"

"How about Richard Grayson, college student?" He stood, flexing his aching muscles. "This conversation is over."

"Screw you, Bruce. I saved your life. You owe me. I'm joining up."

"You're right. I do owe you. I owe it to you to get you to change your mind. Dick . . . I've been dragged into a pit long before tonight. How would I be fulfilling my obligation to you if I let you get dragged into it with me?"

"And how can I fulfill my obligation to my parents, and to myself, if you don't!"

"You're totally out of control. You're going to get yourself killed."

"I'm going to be your partner."

Bruce laughed at the ludicrousness of it. He turned to Alfred, waiting for him to say something.

Alfred simply shrugged.

"That's it? A shrug?"

"If you insist, Mister Wayne," Alfred said, "then I must point out that if it weren't for this lad, you would most likely be deceased. And this lad wold be vowing even more vengeance, set to tear off on his own and very likely wind up just as deceased. All I'm saying, sir . . . is that you might be stronger together than apart."

Bruce shook his head. "There's no way—"

And Dick realized that he had lost interest in the conversation. It was he, not Bruce, who was dealing from strength. "Whenever the call comes, I'll know. Whenever you go out at night, I'll be watching. And wherever there's a Batman, I'll be right behind him." He smiled sadly. "How are you going to stop me?"

Bruce held his gaze, and there was something very flat and very dangerous—a contained animal—in his eyes. "I can stop you."

For just a moment, Dick realized that he had stepped over a line. He skittered back across it and, feeling embarrassed for having to do so, he covered it by turning his back and storming out of the Batcave. Glowering, Bruce watched him go, and then turned to Alfred. "And you're encouraging him."

"Sir," said Alfred with the air of one who knew precisely what he was talking about, "young men with a mind for revenge need little encouragement. They need guidance."

Bruce shook his head, discouraged . . .

. . . and thought about his sinking in the sand . . . thought about how he'd never needed someone to save him before, and now this kid had shown up and it was true, the great Batman owed him his life. . . .

He couldn't keep doing it alone . . . but did that mean that he brought in a partner, a teammate . . . or did that mean that he should . . .

. . . stop . . .

He glanced over at a TV screen, which was playing the news. There was that wonderful station owner editorializing again, and there was the Bat symbol with the red international prohibit sign through it.

Bruce reached for the volume.

"Don't," suggested Alfred.

He turned it up anyway, to be graced by the comforting words, " . . . subway tunnel will take weeks to repair. Batman is a magnet for so-called supervillains. Only when Batman hangs up cape and cowl will Gotham be spared these evildoers' violent vendettas . . ."

Bruce Wayne started to laugh.

Alfred looked at him worriedly as Bruce's laughter drowned out the rest of the editorial.

"I was . . . I was wondering how they'd do it," Bruce managed to gasp out. Slowly he regained control of himself. "That's what our society is all about, Alfred. We build up heroes. We create them. They spring from the media, or movies, or television, or full-blown from our brows. And once we've got our heroes in place, we look at them and see how little we are in comparison. How meaningless our own lives are. And we start to tear them down, bit by bit, drag them 'down' to our level rather than raise ourselves up to the level we've established for them. We always destroy the heroes we create, Alfred. Always."

Very quietly, Alfred said, "Even those we create for ourselves to inhabit?"

Slowly, Bruce nodded. "It seems that way, doesn't it. Are they right, Alfred? Is it time for Batman to retire?" As much to himself as to Alfred, he addressed the question, "Why do I keep doing this?"

Alfred reached over and put a hand on Bruce's shoulder. "Your parents are avenged. The Wayne Foundation contributes a fortune to anticrime programs. Police handle much of the villainy. Why, indeed?"

"Chase talks about Batman as if he were a curse, not a choice. What frightened me the night of my parents' wake? The Bat? Did I create all this"—he gestured around the cave—"just because a little boy was scared of a monster in the dark? I thought I became Batman to fight crime. But maybe I became Batman to fight the fear."

"And instead you became the fear."

He stared at the screen, which was now running photographs of Two-Face. "If I quit, would Two-Face end his crusade? Could I leave the shadows? To spare Dick. To have a life. Friends. Family."

"Dr. Meridian . . ."

Bruce looked up at Alfred, pain in his eyes. "She loves Batman. Not Bruce Wayne . . ."

"Go tell her. Tell her how you feel."

He rubbed the bridge of his nose. "How do I tell her, Alfred? As Batman, knowing she wants me? Or as Bruce Wayne and hope . . . ?"

Bruce stared at the phone, then punched in Chase's number. Alfred watched expectantly as Chase's voice came over the speakerphone.

"Hello? . . . Hello? . . . Who is this?"

Bruce started to reply . . . and then stopped. To Alfred's dismay, Bruce reached over and disconnected the phone.

"Who am I, Alfred? I don't think I know anymore."

"Where . . . are they . . . ?" said Gordon slowly.

The others of Two-Face's thugs whom they had questioned had remained tightlipped, refusing to give Gordon and the other cops standing nearby the slightest hint of Two-Face's whereabouts. This one, though, a burly one named Taylor, seemed to be sweating profusely. "Look, you don't understand," said Taylor. "I'd like to cooperate. I'd like to save my own butt, don't think I wouldn't. But if I spill the deal about Two-Face and Riddler, I'm toast. I'm cooked."

"How? How are you cooked?"

"I dunno, but that's what they said. They said if we ever squeal, we'll regret it. And they weren't kidding. I'm sure of it."

A heavyset detective named Bullock grunted, "Gimme a few minutes with him, Commish."

Gordon ignored him. "We can protect you, Taylor."

Taylor considered it a moment, and then said, "No jail."

"I'm not sure I—"

"No jail, and I go into the Witness Protection Program. In exchange, I give you Two-Face and the Riddler. That's the deal. You don't like it, then that's the end of this conversation. I ask for a lawyer, he tells me to shut my yap, and that's it. This offer has got a shelf life of exactly thirty seconds."

He drummed his fingers nervously as Gordon considered it a moment. "Okay," he said. "I think I can sell it."

"Guarantee it."

"Guaranteed. Providing it pans out."

"Oh, it'll pan out. Because I can tell you that you can find those—"

Suddenly his eyes went wide.

"Taylor?"

He seemed to be looking inward, his entire body shaking.

Then he started to scream, his head snapping back and forth, as if something were inside his head trying to eat its way out.

Immediately Gordon summoned a doctor, but by the time he arrived, it was too late. Not that he would have been able to do much of anything even if he'd been present at the beginning of the attack.

Taylor's head lolled to one side, his tongue hanging slightly out, his eyes staring at nothing. Every so often a slight twitch indicated that he was still alive, but that was all. Word would quickly spread, and anyone else who was even entertaining the notion of ratting out the Riddler and Two-Face got the message loud and clear.

And miles away the Riddler removed the helmet that had connected his mind to the subcutaneous implant that Taylor . . . that all of their henchmen, in fact . . . carried with them, unbeknownst to them. The one that had given Nygma full access to Taylor's entire thought process, not to mention the ability to blow out his neural pathways at whim.

He sighed. "It's *so* difficult to find good help these days."

CHAPTER 20

Pale moonlight shined through the windows of Chase Meridian's bedroom. She lay asleep, chest rising and falling evenly.

A shadow crossed her face. Somehow it seemed to work its way into her mind, causing her to stir slightly. Then her eyes opened in narrow slits, dream and reality blending seamlessly.

The French doors to her bedroom opened, a tall and . . . to some . . . frightening apparition stood framed against the window.

She rose slowly from the bed, moonlight playing along her body clad in a diaphanous gown. She went to him, cape whipping around her.

"It's 2:00 A.M.," she whispered. "I'd given up on you."

His mouth came close to hers, so close, and then their lips met, tasting each other's passion.

They broke.

And she laughed.

The lower half of his face was hidden in shadow, his eyes glittering like polished flint behind his mask.

"I'm sorry," Chase said. "It's just . . . I can't believe it. I've imagined this moment since I first saw you . . . your hands . . . your face . . . your body," touching each of them in turn, letting her hands rest on his emblem. "And now I have you and . . ."

She turned away from him, walking across the room into the living room. He followed her noiselessly.

"Guess a girl has to grow up sometime," she said as she moved to her desk. She pushed the rolltop up, turned on the desk lamp. "I've met someone. He's not . . . you . . . but . . ." She stopped and then, with a helpless shrug, said, "I hope you can understand."

All of the Batman memorabilia on the desk had been replaced by photos and articles about Bruce Wayne.

"He, uhm," she cleared her throat. "He came to me for advice. We didn't have a doctor/patient relationship . . . not exactly, I guess. I suppose we were sort of in a gray area. I suppose you can understand about gray areas." She paused and then, her voice choking slightly, she said, "I . . . don't want to be in gray areas with him. I want to move into the light. Do you understand?"

He never uttered a word. He merely moved backwards and out. He stood in front of a window and seemed to recede out of it. Chase went to the window and watched him swing away, cape flaring out behind him.

She watched until he was out of sight, and then she crossed to her desk. She picked up her hand-held tape recorder and clicked it on. When she spoke, her voice was slow and trembling.

"I was right. I figured it out. I saw Bruce wade into Two-Face's thugs in the circus. I heard his voice, saw his eyes, his chin . . . studied his body language."

She stopped and stared out the window at the moon. "I . . . I don't know what I want. I've gone through my life so obsessed with trying to figure out what makes other people's minds work . . . I don't feel in touch with mine anymore. And whenever I'd spend time with Bruce, I'd see . . . I'd see something there. So much inner strength and, at the same time, someone who needs so much himself. And when I started to figure it out . . . the first thing I thought, God help me, the first thing I thought was what an incredible opportunity this was. To study him, to see 'behind the mask.' He wasn't a person, or a human being, he was just this . . . this thing with a background and facts and figures . . . and . . ."

She realized her voice was choking up even more, and tears were starting to trickle from her eyes. "And then I . . . the other day, when he was here, and I was playing with my suspicions, teasing and pushing at his mind . . . and I looked in his eyes again, and I didn't see him . . . I saw myself, and everything mean-spirited and self-centered, and I'd been so . . . so horrible to him. He needed me." She slammed her fist against the desk, swept material off it onto the floor. "He needed to be loved for himself! He needed me! *He needed me and I was playing goddamn head games with him! What the hell kind of doctor am I? What kind of **human being** am I, for God's sake?!*"

Then the sobs came stronger, and she made no effort to stop it. It took her several moments to recover her voice, and when she did speak again she was holding one of the photos of Bruce in her hand.

"If I told him I'd figured it out . . . and then told him that I loved him . . . he might not have believed it. Hell"—she drew an arm across her nose, sniffling—"I wouldn't have if I'd been him. Thank God . . . thank *God* . . . he came as Batman, so I could speak to the mask instead of to Bruce. Maybe he'll believe. Maybe I've managed to undo the damage I've done up until now. Maybe . . ." She paused and drew in a slow breath. "Maybe now . . . now we can start talking to each other, instead of *at* each other."

She clicked off the tape then, and held the recorder for a time. Then she popped it open, removed the tape, and went over to the fireplace. It was gas-operated, so she turned the controls and watched the flames leap to life.

She could simply have erased it, of course. She didn't even really have to have committed it to tape in the first place. But she just wanted to get it off her chest, just tell someone . . . even if it was herself. It was a cleansing experience, and fire was likewise cleansing. It signalled the end of what was and heralded the time to rebuild.

She tossed the tape into the fire and watched it burn to ashes.

From far, far away, crouched against a gargoyle with the moon at his back, Batman watched Chase Meridian's apartment until the light went out. Then, via his rope, he descended to the waiting Batmobile.

He climbed into the cockpit and touched the communications unit. Despite the lateness of the hour, Alfred answered immediately. "How did it go, sir?"

Under his cowl, he smiled. "Exactly as I thought it would."

"Did it?"

Batman nodded. "She knows. She figured it out."

"Well, sir," said Alfred politely, "it would seem that the two of you are well matched."

"You might be right."

"Sir," said Alfred archly, as if offended, "I do not deal in 'might be's.'"

"I'll remember that," said Batman, and he gunned the Batmobile forward.

CHAPTER 21

Edward Nygma couldn't get Chase's face out of his mind.

Heaven knew he had tried. Seated on his thronelike chair on Claw Island, rivulets of neural energy rippled and danced on his forehead as images of the woman flared on screens all over the control room.

Two-Face entered and, without preamble, yanked the device from Edward's head. He gasped as if kicked in the stomach, Chase's picture vanishing from the screens.

"Our belfry is finally free of Bats," said Two-Face in a pleasant tone that ran counter to his mood. "An end to late-night raids by the man in rubber. No more troublesome explosions of violence from the winged ferret. A cease to all wall-crawling, night-flying, humorless, vitriolic, self-righteous heroics from a man whose belt and footwear don't even match. Ding damn dong, the annoying Bat is dead." And then he grabbed the Riddler by the throat and growled, "So, why do we need you? You only come between us. We're going to be the smartest in Gotham City. We're taking the empire for ourselves. Time's up, laughing boy."

Rasping, trying to squirm out from under Two-Face's grip, the Riddler gasped out, "Bad news, pals. The Bat lives."

Nygma reached to his side and shoved a newspaper into Two-Face's faces. The headline read BATMAN SURVIVES SUBWAY SABOTAGE. It went on to describe eyewitness reports of a battered and dirt-stained Batman emerging from a manhole, accompanied by another individual also wearing a cape and mask.

"Not only isn't he dead," observed the Riddler, "but he seems to be multiplying."

Two-Face threw back his arms and screamed. It seemed to go on for a very long time, and the Riddler jammed a finger in his ear to clear the ringing. "Nice. A little flat. Try a C-sharp."

"Cats have nine lives!" bellowed Two-Face, his fury building. "*Cats! C*, not *B*. The man's refusal to die is really annoying!" Then he pulled his gun, as he usually seemed wont to do when faced with this sort of situation. "Someone is going to die today!"

The Riddler stepped back, looking chagrined. "You want to kill me, Harv? The guy who personally guaranteed adherence by our employees to the nondisclosure agreement? The one where they promise not to rat us out, or else? The one we made them sign three times? You remember."

Two-Face cocked the hammer.

"Kill me?" said the Riddler. "Well, all right. Go ahead. Take the empire. All yours." He grabbed his head and declared, "Hell, Harv, old pals. I'll kill me for you."

He grabbed his hair and started slamming his head into the desk. Two-Face watched him, not entirely sure what to make of it, although he found it amusing in a sadomasochistic sort of way.

In between slams, the Riddler managed to get out, "Too . . . bad . . . about . . . Batman."

Immediately Two-Face grabbed his head, halting the self-imposed pounding. "What about Batman?" he said suspiciously.

The Riddler smoothed out his hair. "What if you could know a man's mind? Would you not, then, own that man?"

He hit a switch, and suddenly every screen was filled with images of Bruce Wayne stepping into the booth at the party.

"A few dozen extra IQ points and my little doggy learned

a new trick. It does more than drain your brain. It makes a map of your mind. Would you like to see what my old friend Bruce has in his head?"

He hit another switch, and something huge and frightening ripped free from the landscape of the schematic brain that had appeared on the screen. A trapped bat, fierce and monstrous. It was the very picture of imagined evil, made live. Bruce's nightmare, given form.

"Riddle me this," said the Riddler so softly that Two-Face had to strain to hear him. "What kind of man has bats on the brain?"

Two-Face stared at him in amazement. "Go ahead," the Riddler urged. "You can say it."

"A Bat . . . man. Bruce Wayne is Batman. You're a genius," said Two-Face, and he meant it.

The two of them began to laugh, loud and long.

CHAPTER 22

Dick Grayson was positive it was a trick. "What the hell do you mean, it's over?"

In the Batcave, Bruce was going from one device to the next, shutting them down. "You were right, Dick. As long as there's a Batman, you'll be behind him. But without Batman, you'll never track Two-Face down. Never get close to him. Never . . . So from this day on, Batman is no more."

He stepped back and looked over his handiwork. Everything seemed pretty much protected from dust. Perhaps later he'd get around to actually disassembling it. Time for that later, though. He threw a switch and the cave went dark.

"You can't quit," Dick said. The arrogance, the anger . . . all of it was sliding away, to be replaced by an almost desperate need to restore the status quo. Like a child begging a parent to tell him that the ugly rumors questioning the status of Santa Claus were, in fact, groundless. "There are monsters out there. Batman has to protect the innocent."

"Dick, I've spent my life protecting people I've never met, faces I'll never see. Well, the innocent aren't faceless anymore. If I let you lose yourself to a life of revenge, all I've lived for will have been for nothing. Batman has to vanish so you can live . . . maybe so we all can."

"You can't decide what I'm going to do with my life. My dad always said every man goes his own way. Well, mine leads to Two-Face. You've got to help me. . . ."

"And when you finally find Harvey? What then?"

Dick looked away from him, and Bruce nodded in confirmation. "Exactly. Once you kill him, you'll be lost, like me." He sighed. "No. You have to let this go. Get on with your life. Trust me. I'm your friend—"

"I don't need a friend," Dick said, temper flaring. "I need a partner. Two-Face has to pay . . ." And then the anger faded, Dick unable to sustain it. Finally, in a voice that sounded like the helpless teenager he was, he simply said, "Please."

Bruce sighed. "Chase is coming for dinner. Come upstairs. We'll talk . . ."

But Dick turned away. Bruce almost reached out for him, but when Dick flinched, he withdrew the hand. Instead he headed up to the house, leaving Dick alone in the dark, still cave.

Dick stood there for a moment. Then he walked slowly to the costume vault. He gazed at it for a time, then opened it up. With a hiss it unsealed. He looked over the array of Batman costumes until he came to a standing figure, separate from the rest.

His Robin costume. His new one; he'd been working in tandem with Alfred on modifications.

"The hell with you. I'll do it myself," he said. He peeled the costume off the mannequin, so that he could pack it.

Half an hour later, carrying with him everything that he cared about, Dick Grayson rode his motorcycle down the mountain road. Far above him, the lights of Wayne Manor twinkled in the night.

Seated in front of the fireplace in the living room, Bruce and Chase nursed glasses of vintage champagne that Alfred had poured for them before discreetly exiting.

"I asked you to come tonight because I need to tell you something," Bruce began.

"I want to tell you something, too."

They hesitated and then, naturally, started to speak at the same time. They stopped, laughed lightly.

"You go first," said Bruce.

"Right," she nodded gamely, and put the wineglass up on the table next to a vase of roses. "Okay. Bruce, all my life I've been attracted to a certain kind of man. The wrong kind of man. I mean, look at what I do for a living. But since I met you—" Her voice trailed off. "God, why am I so nervous?"

She reached for her wineglass and bumped the vase. Two of the roses fell to the floor.

The roses, lying there, and they were wilting before his eyes . . .

She could tell instantly that he was gone again, gone into his past. "Bruce? What's wrong?"

"It's happening again. Flashes. Images of my parents' death."

"Your memories are trying to break through. Let them come."

"I'm not sure I want to remember."

"Bruce"—and she took a giant step in the direction of what she wanted to tell him—"you braved those thugs at the circus, Bruce. Braved your parents' death. You can brave the past."

He gazed at her then, saw the understanding in her eyes. Saw the direction that his life could take, if only he had the nerve to head that way.

He leaned back slightly, closing his eyes. The pictures slowly unspooled themselves in his mind. It was no trouble calling the images to himself; the difficulty had been keeping them away. But now, having made the decision to face them, they came quickly. Slowly . . . both to himself, and to her . . . he spoke.

"My parents are laid out in the library. There's a book on my father's desk. I'm opening the book. Reading. I'm running out into the storm, the book in my hands. I can't hear my screams over the rain. I'm falling into a hole . . ."

"Okay. What hurt so much? What did the book say?"

He did not reply. Instead he stared at his surroundings.

"Where are you?"

"I'm moving through the living room. I'm at my parents' wake. Death is . . . is so still. I'm touching her coffin . . . Mom . . . and there . . . right there. Of course. How did I ever forget? Right where he always kept it, on his desk . . . my father's diary."

"Bruce, you're not that little boy anymore. And you're not alone. I'm here with you."

"Yes. You are. I see you, standing next to the desk."

"What does the book say?"

"The pages are blowing open . . . I can see the words . . ."

"What does it say?" she asked again.

"Oct. 31. The last entry . . . the night they died. 'Bruce insists on seeing a movie tonight.' Bruce insists. I made them go out. I made them take me to the movie. To that theater. That alley . . . It was my fault. I killed them . . . After I read it, I grabbed the book. Ran into the storm. But I couldn't outrun the pain. I tripped, fell into a sinkhole . . . Not the bat?"

"What?" The shift made no sense to her.

"I thought it was the bat that scared me that night, that changed my life. But it wasn't. This is the monster I grew strong and fierce to defeat. The demon I've spent my life fighting. My own guilt. The fear that I killed them."

"Oh God, Bruce, you were a child. You weren't responsible."

And it was at that moment that all hell broke loose. . . .

Alfred opened the door in answer to the ring and never even saw the cane descend toward him.

The thugs stepped over him, two of them picking up his unconscious form and shoving him in a closet. Two-Face looked back and forth, taking in the huge foyer, and snapped his fingers. "Move," he said tersely.

"Remember the plan!" shouted the Riddler. "Seize and capture! No killing!"

The thugs moved in all directions, and the Riddler quickly grabbed Two-Face's arm. "Just a little double check, double-face . . . you didn't tell them, right? Bat Wayne is our little secret, right? We tell any of the g-u-y-s, they might just shoot to kill, which *isn't the plan!* Riiiight?"

Two-Face looked at him balefully. "You patronize us one more time, that cane of yours becomes a rectal probe. Got that?"

He moved off and the Riddler said cheerily, "I'll take that as a yes." And then he headed off through the mansion on his own little treasure hunt. Because, while sitting outside in the van, waiting for the right moment to make their entrance, he had spotted the lovely Dr. Chase Meridian stepping out of a cab, apparently there for a little dining and dancing pleasure with Monsieur Wayne.

"And here it's not even my birthday," the Riddler said joyfully.

Bruce headed into the dining alcove, Chase right behind him, as he heard the commotion. "What the hell?" he demanded.

He ran straight into two of Two-Face's thugs.

Quickly he grabbed up a silver serving tray, flipped it into one of the thug's faces, and kicked him in the stomach. Without breaking motion he slammed the platter into the other thug's head. Two of them were down, and Bruce quickly grabbed Chase's hand. They dashed out the door, several more henchmen in close pursuit.

The Riddler moved slowly through the mansion, holding up his cane in this direction and that, checking the sounding signals being issued from the head. He'd known going in that the most likely means of entrance to Bruce's secret Bat-headquarters would be behind some hidden wall somewhere. It was just a hunch. So he'd equipped his cane with a device to bounce sound waves off the walls. It would register any place where there was a hidden panel . . . something that appeared to be solid but had a drop behind it.

And, in short order, he found it.

Two-Face sat in a chair, disconsolately flipping his coin. Each time Wayne and his lady friend dashed by, pursued by several thugs, it provided a new opportunity for a coin toss. He cocked and uncocked his gun nervously, and each time the coin landed in his hand it was with the clean side up.

In derisive imitation of the Riddler he said, "'No killing. Torture him. Make him suffer.'" He snorted disdainfully. "Whatever happened to old-fashioned murder? Kids these days . . ."

Charging up a stairway, Bruce overturned statues as he went, blocking their pursuers' path. Every path he took, he kept running into thugs. The house was crawling with them.

The Riddler had found heaven, or at least his own little piece of it.

The Batcave was dark, with drop cloths over the equipment. He wasn't sure why, nor did he care. So, Brucie was painting or redecorating or whatever it was.

He started removing small green bombs from his pouch, revelling in the irony of it. He and Bruce. Both unappreciated. Both given hard knocks. Both certifiable geniuses. Both taking on costumed identities. Every step of the way, they had mirrored each other, even if it had been a fun house mirror.

Without even realizing it until just recently, Edward Nygma and Bruce Wayne had been in a contest in every aspect of their lives. And now that he understood that, it was, in fact, Nygma—the Riddler—who was going to win.

The green bombs he had produced were in the shape of bats. With demented glee he twisted each of their little heads, enjoying every single screech. He picked up the first one, its wings flapping furiously, and hurled it into the air.

"You know, it's always risky introducing a trained animal into the wild. They often have trouble acclimating to the new environment."

The bat struck the video wall, and a tremendous explosion rocked it. The next one blew the costume vault to hell and gone, and the third detonated in the crime lab.

He spotted, in the near distance, the Batmobile on the turntable. He tossed the bat under his arm and it zeroed in on the car's cockpit. And as he headed out of the cave, the Riddler shouted to any stray bats who might be listening, "Tell the fat lady she's on in five."

And the moment he was clear of it, the Batmobile exploded. From the outside it was virtually impregnable. From the inside it was less so, and within seconds it became a huge, flaming slab of black metal.

Within the closet into which he'd been tossed, Alfred—still woozy from the blow to the head—tried the doorknob. Locked. Undeterred, he then activated his wrist-comm device.

"Nine-one-one," he said, and the autodialer went to work.

Bruce and Chase fled up the giant staircase, the thugs one step behind. One of the thugs leapt forward, getting a fistful of Chase's dress. She went down and then lashed out with a mighty kick, knocking the thug backwards down the stairs.

"It's therapeutic," she tossed off.

Bruce, meantime, was holding off a couple more attackers, closing near the top step. He spun, a powerful roundhouse kick clocking one in the head, sending him backwards down the stairs. "Go!" he shouted to Chase.

Chase moved behind him, up the landing, turning to see Bruce fell another with a spinning back kick, a third with a flying back fist. They started again toward the top of the stairs, and it looked increasingly as if they were going to make it.

And Two-Face approached the bottom of the stairs, flipping the coin. "A chance to live, a chance to die," he intoned. "Lady Luck makes her decrees and we can do naught but slavishly follow."

The scarred side of the coin winked up at him.

"Finally," he said, then pulled out his gun, aimed, and fired.

At the top of the stairs, the bullet grazed Bruce Wayne's head. Chase shrieked as Bruce pitched back and tumbled the length of the stairs to the bottom. An instant later several thugs had closed in behind Chase and had her arms pinned.

Bruce lay unmoving on the floor. Two-Face stood over him and said, "Bruce, my boy, you sure know how to throw a party."

The Riddler came dashing in at that moment and let out a screech of protest. In the distance police sirens could be heard, but that was the least of the Riddler's problems. "No! You killed him!"

Two-Face aimed the weapon at the unmoving Bruce. "Not yet. But give us a second . . . or two . . ."

But the Riddler swept in behind him, urging him toward the door gently but firmly. "Okay, let's review. We were not going to kill him. We were going to torture him, remember? Wreck and ruin all he holds dear? Leave him broken, knowing his secret is revealed and death will come, but not where or when? Any of this ring bells? You *really* passed the bar?"

Two-Face spun, his guns at the ready. Knowing when he'd gone as far as he could, the Riddler put up his hands. "Kidding. Ha-ha. Joke?"

"Okay." He nodded his head toward Chase, who was struggling with the thugs. "Just grab the bait."

The Riddler grinned as Chase was dragged out, and then walked over to the unconscious Wayne as if he had all the time in the world. He dropped a riddle on top of Bruce's body, and then sauntered out the door.

The riddle read, "We're five little items of an everyday sort. You'll find us all in a tennis court."

But there was no one conscious to read it.

And somewhere far below, as fire licked through the costume vault, the Bat emblems began to burn.

And from out of the fire, a huge bat staggered. It staggered, enveloped in flame, its red eyes blazing . . . and then fell forward and moved no further . . .

"The injuries are relatively minor. The shot did cause a concussion. Watch for headaches. Memory lapses. Odd behavior. I'll check back in a few days."

Alfred smiled thinly at the doctor, easily repressing the urge to inform him that the term "odd behavior" was a fairly elastic one when applied to Bruce Wayne.

Seated upright in his bed, Bruce blinked against the morning sun as the doctor finished packing up. Alfred had been less than ecstatic with the presence of the physician, in the event that the battered and dazed Bruce might say something "incriminating." But he'd had no choice. When the police had arrived, with Gordon in the lead (considering that it was Wayne Manor under assault), Alfred had felt constrained to say that it was indeed Two-Face and the Riddler who had led the assault. Again, no choice: If Bruce had blurted something out in his semiconscious state, Alfred would have been questioned as to why he was covering up. Besides, he reasoned, Dr. Meridian's kidnapping really did warrant alerting the constabulary.

Ironically, Gordon's confident, "Don't worry, Mr. Pennyworth. We're going to call in Batman on this one," had less than the comforting effect Gordon clearly thought it would.

Gordon also wanted to take Wayne to the hospital, which Alfred managed to avoid by promising to bring a doctor to the house immediately. He reflected at that moment that perhaps the single most significant thing about the Wayne fortune was that it had actually prompted a doctor to make a house call. He led the physician out, then quickly returned to Bruce's bedside.

"How are you feeling, young man?"

Bruce smiled wanly. "Not that young. It's been a long time since you've called me that."

"Old habits die hard. Are you all right?"

"As well as can be expected, I guess. And you?"

Alfred rapped his head a couple of times. "Oh, I've had the odd cricket ball or two ricocheted off my skull on occasion. Compared to that, my current stress was minimal."

"Okay. Give me the bad news."

He'd rather not have gotten into it so quickly, but it was unavoidable. "Master Dick has run away. They have taken Dr. Meridian. And . . ." There was no delicate way to say it. "I'm afraid they found the cave, sir. It's been destroyed."

Bruce looked up at Alfred with puzzled, narrowed eyes. "The cave? What cave?"

CHAPTER 23

Gordon stood next to the signal, staring up at the Bat-shaped light against the sky. "Where is he?"

Detective Bullock swayed out onto the roof. In his gravelly voice he announced, "The mayor's called again." But before he continued, he looked up at the signal, and then back at Gordon. "He's not going to show. Maybe he's hurt, sir. Maybe he's . . ."

"Don't even think of it."

Bruce stared in wonderment at the cave, or what was left of it. There were melted ruins and rubble as far as he could see. Alfred stood silently next to him.

"I remember my life as Bruce Wayne. But all this. It's like the life of a stranger." Then he paused. "There's one other thing. I feel . . ."

"What?"

"Afraid." It started to tumble back for him. "The cave. I remember the cave. Something chasing me. A demon . . . Oh my God, Alfred."

"No demons, son," said Alfred tenderly, and touched the side of Bruce's head. "Your monsters are here. And until you face them, I fear you will spend your life fleeing them."

In the Riddler's control room on Claw Island, Chase had

been chained to the floor of his throne. Riddler sat upon it, pulling in pulses of neural energy.

"You really should have considered therapy, Mr. Nygma," Chase said gamely, fully aware by this point of precisely who was her captor.

"Sorry. Not in the Nygmatech health plan. Maybe next year," he said, without looking at her.

She looked out the skylight, saw the signal in the air. "Batman will come for me," she said firmly.

"Your Bat's gonna come, your Bat's gonna come." He leaned forward, his voice low and lethal. "I'm counting on it." Then he studied her. "You got a thing for him, don't you? I can tell. I can tell everything."

"There's a reason we only use a fraction of our brains, Mr. Nygma," Chase said evenly. "You're cutting neural pathways faster than your consciousness can incorporate them. You're frying your mind."

He moaned loudly. "Major buzz kill. Spoil the mood, why don't you?" Irritated at having his good mood ruined, he pulled a hypo from his jacket pocket. It was filled with green liquid. "Nap time, gorgeous." He plunged it into her and she passed out.

Bruce stood in front of the dark, rocky mouth that led to the smaller part of the cave . . . the part that he'd first fallen into those many years ago. The part that he had never been back to, even after he had clambered to safety . . . even after he had explored every other portion of the Batcave . . . because of the monsters that dwelt within.

He insinuated his body through the narrow opening and climbed slowly up into it.

Bats. Bats everywhere, just as he had remembered. Their wings fluttered and they were moving all the time, making the walls and ceiling look as if they were throbbing with life themselves.

The infrared goggles were fitted over his face, the cave

looking like daylight. He looked to the left and right, his every sense alert.

He spotted it in far less time than he would have thought.

It was there, under an alcove, a large piece of rock that extended and covered it, as if protecting it against the possibility of his eventual return. Slowly, terrified of what he would find but unable to stop himself, he reached for the book.

He picked it up, held it close to his face. Through the goggles it was suffused with red. The red of blood. The red of roses.

He turned the pages to the last entry. And there it was, just as he had remembered. "Bruce insists on seeing a movie tonight . . ."

He paused and then noticed that the page was stuck back-to-back with the next one. Moisture had done it. Moisture from the cave? From tears spilled long ago that he had forgotten about? Carefully he separated the pages and turned them . . .

. . . and found more writing.

" 'But Martha and I have our hearts set on *Zorro*, so Bruce's cartoon will have to wait until next week.' "

He stared at the book in disbelief. "Not my fault," he whispered. "It wasn't my fault."

Suddenly, in the dark ahead of him, a shape moved. It separated itself from the rest of the shadows but with his goggles, clear as day, he could see it.

Even in day, it was terrifying.

Mouth wide open to reveal hideous fangs, head moving slowly from side to side and watching him through red slits, wings huge, and suddenly the monstrosity was airborne . . .

. . . *and it was coming for him, and Bruce turned to run, the bat's wings flapping like beating drums, closing fast . . .*

. . . *and he suddenly stopped in his tracks, turning, resolved to meet the thing head-on. He turned and faced the monster as it screeched toward him, glistening fangs barely inches from his face . . .*

. . . *and something remarkable happened. The bat held its*

position, staring straight into his eyes, wings still spread wide. And Bruce raised his arms to match the aspect of the bat. They faced each other, living mirrors, man and bat, neither entirely sure how much of the other was real.

. . . and in the unreality of the cave, they came together . . .

Bats exploded from on high.

In the main chamber of the Batcave, Alfred reflexively put up his arms to ward them off. But they weren't coming for him. Instead they arced all over the ceiling, smashing into each other, as if they couldn't move quickly enough. He watched in stupefaction.

And then a shadow was cast down at him.

He looked up and whispered, "Master Bruce."

A voice spoke to him, familiar and yet unfamiliar. And it said, "Batman, Alfred. I'm Batman."

. . . AND FOREVER . . .

CHAPTER 24

Bullock ran into Gordon's office and said, "Commish . . . you better see this."

Gordon was on his feet. "Has there been an answer to the signal?"

"Yes and no." And Bullock would not elaborate. Gordon followed him up to the roof and immediately saw it.

Indeed, it was fairly hard to miss.

A gigantic green question mark had positioned itself over the Bat-signal, reducing the once impressive image to a small dot at the bottom.

"I'm really starting to hate that guy," said Gordon.

In Bruce Wayne's bedroom, Bruce and Alfred stood over the four riddles. "Five little items of an everyday sort. You'll find them all in a tennis court."

He picked up a pen and started circling letters in the words "A tennis court."

And Alfred saw immediately. "Vowels. Not entirely unclever, sir. But what do a clock, a match, chess pawns and vowels have in common? What do these riddles mean?"

Bruce stared at it for a moment . . . and then something clicked. "Maybe the answer is not in the answers but in the questions."

"I shan't be saying that several times fast, shall I?"

"Every riddle has a number in the question." Quickly he wrote them out on a sheet of paper.

"But 13, 1, 8, and 5. What do they mean? For all we know, these are his stab at next week's Lotto picks."

Bruce shook his head. "What do maniacs always want?"

"Recognition?"

"Precisely. So this number is some kind of calling card."

He started recombining the numbers. Adding them gave him 27. Squaring them gave him 16,916,425. Neither seemed helpful. Then he started separating and rearranging them . . .

"Thirteen . . . eighteen . . . five . . ." He turned and looked at Alfred, and the butler could tell that Bruce already had it. "Letters in the alphabet."

"Of course. Thirteen is M . . . MRE? MRE?"

Carefully, and trying not to sound patronizing, Bruce said, "How about Mr. E?"

"Mystery?"

"And another name for Mystery?"

"Conundrum? Puzzle? Enig . . . ma," he said, realizing.

"Exactly. Mr. E. Mister Edward Nygma. What wasted genius." He gave a moment's thought and then guessed, "The video of Stickley's suicide must have been a computer-generated forgery. That must have been the night that Nygma first realized what his devices could do . . . and that poor bastard Stickley was in the wrong place at the wrong time."

"You really are quite keen," said Alfred approvingly, "despite what others say."

They moved through the charred remains of the Batcave, trying to determine what options they had left to them. Bruce looked at the twisted metal wreck that had once been the Batmobile.

"Pretty bad, huh, Alfred?"

"We've repaired worse, sir."

"No, we haven't."

"True," acknowledged Alfred. "I was hoping to provide some small comfort."

"The small comfort we can take, Alfred," he said, pushing a button on the platform on which the Batmobile's charred frame sat, "is that Mr. E. didn't know about the cave under the cave."

The platform started downward, slowly descending into the subterranean depths where, decades before, young Bruce Wayne had heard water running. It had been the next area that he had explored before discovering the higher portions, eventually settling on the upper sections for his main headquarters, and the lower regions for the storage of the Batboat and Batwing. Plus he also used that area for the testing of some of the larger equipment; working out the kinks in flame throwers, for example, was not a particularly viable idea in the upper reaches.

"What now, sir?"

"Claw Island. Nygma's headquarters. I'm sure that's where they're keeping Chase." He paused and said, "Are all the Batsuits destroyed?"

Alfred seemed reluctant to bring it up, but he pointed to a darkened area of the cavern. "All except the . . . prototype . . . with the radar modifications you've invented. But we haven't had a successful test yet."

Bruce smiled. "You know what, Alfred? I'm feeling lucky tonight."

The young man stood in the cave, looking around at the wreckage. His black cape was draped around him as he surveyed the wreckage. He was wearing a red armored vest, green tights, and knee armor. A Utility Belt was buckled around his middle, and he wore flexible black boots. A small stylized "R" decorated his chest plate, and a mask covered his features.

"So this is why he hasn't answered the signal," he said. He felt dread creeping through him. There had been no sign of Bruce or Alfred upstairs. But certainly there would have been a news report if someone as prominent as Bruce Wayne had been killed. It didn't make any sense.

Then he noticed the platform for the Batmobile was gone entirely. He walked over to it and looked down. No, not gone. Lowered. And he heard voices from below, echoing up to him.

He unsnapped a grappling hook and length of cable from his Utility Belt, anchored it firmly, and then jumped down into the darkness.

Batman emerged from the shadows, his armor bulkier, his cowl more fearsome-looking. The Bat symbol now ran the width of his chest. Alfred stared at him with distress. He certainly looked more intimidating. Now if the blasted armor didn't kill him in the process . . .

"What do you suggest, Alfred? By sea or by air?"

"Why not both?" But the response had not been from Alfred. They turned to see the red-and-green-clad form of Dick Grayson drop down a few feet away.

The two costumed individuals studied each other. Alfred felt somewhat underdressed.

"Dick . . . Where did you get that suit?" he asked finally.

It was Alfred who said, "I . . . um . . . took the liberty, sir."

Batman nodded slightly, although it was difficult to tell in the mask. "What's the R stand for? Richard?"

"Robin." He hesitated, trying to decide whether to explain it, and decided there was no point doing so at the moment. "Riddler and Two-Face look like a pretty lethal combination. I thought you could use some help."

"Two against two are better odds," Batman allowed. "But your attitude—"

"—has changed," Robin put in. "Whatever happens, I won't kill him." He hesitated, then went on, "A friend taught me that."

"Not just a friend . . ." Bruce extended his hand. "A partner."

Dick stared resolutely into Bruce's eyes. It was the hardest thing Dick had ever done because he knew, deep down, that he was still plagued with doubts. He had said what he had to say to get Bruce to accept him. But there was still the rage burning within him, the rage that blazed more brightly every time he envisioned Two-Face's leering visage. The rage he was not altogether sure he could control. In order to function as Robin, had Dick's first official act as Bruce's partner been to lie? Had he become two-faced himself?

Who knew for certain? Perhaps Bruce was aware of his qualms, but was positive that Dick would do the right thing.

Now if only Dick could figure out what that was. . . .

The walk up to the rooftop of police headquarters had been the longest Gordon had ever made. He stood next to Bullock and tapped the signal.

"He's not coming. Shut it down."

Bullock reached for the switch, and suddenly a roar cut through the night.

The Bat-Signal was coming closer.

It was impossible, but nevertheless it was happening. The great black shape, getting closer and closer, and then all of a sudden the Batwing burst through it, buzzing police headquarters and dipping a wing to Gordon.

A triumphant Gordon saluted as the Batwing, with Batman at the controls, arced up and in the direction of Gotham Harbor.

And in the waters of the harbor itself, Robin steered the Batboat across the still waters. His mind raced with infinite possibilities, infinite plans. And none of them included losing.

He cut back the engine noise, running silent and almost invisible in the darkness.

Claw Island loomed before him.

CHAPTER 25

Atop Claw Island, searchlights popped on one by one, flooding the water with light.

Within, the Riddler and Two-Face were playing electronic Battleship. The Riddler studied the board. "A-14."

"Hit!"

Mortars exploded from the top of Claw Island, angling down toward the Batboat. Robin cut the ship hard to starboard and water spouted high in the sky behind him.

"B-12," said Two-Face.

"A hit. And my favorite vitamin, I might add."

Another explosion to stern. They were getting his range and Robin knew that he was in serious trouble. Then the water right in front of him erupted in a mountainous geyser, and Robin was blown back and out of the Batboat. The only thing he could think of was, *Bruce is gonna kill me.*

A mortar struck the Batboat square amidships and blew it to bits.

"A hit," said Two-Face, looking disappointed. "You sank our battleship."

* * *

Beneath the waters of Gotham City, Robin shoved a re-breather in his mouth and started to swim toward Claw Island. He had about three seconds to think that things were going to get better, at which point a stream of armed frogmen started converging on him from all sides. He twisted frantically out of the way as a spear shot past him, leaving a tiny trail of bubbles behind it.

Robin figured that maybe he had one or two more good dodges in him before he got shish-kebabbed.

Then he looked up as the roar of an engine alerted him to the presence of the Batwing.

The air vessel angled down toward Robin, and once again he allowed some measure of hope to bubble up within him. This fleeting hope lasted a good ten seconds, until laser beams from the top of the Riddler's stronghold blasted outward, neatly severing one of the plane's wings.

The plane spiralled downward, crashing into the water and sinking without a trace.

And that was when the frogmen caught up with Robin. They dragged him under, the water swallowing him, and he struggled furiously, lashing out with his hands, kicking desperately. But it was like moving in molasses, and the frogmen were far better equipped to maneuver in the water than Robin was.

Robin twisted, ripped the mask off one of the frogmen, and yanked the breathing tube out of another's mouth. But more converged on him, grabbing his arms and legs, and now more were approaching with knives. And as if cutting him to pieces was going to be insufficient penalty, one of them managed to get his hand on Robin's face and yank off his re-breather.

Suddenly one of the frogmen gestured frantically, and they all turned to see what he was indicating.

It was impossible to miss.

Speeding toward them through the water were the remains

of the Batwing. Except that incredibly, even miraculously, it had transformed into something else. The other wing had telescoped inward, and sleek fins had slid into place. The Batsub, for want of a better name, approached at top speed to aid the beleaguered teen.

The frogmen hesitated, the next move belonging to the sub.

With a roar and rush of water, a black torpedo streaked toward them, shot out of the Batsub.

A torpedo with arms.

That's what one of the frogmen adjudged it to be as a capeless Batman shot past him, snagged the struggling Robin with one hand, and with the other released a large net. The guided net ensnared the frogmen. They tried to slice it open with their knives, but didn't even come close to cutting through it.

Batman and Robin shot straight toward the surface. When they broke the water, Robin gasped for air, sucking in great lungfuls of it. Batman, meantime, hooked the net cable onto a nearby buoy to keep the net from drifting.

Moments later Robin had clambered up to the rocky shore of Claw Island. Batman came up several yards behind, refastening his cape to his armored shoulder plates. As he did so, he heard Robin exclaim, "Holy rusted metal, Batman!"

His partner frowned. "What?"

Robin took a few steps forward, kneeling. "The ground. It's metal, and it's full of holes. You know. Holey."

"Oh." He looked around. "This place was a refueling station for subs during the war . . ."

And just as Batman started to climb out of the water, he heard a grinding of motors and a horrible crunching noise. He looked upward as Robin started to rise into the air.

The cylinder in Nygma's illustration of Claw Island now made terrifying sense. The island was situated atop a tremendous cylindrical oil tank, rising quickly out of the water. Batman was left behind on a necklace of jutting rocks as Robin, with the rest of Claw Island, ascended higher and faster. It was already higher than his wirepoon gun could shoot a grappling hook. Looking around desperately for some means of access, he spotted a rusted panel on the giant metal structure. He moved quickly to it, ripped it free, and climbed inside.

Robin looked down at the water surging far below him. That was when a silky voice said, "The Bat or the Bird. We couldn't decide who got to kill who."

He spun and looked straight at Two-Face. "Or is it whom?" said Two-Face thoughtfully. He had a knife in his hands, flipping it casually from one hand to the other. "We flipped for it. We got you. We'd be angry—furious, even—if we thought we'd be out of the loop in killing Batman. But we don't anticipate your demise taking more than a minute or so. Plenty of time for us to get back for the main event. Indeed, the coin toss favored us. The Riddler, after all, only gets to focus on the Bat. We, however, will have the Bat *and* you. Two for the price of one."

They faced each other, circling. "The circus-boy, right?" asked Two-Face. "Makes sense, after all. If Wayne is the Bat . . . then it makes sense that you're . . . what? What are you supposed to be?"

Tightly, Robin didn't answer immediately. Instead he said, "You flipped for me, huh?"

"That's right. As we said, for the moment, Riddler got the Bat."

"Great. Well, you're going to get flipped . . . the Bird!" And Robin leapt at him.

Two-Face easily sidestepped. His own lunge was savage, catching Robin by the throat. Robin hit the ground hard, the metal shaking under him. Two-Face landed on top of him, slamming him viciously in the head. Light exploded behind Robin's eyes.

"What's wrong, circus-boy? No mommy and daddy to save you?"

Two-Face raised his blade over the dazed Robin, and brought it down fast. At the last second Robin rolled clear, the blade wedging into the rusted metal surface. It was the brief instant that Robin needed. He backflipped, kicking Two-Face hard in the head.

"For my mother," he shouted. As Two-Face staggered, Robin kicked him again and again, moving so quickly that Two-Face couldn't mount a defense. "For my father! For Chris!"

He knocked Two-Face to his knees, and said tightly, "For me." He smashed Two-Face in the chin, sending him rolling down the slope. His fingers found dirt and stone, but no other grip. At the last second, Two-Face grabbed a jagged outcropping of rock on the island's edge, hanging on for dear life, feet kicking wildly over the abyss.

To Robin's confusion, Two-Face was grinning.

"The scales are tipped. The blindfold torn from the lady's eyes. Justice will be served." The rock he was clutching began to slide. "You're a man after my own heart, son. See you in hell!" The rock ripped free, and Two-Face started to fall.

He dropped only two feet, and then Robin's hand grabbed him. His other hand had a grappling hook buried solidly into the rock.

He stared into the visage of Two-Face and saw himself. And more than all of Bruce's words, more than all of his own twisted emotions . . . that face laid out for him the conflict within him.

He saw the part of him that wanted the death of Harvey Dent. It looked up at him with an unblinking, glaring eye from a scarred and distorted soul.

"No. I'd rather see you in jail." And with that, he hauled Two-Face to safety.

"The Bat's taught you well," said Two-Face, catching his breath. And suddenly there was a gun in his hand, pressed against the flesh between Robin's eyes. "A mistake. But definitely noble. I underestimated you after all, kid. You didn't have the guts to do the right thing."

Two-Face cocked the trigger.

CHAPTER 26

The interior of the cylinder was a world of spinning, glowing question marks.

A series of steel gratings at intervals of roughly a hundred feet rose the height of the cylinder. Each grating was flush against the walls, and Batman had been using them to make his way up. He would fire his wirepoon, hook onto a grating, clip it to the winch on his belt, and hoist himself up. Each grating had a trapdoor that he would ease through. Then he would repeat the process.

Far below him the surf crashed against the rocks.

There seemed to be only one more grating between himself and the top. Unfortunately, Batman could see from where he was standing that there was no trapdoor on that final one, for whatever reason. He tried to ignore the array of moving question marks as he planned his strategy. He'd have to haul himself up, and then dangle there as he sliced through it with a laser torch. . . .

Was the grating closer?

Then he heard the grinding of motors. Sure enough, the upper grating was moving toward him. And it was doing so very quickly.

He knelt to pull open the trapdoor in the grating on which he was standing. It didn't budge. It had sealed behind him electronically.

He looked up again, and the grating was moving so fast

that he quickly realized he was not going to have time to cut through with the laser torch.

It left him exactly one option. He thumbed a button on his Utility Belt, painfully aware that the last time he'd tested the device, he'd almost set himself on fire.

His costume vibrated, building up in intensity, and seconds later his boots flared. The thrusters hurled him upward toward the descending grate. He crisscrossed his arms over his head, becoming what Robin would undoubtedly have termed a "Bat"-tering ram.

The descending grating and ascending Batman collided, Batman smashing through it. The metal wrenched free of the cylinder sides, clattering downward.

And the thrusters sputtered and cut out.

Batman reached out desperately and snagged an old access ladder set into the cylinder wall. He hung there for a moment, listening to the grating crash downward. Then he hoisted himself upward, shoving his way through a rusting access hatch to face . . .

. . . a weird haircut.

The head belonged to the Riddler, and the haircut consisted of a question mark shaved into the back of his head.

He was seated on his throne, which was slowly rotating. Extending from the back of his throne was a huge antenna, stretching up into the night sky. A ring of light encircled him, feeding even more brain power into him.

Batman quickly saw that the Riddler was substantially different from when he'd last seen him. Whatever he'd been doing to his brain had apparently spread to his body. Immense muscles bulged like a steroid-pumped bodybuilder's.

Batman moved slowly through the Riddler's control room, staring in bleak despair at what the poor, demented creature had done to himself. For his part, the Riddler grinned down at him. He indicated his overly muscular body. In a thick Austrian accent, he said, "*Hasta la vista*, baby. It's me. Arnold Schwarzenygma." He awaited a reply, but there was none. So he made his own. "Riddle me this. Riddle me that. Who's afraid of the big, black Bat?"

"No more tricks, Edward. Release Chase. This is between you and me."

Two-Face stepped from behind the Riddler's throne. "And me . . ." and he added, "and me."

Batman was looking up at the antenna. "Of course. The Box does more than enhance neural energy. You've been sucking Gotham's brain waves."

"And now it's new," chirped the Riddler. "Improved. Better than ever."

On the screens occupying the control room, he saw screens with schematics of flickering brains. "The disorientation I felt in the beam at your party. You've devised a way to map the human brain. To read men's minds."

"Oh, Batman, you are clever," the Riddler said with child-like glee. And then his voice started to rise, becoming louder, more demented. "How fitting that numbers led you to me. For numbers will crown me king. My Box will sit on countless TVs around the globe, mapping brains, giving me credit card numbers, bank codes, safe combinations, numbers of infidelities, of crimes, of lies told. No secret is safe from my watchful electronic eye. I will rule the planet. For if knowledge be power, then tremble, world. *Edward Nygma has become a god!*" His voice echoed throughout the room.

He waited until the reverberations stopped and then he turned to Two-Face. "Was that over the top?" he asked in earnest concern. "I can never tell . . ." Then, as if Batman were an afterthought, he said, "By the way, B-man, I got your number."

The images on the screen changed, becoming pictures of Bruce Wayne . . . and then of Batman . . . and then the two of them flickering, superimposing one over the other.

"I've seen your mind, freak," thundered the Riddler. "Yours is the greatest riddle of all. Can Bruce Wayne and Batman ever truly coexist? Ring a bell?"

The Riddler's hands were resting on small statues of the

Thinker. He twisted the two statues and suddenly his muscular physique split right in half. It was simply a solid formfitting body suit built right onto the chair. The Riddler, dressed in his customary skintight question mark–covered leotard, trotted out of it. He stood in the center of his glowing white ring.

"I know who I really am. Let's help you decide, once and for all, who you really are. Behind curtain number one . . ."

Sugar appeared on the edge of the room, pointing toward a curtain-draped cylinder suspended overhead. The curtain rose to reveal Chase within the tube, bound and unconscious.

"The captivating Dr. Chase Meridian. She enjoys hiking, getting her nails done, and foolishly hopes to be the love of your civilian life."

Spice appeared on the other side of the room. She gestured toward another cylinder. Batman knew even before the rising curtain displayed it that within the tube would be . . .

"Batman's one and only partner," the Riddler said, continuing in his best emcee voice. "This acrobat turned orphan likes looking his best despite an endless series of bad hair days. And below our contestants, my personal favorite . . ."

Trap doors slid open beneath Chase's and Robin's cylinders.

"A watery grave!" declared the Riddler, and paused a moment for the applause that he no doubt heard in his head. Then he pointed to a button that was on the armrest of his chair.

"A simple touch and five seconds later these two day-players are gull feed on the rocks below. Not enough time to save them both. So who will it be? Your love? Or your partner?"

"Edward, you've become a monster," said Batman.

"No," he replied with shrug. "Just the Riddler, and here's yours. What is without taste or sound, all around, but can't be found?"

He began humming the music from "Jeopardy!" to pass the time.

Slowly Batman began to walk towards the two cylinders, his mind racing furiously. He heard a soft chuckle from Two-Face. . . .

And froze.

As the answer sprang into his head, he suddenly became aware of what might be waiting in front of him. He studied the floor carefully, closed his eyes—and felt a very gentle breeze wafting from in front of him.

"Death," Batman said softy, aware now that there was no floor in front of him, but only a holographic representation of one. One more step would have sent him plummeting into an abyss. More loudly and with a sudden awareness he repeated, "Death. Without taste, sound, and all around us. Because there is no way for me to save them or myself. This is one giant death trap."

"Bzzzz. I'm sorry," said the Riddler, sounding tragic, "your answer must be in the form of a question. But thanks for playing." And his finger went toward the skull button.

"Wait. I have a riddle for you."

The Riddler seemed enchanted with the notion. "For *me*? Really? Tell me."

"I see without feeling. To me, darkness is as clear as daylight. What am I?"

Immediately the Riddler's joy turned to disgust. "Oh, please. You're blind as a bat."

"Exactly!"

Batman slammed his Utility Belt, released a Batarang with a high-energy charge, and hurled it at the antenna. The Batarang smashed into the antenna and a massive charge of electrons fed into the transceiver, overloading them.

"Noooo!" screamed the Riddler, as he was bombarded with massive pulses of neural energy. His entire head started to distort, fluctuate in size, and waver. His brain actually seemed to grow, skin stretching for a second over his expanding skull before snapping back into place. It didn't, of course, since the result would have been massive cerebral hemorrhaging and instant death. But that was what it felt like to the Riddler, and thought became holographic representation. He staggered, searching for something intelligent to say . . .

. . . and nothing came to mind.

"Bummer!" was all he could get out, and then the room went black.

The Riddler collapsed, slumping against the button. . . .

And Robin and Chase Meridian fell through their cylinders, the drop yawning before them.

But the tubes hadn't opened simultaneously. They'd opened sequentially: Chase's first, then Robin's. No more than a second between the two . . . but it might be all Batman needed.

In that instant, two metal lids slid shut over Batman's eyes. Small radar screens appeared on the back of his eyepieces, revealing the phantom floor and the wild crisscross of interconnected steel beams between the Riddler's lair and the crashing ocean below.

He leapt forward and hurled a Batarang all in the same motion. As the Batarang cable snapped taut, he swung down and caught Chase, depositing her on a steel beam while preparing to leap after Robin.

He looked down.

No sign.

My God . . . he couldn't have fallen that far, that fast . . . he couldn't be gone . . . he . . .

"Robin!" he shouted over the crashing of the surf.

"What'cha want?"

He looked up, his radar tracking and zeroing in.

Robin was wedged in the bottom of the tube, his arms and legs pushing against either side.

Batman started to climb the girders toward Robin when suddenly the world went white. Staggering back, Batman nearly slipped off the girder. He grabbed out and clung desperately.

Robin, craning his neck from his vantage point, spotted Two-Face on the beam in front of Batman. He had a halogen light strapped around his head, blinding Batman's sensors. He brandished his gun.

"All those heroics for nothing. No more riddles, no more curtains one and two. Just plain old curtains." He actually sounded disappointed.

"Haven't you forgotten something, Harvey?" called out Batman. "You're always of two minds about everything . . . "

To Two-Face's chagrin, he realized that Batman was right. "Oh. Emotion is so often the enemy of justice. Thank you, Bruce."

He took out his coin and flipped it.

And Batman threw a Batarang.

It was purely guesswork. He could hear Harvey's voice. He knew which hand Harvey threw with. He knew how high Harvey threw it. The rest was hanging on faith.

The Batarang clipped the coin and sent it off its arc.

Batman's intention was to knock the coin away and down, hoping that—without it—Harvey would be stymied, unable to decide.

Instead he lunged for it.

He snatched it out of midair, still clutching his gun, and then he fell.

Two yards. .

Two-Face slammed against one of the lower girders. It was bone-jarring, but his crazed strength and determination were enough to enable him to cling both to the coin and the gun. He twisted himself around, bracing his feet, clinging tenaciously . . . like a bat.

"Did you think it would be that easy? *Did you?*" he howled. "After everything that was between us, Batman! After the promises you made! You, the hero, the upholder of justice . . . and look what you did to us! Look!"

And from above, Robin shouted down, "And look what you did to *us*!"

Two-Face peered up at him. "What?"

"You go around acting like that coin is making all the decisions. But it's all bull. It's not the coin. It's you! You called me gutless? God, you are so damned gutless, I feel sorry for you!"

With a snarl, Two-Face brought his gun up and aimed at Robin.

Robin pressed on relentlessly, his arms and legs starting to tire. "You don't have the guts to admit Batman was human and couldn't do everything. He's a better man than you'll ever be, and you're passing judgment on *him*? How about you, hotshot? What's that coin say about you, huh? You're so busy passing judgment on everyone and everything except the guy who's really on trial here! I bet you don't have the nerve to try challenging the hand of fate yourself for once! See if it pats you on the back, or slaps you down! Go on! Do it! Forget about your coin. Decide for yourself, about yourself, you pathetic monster! Do it! *Do it!*"

Two-Face stared up at him for an eternity, as the water crashed below.

Then he flipped the coin.

It spun, hanging there in the night, and then descended. Two-Face plucked it out of the air, looked at it.

He shook his head. Without looking at Robin, he said, "It seems . . . we were right the first time. You are a man after our own heart. And you managed . . . you managed to rip it out." He chuckled softly. "You owe us, kid."

And he released his hold on the girder.

He made no sound as he descended. None at all.

There was dead silence.

"I didn't want to do that," said Robin slowly. "I . . . I killed him."

"No. You just showed Two-Face his real face. The rest was his decision. Maybe his first genuine decision in years. Robin . . . give me a moment to get these radar lids off line. Then I'll help you out of there . . . and attend to unfinished business."

Inside the Riddler's control room, Sugar and Spice—surrounded by a smoke-filled world of sparks and flame—held a quick confab.

"Girl, can you swim?" asked Sugar.

"And ruin this hair?" sniffed Spice. "Hell no." As they headed for a secret exit, Spice flipped open her portable phone. "I know a guy with a yacht."

They disappeared into the exit, still unclear on everything that had happened. Batman's salvation was that the Riddler and Two-Face, considering knowledge to be power, had told no one else of the connection between Batman and Bruce Wayne. Nygma had it in for his former employer, but so what? Chase Meridian was hot on Batman, but again, so what? Sugar and Spice themselves found him kind of hot.

Unfortunately, a proposed romance with Batman didn't seem conducive to continued freedom. And so they made their escape, vanishing from Gotham entirely.

None of this was going to be of any particular interest to Edward Nygma, a lonely figure trying to piece together the charred fragments of his machinery. His voice was small, lost. Batman stood next to him, and Nygma was speaking to him . . . but it was as if he was unaware that Batman was in the room.

"Why can't I kill you? Now, there's a riddle. Not smart enough. Find a way. Fuse the transceiver to . . . what? Can't remember. Too many questions. Why you and not me? Why me? Why??!!"

His scalp was blistered and burned. Pathetic, whimpering and mad, he stared at the pieces of his machinery as they crumbled in his hand.

"Poor Edward. I had to save both Chase *and* Robin. You see, I am Bruce Wayne and Batman. Not because I have to be. No, because I choose to be. However . . . it would have been nearly impossible to accomplish rescuing both of them. Fortunately," and he looked to Robin, who was standing nearby, holding the unconscious body of Chase. "Fortunately . . . I had help."

He reached down for the Riddler, who turned and looked up at him, and shrieked.

For descending towards him was the ravenous face of a hideous, demonic giant bat. . . .

CHAPTER 27

Surprisingly, it was a quiet night at Arkham Asylum, except for the screaming of one inmate. Actually, the inmate had been screaming ever since his apprehension at Claw Island. Every so often the noise would fade as his vocal cords grew strained. But then from somewhere he would regain strength and start howling again.

Lately, though, he'd started shrieking something new.

Dr. Burton walked down the hallways of the maximum security wing, Chase Meridian at his side. "Edward Nygma has been screaming for hours that he knows the true identity of Batman," Burton informed her.

"Really?" said Chase, her voice neutral.

They reached cell 22 and Chase peered in through the small barred window set into the heavy door. "Edward . . ."

The screaming cut off abruptly. "Who is it?"

"It's Dr. Chase Meridian. Do you remember me?"

"How could I forget?"

"Dr. Burton . . ." She paused. "Dr. Burton tells me you know who Batman is."

Edward giggled gleefully. "Yessss. I know!"

She steeled herself. "Who is the Batman, Edward?"

"Can't tell if you don't say please."

Gamely, she said, "You're right, Edward. I didn't mean to be impolite. Please."

Nothing.

"Edward, please. Who is Batman?"

Suddenly a huge silhouette of a bat appeared on the cell of the padded wall. Into it leaped Edward, the sleeves of his straitjacket madly flapping like the wings of a bat.

"I AM BATMAAAAANNNN!!!"

And now the other inmates, hidden away in their cells, began to laugh and howl, cackle and shriek, matching Edward Nygma's demented glee. Drs. Burton and Meridian walked quickly away, the laughter ringing behind them.

Chase emerged from Arkham Asylum to find Bruce waiting with the Bentley, holding the rear door open.

"He's lost all contact with reality," she said, and was pleased to see him relax a little. "Your secret is safe, Batman, or do I just call you Bats?"

Bruce smiled, and then reached into his coat and handed her a small wicker figure. The dream doll.

"Thank you," he told her. "I don't need it anymore. My dreams are all good dreams. Now."

They climbed into the Bentley, pausing to kiss. The car rolled away from Arkham and down the hill . . .

And that was when the Bat-Signal flared in the air.

Bruce looked up and sighed, exchanging glances with Chase. He started to speak, but she simply shook her head and smiled. "Don't work too late," she said.

Minutes later, Chase Meridian was the sole passenger in the car, with Alfred at the wheel. She stared up at the Bat-Signal, burning against the sky. "Does it ever end, Alfred?"

Alfred chuckled softly. "No, Miss. Not in this lifetime."

And high above the city, crouched on the edge of a gargoyle-lined building, Batman looked out over his city. He didn't even have to glance behind him to know that Robin was nearby. Their capes billowed in the breeze as they swung off across the skyline, twin guardians of the night.

The darkness opened up to them, and they were gone.

PETER DAVID is a prolific author, having in the past several years written nearly two dozen novels and hundreds of comic books including such titles as *Aquaman, The Incredible Hulk, Spider-Man, Star Trek, X-Factor, Sachs & Violens, Soulsearchers & Company, The Atlantis Chronicles, Dreadstar, Wolverine,* and *The Phantom.* He has written several popular *Star Trek: The Next Generation* novels including *Q-Squared, Rock and a Hard Place, Vendetta, Imzadi,* and *Q-In-Law,* which have spent a combined six months on the *New York Times* Bestsellers List. His other novels include *Knight Life,* a satirical fantasy in which King Arthur returns to contemporary New York and runs for mayor, *Howling Mad,* a send-up of the werewolf legend, the "Psi-Man" and "Photon" adventure series, and novelizations of *The Return of Swamp Thing* and *The Rocketeer.* He has written two episodes of the acclaimed TV series *Babylon 5,* and is the sreenwriter of the award-winning SF film spoof *Oblivion.* He also writes a weekly column, "But I Digress . . ." for *The Comic Buyers Guide.* David is a long-time New York resident, with his wife of eighteen years, Myra (whom he met at a Star Trek convention), and their three children: Shana, Guinevere, and Ariel.

WATCH FOR

BATMAN
THE ULTIMATE EVIL
By Andrew Vachss

"Batman and Andrew Vachss. . . . If Batman were real this is exactly the sort of mission he would be undertaking. Hardboiled and adventurous, as well as important fiction, it doesn't get any better than this. THE ULTIMATE EVIL is a perfect marriage of reality to myth."

—Joe Lansdale,
author of *Mucho Mojo*

"If ever a work of fiction featuring a comics character deserved to be compulsory reading, this is surely it . . . [THE ULTIMATE EVIL] is a book no Batman fan should miss."

—Alan Grant,
writer, *Batman: Shadow of the Bat*

Coming in hardcover from Warner Aspect
November 1995